# THE NEW MARRIAGE

# BOOKS BY L.G. DAVIS

*Liar Liar*

*Perfect Parents*

*My Husband's Secret*

*The Missing Widow*

*Stolen Baby*

*The Stolen Breath*

*Don't Blink*

*The Midnight Wife*

*The Janitor's Wife*

THE LIES WE TELL SERIES

*The New Nanny*

*The Nanny's Child*

BROKEN VOWS SERIES

*The Woman at My Wedding*

*The Missing Bridesmaid*

# THE NEW MARRIAGE

## L.G. DAVIS

Bookouture

Published by Bookouture in 2025

An imprint of Storyfire Ltd.
Carmelite House
50 Victoria Embankment
London EC4Y 0DZ

www.bookouture.com

The authorised representative in the EEA is Hachette Ireland
8 Castlecourt Centre
Dublin 15 D15 XTP3
Ireland
(email: info@hbgi.ie)



ISBN: 978-1-83618-323-5
eBook ISBN: 978-1-83618-322-8

# PROLOGUE

Something is coming. Something bad.

Outside the car window, the last traces of daylight fade, and a few warm lights flicker on in the houses lining the quiet streets of Stoneview. There's a heaviness in the air as though the world itself has paused to watch what happens next.

I distract myself by daydreaming about the future. I see myself standing in our kitchen, baking cookies or cakes for birthdays and anniversaries, making lemonade on hot summer days. I imagine weekends spent in our backyard, the aroma of barbecued meat wafting through the air as laughter echoes around me and my family.

But then, something disrupts my thoughts. It's barely noticeable at first, a slight hesitation in the engine, a shift in the car's behavior.

Frowning, I glance down at the dashboard, but the lights are all normal.

"Is everything okay?" he asks from the passenger seat.

"Yeah, I think so." I try to keep my tone light.

But now the car seems to be pulling slightly to one side.

I grip the wheel tighter and it resists.

A prickle of fear tingles at the base of my neck. I press down on the brake pedal, but the response is sluggish.

Full-blown panic bubbles up inside me now.

"Okay, no. Something's not right," I say in a strained voice just as the car swerves again, more violently.

There are gasps of alarm as I struggle to regain control. The road blurs in front of me and soon we're veering off course.

"What's happening?" A terrified voice comes from the back-seat and my heart stutters. I can't let anything happen. Not now.

Not after everything we've been through to get here.

"Don't worry. I... I'm trying to fix it," I manage, but my mouth is dry, my breath coming in shallow gasps. "It'll be okay."

Even as I try to reassure him, I know this is beyond my control. Terror claws at my chest as the world outside the windows spins in a dizzying dance of blurry lights.

A single, terrifying thought crystallizes in my mind: we may not survive this.

Then there's a sudden jolt, everything lurching sideways. The tires screech loudly against the asphalt as I desperately try to turn the wheel and bring the car back under control, the steering wheel nearly ripping out of my hands. I fail and now we're in the wrong lane and a truck is barreling toward us at great speed.

Then it happens. It ends with a deafening crash, a whirl of glass shards, and the sickening crunch of metal against metal.

There is one thing on my mind before I close my eyes: this was no accident. And I know who did it.

# ONE

## DREW

I'm sitting cross-legged on the floor with books spread out in front of me, some in piles, and some scattered haphazardly around the room. Most people would find it daunting, but not me. I've been a bookworm since I was five years old, with a love for reading that I inherited from my mother, who was a part-time librarian.

"What in the world! How many books do you have, Drew?" My husband, Mark, has just returned after his swim in the ocean, something he does most mornings, even when the weather is on the chilly side. If I'm a bookworm, he's a water rat through and through.

Water drops glisten as they fall from his dark-brown hair onto the tips of his broad shoulders and I stifle a giggle at his widened eyes, the color of rich caramel.

"Not nearly enough, my darling. Never enough." I push to my feet and step over the books toward him. Wrapping my arms around his neck, I press a kiss to his lips, which still taste salty.

Mark shakes his head and chuckles as he tightens his arms around me, pulling me close enough that I feel the muscles under his white t-shirt, evidence of years of working out in the gym.

"Have you seen the price of books these days?" His lips curl in a playful grin as he presses his forehead to mine. "We will have to rob a bank if you want to build your dream library."

I return his smile, but deep down I'm thinking we might have to rob a bank period, and that's just if we want to keep this house. When many couples get married, they either move in and rent together, or they start afresh and make their own imprint on a home that is just theirs. But this beautiful brick-stone house was bought by Mark and his late wife, Melody. When they moved in, they planned to raise a family and grow old here, to watch hundreds of sunsets through the windows that overlook the ocean. This place is still filled with memories they made together, just as much a part of its foundation as the walls.

Mark and I got married a year ago, and sometimes I feel like a character in a story that doesn't quite belong or was written in a little too late.

I force myself to just be here in the moment. Mark is my husband now and I should focus on making our own memories. I lean my head against his chest, my head fitting perfectly in the space under his chin.

But it's hard not to think about the past. As we stand in a comfortable silence, my eyes pause on the cherrywood mantelpiece at the far end of the room. Just yesterday, a photo of Melody on her wedding day was there. I've packed it away, but I can still see it. The light is bouncing off her golden hair and her eyes are looking back at me, judging me, the stranger in her home, the woman who dares to step into her shoes.

"Penny for your thoughts?" Mark pulls away a little. "You're very quiet. Is everything okay?"

I nod first, then shake my head. "I was just thinking... Mark, are you sure this is okay with you?"

Melody was an artist and this room was her home studio. It's beautiful, with an entire wall made of glass that overlooks the sea. And now here I am, about to turn her personal space into my library. It has always felt like some kind of shrine and I wanted Mark to be the one to decide what happened to it. Then yesterday, he suggested I turn it into a library for all my books that until now had been boxed up in the garage. I was exhilarated, despite the shadow of guilt. Then again, after what I did, guilt is an ever-present companion in my life.

Now, Mark places a finger under my chin and tilts my face upward so I can look into his eyes. "Drew, this is your home as much as it's mine. Melody would've wanted you to feel at home here, as do I."

Beneath the firmness in his tone, I hear a tremor of something else. The pain is still there, torturing him. Every time he says her name, I feel it radiating off him. The love they shared before she died, before I came along to take her place, was immeasurably great.

I really want to believe him, that he doesn't mind me turning this room into something else, that Melody would understand.

But to be honest, if Melody knew who I am and what I did, she wouldn't want me anywhere near Mark. Let alone in her home.

"Mark..." my voice trails off.

"What's on your mind?"

"Thank you."

He kisses the tip of my nose then walks to the door. "I'm heading to the gym."

When Mark says he's going to the gym, he's actually going to work. At thirty-nine—two years older than me—Mark Reynolds is already the owner of Shoreline Fitness Centre, the only gym in Stoneview, Florida. It's a business inherited from his wealthy parents, who died in a tragic boating accident, six months after he graduated from college with a degree in sports medicine. The gym is a beautiful property right by the sea, complete with top-of-the-line equipment, a spacious sauna, two steam rooms, an infinity pool with a view of the ocean, and any other amenities that a fitness enthusiast could dream of.

It sounds fancy, but the business is barely keeping afloat these days. In fact, it's bleeding money we don't have. And it all started with Melody's death, two years ago. Mark fell into a deep depression that completely consumed him. The gym was the last thing on his mind, and he neglected it. That led to a decline in memberships and staff turnover increased. That's how much Melody meant to him, how much her death affected him. He'd already been through so much in his life, he was no stranger to grief, but losing Melody broke him.

Even when he got back on his feet, things never really improved financially. In fact, things are worse now than they've ever been and due to too many missed payments we are on the verge of losing this house. As of today, July fifth, we have exactly eight months before we're homeless.

Unless, of course, we decide to move in with his sister, Sarah, who lives just a few doors down in a three-bedroom townhouse left to her by their parents. But the mere thought of living with that woman makes me feel as if the walls are closing in on me. She has never accepted me into her family, and I don't see that changing.

I wish I had a job that could help take off some of the load, but being a hairstylist at Locks Lounge doesn't bring in enough to make a difference in our mountain of debt.

Half an hour later, Mark leaves the house and I glance at the time on my phone. It's half past seven and I don't have to be at the salon until nine-thirty, which gives me enough time for my jog and a quick coffee at the Sip & Snack Café. That's where Jason, my twenty-year-old son, works as a barista.

He thinks I go there for the coffee, but actually, I like checking up on him, making sure he shows up for work and stays out of trouble. I know I have nothing to worry about anymore, but I can't help it. I'm a mom and it's my job to worry, especially after what Jason and I went through.

Having slipped into a gray tank top and matching yoga pants, I'm heading back to my future library to get my phone, when the doorbell rings. I know it's Sarah. I keep walking because she has a key and she will let herself in anyway. I don't understand why she even bothers ringing the bell.

A visit from Sarah is never a good thing; she's the last person I want to see in the morning when I'm tanking up energy for the day. She always leaves me so drained and upset. But she's Mark's sister and asking her to stay away is as impossible as asking the sun not to rise.

"Mark?" she calls, her voice sharp and demanding.

She has never once called for me when she comes over; she acts almost as if I don't exist. It's understandable, given that Melody was not only her sister-in-law but also her best friend, and to Sarah, any woman who isn't Melody simply doesn't belong in Mark's life or in this house.

"In here," I call back, trying to sound warm and confident. "In... the studio."

The moment she fills the doorway, her eyes widen in shock and her ruby lips stretch until they form a thin line.

Sarah is thirty-two and works as a journalist for the *Stoneview Gazette.* She's dressed and prepared for work in a tailored charcoal gray pantsuit; the edges are razor-sharp and underneath the suit is a fitted blouse made of crisp white silk. Her short black hair is styled to look feathered and her green eyes coldly sweep across the room.

"What are you doing?" Her tone could cut through steel. "You shouldn't be in here. Where are Melody's things?"

"In the garage. We are turning this room into a library."

I brace myself for the war I know is about to start.

TWO

If looks could kill, then Sarah's glare certainly would have done the job. I watch as her normally flawless complexion turns puce from the neck up and her hands clench into fists at her sides.

"A library?" she sputters. "Over my dead body, Drew."

"Mark said it was okay." It's so hard not to keep my voice from wavering especially since Sarah looks like she's about to claw at my face with her oval, rose-tinted nails.

"Oh, did he now?" She raises a perfectly manicured eyebrow, fitting for someone with past experience as a model, even if it was brief. She steps so close I can smell the coffee on her breath. "Melody's things belong here. In this room, *her studio*, and not in some damp garage."

I part my lips to fight back, to remind her that I'm the woman of the house now. But my words die before they leave my throat. I snatch a deep breath of the lemon-scented air and push back my shoulders. "I know this is hard for you, Sarah, and I understand, but Mark needs to move forward."

"With you?" Sarah laughs bitterly. "You think you can just replace her like a pair of socks? You really think it's that simple?" She looks so intimidating right now, so different from the way she is when Mark is around. He never gets to see this side of her.

"Sarah, I—" My voice cracks, and I hate myself for it. Why do I always become a weak mess around this woman? No wonder she doesn't respect me. From the moment I walked into her brother's life, she knew that she could walk all over me.

In a nearby mirror, I catch my reflection, and I do look weak. My lack of makeup makes me look even more vulnerable next to Sarah who never leaves the house without at least a coat of lipstick and a perfect sweep of mascara.

"I'm not trying to replace her," I say softly. "I'm just... Mark—"

"Doesn't know what he wants." Her words are final, as though she's the one in charge of his life.

Accepting defeat, I take a step back as she continues shooting her arrows, trying to hit the bull's-eye.

"Melody hasn't even been gone for that long." She folds her arms across her chest. "You need to stop playing house, redecorating as if... as if..."

"Melody has been gone for two years, Sarah." My pulse beats hard against the side of my neck and I can feel the rush of blood in my head. "*You* need to stop—"

She cuts me off. "You think you can just walk into her life and home? You're nothing like her. You will never be her." She pauses. "Mark is vulnerable. He doesn't see what I see. How you're just waiting to take everything she had."

Each of her words cuts me deeper than the last. But I need to say something, anything. So, I take a deep breath and try again. "I'm sorry you feel that way, Sarah."

"Well, I do. Melody was and always will be the love of Mark's life. Never forget that." With those final words, she walks away and seconds later, the front door slams shut.

I stumble to a nearby chair and drop into it, trying hard to calm myself. I sit there for fifteen whole minutes until I pull myself together and leave the house.

My jog is normally calm, but not today. The houses blur into streaks of color as I push myself faster and harder until my legs are burning and my lungs are screaming in protest. The lump inside my throat is still there, but I ignore it. I will not cry. I will not let Sarah win.

I only slow down when I reach Sip & Snack.

The café is situated on a quiet corner three streets from us with inviting wooden tables and mugs hanging from rustic hooks on exposed brick walls. When I step inside, I see Jason immediately. He looks up from the counter where he's brewing a pot of coffee and offers me one of his crooked grins, revealing the small gap between his two front teeth. Jason used to live with us at the house, but when he got this job, seven months ago, he decided to move out.

"Morning, Mom. Rough start to the day?" he asks as I approach the counter and already gets to work making me my favorite drink.

I collapse onto a stool at the counter, too drained to even put on a brave face. "You could say that, but it's not worth talking about, trust me."

From the way he's looking at me through the locks of sandy hair that have fallen over his forehead, I can tell he already knows. He's well aware of the tension between me and Sarah, and even though she's supposed to be his aunt through marriage, he keeps as much distance from her as he can.

"Yeah, let's not talk about it." He soon hands me an ivory mug filled with steaming mocha and a generous helping of whipped cream on top.

"Thanks, love. Get back to work, ignore me and my bad mood." I'm happy to just sit here and watch him work.

With one last comforting smile, he gets back to his tasks, serving hot drinks and dazzling customers with a trivia fact about the origin of arabica beans. That has always been his thing: he loves to memorize random interesting facts and share them with anyone who will listen.

"Did you know that arabica beans are one of the oldest coffee species in the world?" he asks a young woman at a nearby table while he froths milk.

"No, I had no idea," she says, her face lighting up.

"They've been cultivated in the Arabian Peninsula for over a thousand years." He gestures excitedly with a spoon, creating ripples in the milk. "They make up about sixty percent of the world's coffee production."

As I watch my son, my thoughts drift to Dean, his father. Dean got me pregnant at seventeen and married me two years later. When Jason would get excited like this and start spewing off facts that were honestly too complicated for a small child to understand, Dean would ruffle his hair and keep asking questions. His nickname for Jason was Little Professor.

Dean and I were so very happy, at least at the start. We grew up together and supported each other in our individual endeavors, while caring for our son. He became a policeman and I became a professional photographer. But Dean died in a car accident four years ago and Jason and I were left reeling and alone as we picked up the pieces.

Jason was sixteen at the time and the death of his father hit him so hard that he dropped out of school and started drinking before he was legally allowed. I watched his life crumble right before my eyes.

So now, I'm so proud of the man he has become. He may not be where I wished he would be at this age, but he's sober, talking to people, and standing on his own two feet.

Jason catches my eye then and smiles, but something flickers in those expressive eyes, a shadow of our shared secret.

I smile back, pride swelling in my chest for this young man who fights his demons every day and wins. His journey wasn't easy. There were days of slipping, nights of relapses, and countless morning promises. But we did it, one sober day at a time.

Still, deep down, the memory of that other life—the one we both want to forget—flickers. I can't help but wonder, as I sip my mocha, if Sarah senses it and that's why she doesn't trust me. That there's something I'm hiding, that I've run away from. If she does, it's only a matter of time before she finds out and tells Mark.

And Mark is the one person who must never know the truth.

# THREE

I walk quickly away from Sip & Snack, my mocha warming me up from the inside, and make my way to the nearby pond. I love this spot; it's a beautiful little oasis with lush bushes and daisies surrounding it like a crown. Normally, I would have a handful of seeds to feed the ducks, but today I left the house in a rush.

The only sound is the gravel crunching underneath my feet and soon I spot my favorite bench in front of a weeping willow, with a good view of the café. Sometimes I'm still able to see Jason through the glass or when he comes out to serve people who are seated outside.

I'm steps away when something catches my eye. There's an unmarked envelope on the bench.

Sitting down beside it, I vaguely wonder if someone forgot it here or if it's a piece of litter. If there's one thing that really gets under my skin, it's people littering. But someone probably left it by mistake; it's pristine, not crumpled or stained. My curiosity piqued, I pick it up and turn it over in my hand. It's light and unsealed, but it looks like there's something inside.

Glancing around and seeing no one, I open it.

It's a single lottery ticket, how odd.

Maybe someone checked to see if they won, were disappointed and left it behind. I'm not sure why they'd put it in an envelope, though.

I push the ticket back into the envelope and pocket it, planning to recycle it when I get home. The breeze rustles the leaves above me and I spend the next few minutes watching the ducks swim languidly around. The water, like liquid glass, ripples around them and dances with the reflection of the sky.

Finally, with a sigh, I push up from the bench and glance one last time at the pond, wishing I could draw enough calming energy from it to last me through the day. Then I jog back to Elm Grove, our street, making a quick stop at the memorial of someone who died here. It's just a pause to tidy things up, a ritual I've adopted. It's a makeshift altar of sorts, decorated with pictures, candles, and wilting flowers.

The woman in the picture mounted on the tree watches me as I rearrange the flowers. She has high cheekbones and dark, piercing eyes surrounded by thick lashes. Her long, flowing hair cascades like a waterfall. I wonder if she's really watching me now, if she appreciates these small gestures from a stranger.

Taking a step back, I snap a photo of the memorial. Even though I no longer do it for my job, I'm a photographer at heart. Each day I stop here, I take a photo and wonder when people will stop leaving keepsakes behind, memories of the woman who is fading away.

When I get back to the house, I toss the lottery ticket into the recycling bin under the kitchen counter, then head upstairs to the bathroom to shower. Our en suite bathroom is a blend of stone and glass, an echo of Melody's style. The edges of the glass shower are frosted, and the stone tiles beneath my feet resemble the rustic cobblestone streets of old European towns.

As I let the water slide down my body, my mind starts to wander back to the numbers on the ticket and when I'm dressed, I find myself heading back to the bin and pulling out the envelope. I draw the ticket out and the numbers stare back.

"Stupid," I murmur, but then a question drops into my mind. What if?

It's ridiculous, and I nearly laugh out loud.

"You're being silly, Drew," I say to myself as I head back to the bedroom and pick up my phone, pulling up the lottery website. I wait for the page to load. The first thing I see is the set of winning numbers. Holding my breath, I glance at the ticket and read the numbers out loud.

Once, twice... by the third match, my breath hitches inside my throat. Four, five... a silent gasp escapes as the sixth number aligns.

I'm holding a ticket with the winning numbers and the prize amount is nine hundred thousand dollars.

My vision blurs and my hands start trembling.

"Nine hundred... thousand..."

This can't be real. In my experience, life doesn't give, it takes. It took Melody from Mark, Dean from me.

Now this.

The numbers start blurring in front of my eyes.

These are winning numbers, yes. But this ticket doesn't belong to me.

Nine hundred thousand dollars.

I sink down onto the bed, the piece of paper quivering between my fingers.

My mouth is dry, my head spinning from staring at all the zeros on the screen. Never in my life have I won anything close to even ten dollars. And now this, out of nowhere and without me even buying a lottery ticket?

I'm in shock, but I should really get myself to work, or I'll be late.

I've never been late once since I started working at Locks Lounge—or the Lounge as we all call it—and I pride myself on that. I like to respect other people's time and, in turn, I like them to respect mine.

But I can't get myself to move just yet; I'm rooted to the spot. It's as though this one single piece of paper is made of actual gold bars that are weighing me down. I can't help wondering how much nine hundred thousand dollars' worth of gold bars would weigh.

Everything has narrowed to this moment, this tiny piece of paper in my hand. What do I do now? What do people normally do?

Still holding onto the ticket, I go to my contacts. I need to call Mark. As I wait for him to answer, my breaths come in short, shallow gasps and I feel dizzy, like there's not enough air reaching my brain. I force myself to take deeper breaths.

Mark doesn't answer, which is not surprising. Aside from being the boss at Shoreline, he's also a personal trainer and he is probably busy with clients. I switch off the phone and drop it into my handbag. Funny how when one has good news to share, people are suddenly not reachable. Not that I've had a lot of good news in my life.

But then maybe it's a good thing he didn't pick up. I mean, this is not something I can just blabber out over the phone, right? It's too massive, life-changing. And I'm still trying to figure out exactly how it happened and what it means. I need to wait until he gets home tonight.

I stare at the ticket. I don't think it's a good idea to carry it in my purse with me. There are way too many people who walk in and out of the Lounge and there are no keys on our staff lockers. Helen Walker, the salon owner and my boss, has been saying for months that it's one of the things on her to-do list.

Without thinking I find myself lifting one side of the mattress and sliding the ticket underneath. Then suddenly, my skin cools as though the temperature in the room has dropped a few degrees, like it too is aware of the magnitude of the secret it now holds: nine hundred thousand dollars' worth.

I rub my arms to make them warmer.

"Stop being silly, Drew," I scold myself again and blow out a breath, before grabbing my purse and heading to the door.

Inside my car, I tell myself to pretend it's just another, ordinary day. But it's not. Nothing is the same.

One question nags me. Who would leave nine hundred thousand dollars unclaimed? Why wouldn't they guard it with everything they've got?

Maybe they forgot it on the bench for some reason, or it fell out of their pocket?

I know I found that ticket innocently, but deep inside, I feel like a thief.

A thief. The word tastes sour. I know I didn't steal that ticket. It was abandoned, forgotten. I'm a lot of things, but I'm not a thief.

And yet I didn't exactly run to hand it in to the police. I put it under my mattress, hidden away. Is someone searching for it now?

# FOUR

I had ten clients in the salon today and I was rushed off my feet, so I barely had any time to think about the lottery ticket. But now, as I drive off, anxiety hits me hard.

What if someone got into the house and found the ticket? Sarah has a key.

I'm being silly. People don't just flip over mattresses for no reason. I guess I'm just nervous because this is a life-changing amount of money for anyone, let alone someone like me.

Stoneview's charm blurs past me unnoticed as I drive. Finally, I pull into the driveway and turn off the engine, noting that Mark's car isn't here. I get out and my shaking legs carry me to the front door. The moment I enter the house, it's as though adrenaline has been shot into my veins, and I race up the stairs, taking two at a time.

Inside the bedroom, I drop to my knees and lift the mattress. The ticket is there. I swallow hard and press it to my chest.

After a while, I get up and decide to get dinner ready. When Mark arrives we can sit down and talk about this.

Soon his black sedan rumbles as it enters the driveway, and not long after, his key turns in the lock.

Taking a deep breath, I put my quick meal, a vegetable stir fry, on the kitchen table, and by the time he finds me in the kitchen, I'm wiping my hands on the apron, feeling a little more composed. The room smells deliciously of chili and garlic.

Mark draws me into a hug and kisses me before dropping into a chair. He looks exhausted with dark shadows forming bruises under his eyes.

"Rough day?" I pull out a chair and reach for his hand.

"Pretty much. Lots of clients, and the last one was quite demanding." He pauses and suddenly seems to notice the food. "Wow. That looks good."

"Thank you. It's nothing special. I'm sorry you had a bad day, darling." I'm sure there is something else he is not telling me. Mark rarely ever complains about his work. The business is struggling, but he still loves what he does.

He doesn't say much as we start eating, and the atmosphere is so strained I can't quite bring myself to share my news just yet.

I dab my lips with a napkin. "Baby, are you okay? You seem to have a lot on your mind."

Mark lets out a breath. "I got a call from the bank today."

"What did they say?"

"That we only have six months before we have to give up the house."

"Six months? That's... Woah. I thought we had eight." It's not like there's much of a difference, but those extra two months were something, at least.

He buries both his hands into his hair and tilts his head back, staring up at the ceiling. "Things are even worse than I thought," he says and then suddenly he forces himself to put on a brave smile. "But at least we won't be on the streets. Sarah said we are welcome to stay with her until we get back on our feet. Whatever happens, we'll be fine."

Mark always does his best to look on the bright side. But

everyone has their limit and I know how he gets when the light inside him goes out. I've seen it with my own eyes. I witnessed him hit rock bottom when Melody died.

I remember the first time I saw Mark at Stoneview General Hospital. I was there with Jason at the time, who had broken his leg.

Mark was sitting alone in the hospital waiting room, holding onto a cup of steaming coffee while his eyes stared into space and tears streamed down his cheeks. His hands were shaking so hard I was afraid he would spill hot coffee on himself, so I approached him and reached for the cup. My heart fell apart at the pain that bled out of him when he talked about his wife possibly never waking up from that coma.

We connected and soon became friends, and even after Jason was released from the hospital, I stayed by Mark's side, offering whatever comfort I could. When his wife passed away, I was there for him, knowing first-hand the anguish of losing a spouse. We bonded over our shared grief. I never expected what happened next. I never planned on falling in love with him, so hard and so fast.

I never planned on getting married to him—or anyone else, for that matter. And I certainly never planned on being here, in the house he had shared with the woman he had loved first. And yet, here we are.

I can't imagine moving out of this house and living with Sarah. That woman will make my life hell. She will scrutinize my every move, waiting for me to mess up so she can find a reason to push me out of Mark's life. There's no way I'm going to let that happen.

I have no idea how that winning lottery ticket ended up on the bench but it certainly came at the right time. That money would fix everything for us.

"Mark, there's something I need to tell you."

The furrow between his brows deepens and the moment stretches, taut as an elastic band about to snap.

"I bought a lottery ticket."

"What?" He shakes his head as if he must have misheard then leans forward, placing his hands on the table.

Once I tell him about this, there's no going back. "I bought a lottery ticket. And I won."

"But you don't ever play the lottery. How—"

"I know, but this time I did and the crazy thing is, I got lucky."

Mark is such a straight, decent human being. If I told him the truth he would insist on finding a way to get the ticket to its rightful owner. But the idea of losing this house and moving in with Sarah is haunting me. And it's not just about us, I also desperately want this money to help my son. More than anyone, Jason deserves a good life, and if ever things get bad again, that money might be necessary to get him the help he needs.

"Right." He presses a hand to his brow. "Wow, okay. How much did you win?"

"Nine hundred thousand dollars."

I wait for the words to sink in.

"You're joking, right?" he says in disbelief. "Nine hundred thousand?" He says each number slowly as though weighing it before setting it free, and his jaw drops as I blink in response. "Are you sure?"

"Yes. I'm sure. I won nine hundred thousand. This will change everything for us, darling."

"Nine hundred thousand..." he whispers again, a slow smile spreading across his face. "I can't believe it. Can I see it? The ticket?"

"Sure." I'm starting to feel a little dizzy. Now that I've put it out there, I will have to deal with whatever consequences will follow. "I'll go and get it."

I leave him standing there, his excitement palpable, and

head upstairs. A few minutes later I come back into the room. "Here." I hand him the ticket and I notice his hand shaking. "It's right there. Everything is going to be all right now, my love."

His eyes scan the numbers, disbelief etched on his face. Then suddenly, something shifts and he jumps to his feet, sending the chair clattering to the floor with a thud.

"Is this real? Drew, is this—"

"It is. It's real, Mark." I've been anxious from the moment I found out those numbers on the ticket are winners, but Mark's excitement is starting to rub off on me. I try to let myself go as he pulls me into his arms, lifting me off the ground. His body vibrates with joy.

This should be a happy moment for both of us, but for me this joy also comes attached to a lie. Yet another one.

"Baby, do you realize what this means?" Mark's voice is urgent, breathless. "We can keep the house. We can pay everything off. No more worrying about money, we're free."

I nod against his shoulder. "It changes everything."

As I take in the joy on my husband's face, for one tiny moment, I allow myself to forget everything but the here and now.

He stares at the ticket again and looks up at me with damp eyes. "I can't believe this is happening. Imagine... no more sleepless nights! No more scrimping and saving, no more bills hanging over our heads and debts we can't pay off."

After all the jumping around, we finally sit back down at the table and are just numb, unable to believe our luck. Then Mark goes over to the sink, splashes water on his face and turns to me with a huge grin on his face.

"Go ahead, babe. Find out what we need to do to get the money paid out."

"Right." My voice wobbles slightly as I pull out my phone and visit the website again, and this time, I scroll past the winning numbers to the information section just as Mark comes to sit heavily in his chair.

"Largest amount ever won in Stoneview," I read aloud, but my mouth is so dry it's hard to pronounce some words correctly. Then I move on to the next paragraph and I feel the blood drain from my face. I scan it instead of reading it word for word. "Background check. Public identity revelation..." The words blur before my eyes, each letter a silent scream.

"Come on, read on," Mark urges. "Looks like they'll want to verify who you are. Make sure you're not a fraud. I'm sure it's just routine. Shouldn't be too hard, right?"

My stomach plummets and my throat goes dry. "Right."

FIVE

After a lot of tossing and turning, I finally drift off into a dream where I'm holding the winning lottery ticket and someone is frantically pursuing me. Just as they catch up with me and grab my arm, I jolt awake, gasping for air.

In the darkness of the room, I'm careful not to wake Mark as I lift the corner of the mattress on my side of the bed and reach beneath it, pulling out the ticket. Then I tiptoe across the room to the walk-in closet, making sure not to make a sound. I shut the door quietly behind me. My hands are shaking as I flick on the light and stare at the ticket, its weight pressing on me.

How will I ever be able to claim the money without undergoing a background check? I can't risk anyone finding out who I truly am... what I did.

With the ticket in my hand, I sink down onto a padded stool. If I ever get the money, one of the things I would do is change this closet to make it more mine and less Melody's. Instead of the white and gold palette she chose, I'd be inspired by the deep blues and greens of the ocean nearby. I'd ditch the gold-rimmed vanity, replacing it with something more rustic, made from driftwood perhaps.

I'm also not a huge fan of open shelving, so I'd install cupboards with solid doors of distressed wood, painted a faded sea-foam green. The floors would be treated with a cool sandy beige, so that when I walk in, I'd feel like I have the sandy beach underfoot. The crystal chandelier would go too and would be replaced with vintage lanterns that release soft, inviting light.

I don't care what Sarah says. If I could afford it, I'd make our bedroom, and this entire house, a place where I can truly be myself rather than live in Melody's shadow.

When I moved in, Mark removed many of her personal belongings, but sometimes when I close my eyes, I feel like I smell her perfume. It's a light but persistent scent, floral and sweet. I even smell it now, I think. It definitely feels like someone is watching me as I sit here, holding this ticket like it's a live bomb.

There's a gold and white clock above the door and as it ticks, I feel like it's mocking me, reminding me I'll have to make a decision soon.

The thing is, there is another way I could get the money without exposing myself or Jason: Mark could claim it. But I'm stalling, because first and foremost, I'm a mother. My son means everything to me and if Mark claims that money, the brutal reality is, it's his alone. If anything happens to me or our marriage, he could take it all. And if my secret comes out, he most certainly won't want anything to do with us. If it's in his name and everything falls apart between us, Jason would get nothing.

No, if the money is to be claimed, it has to be by me.

But I'm stuck. I can't let Jason claim it either, he's too connected to my past and there's a risk my secrets could still come to light. If I claim it, it would certainly destroy everything. Jason would end up with his mother behind bars. What would that do to him, just as he's got his life back on track?

I just don't know what to do. So for now I need to delay

claiming the money until I figure out some kind of plan that keeps me out of handcuffs and protects my son's future.

I stiffen as the floorboards creak outside the closet. Before I can put the ticket away, the door opens. Mark is standing there wearing gray pajamas and a confused expression. His eyes are sleepy but slowly coming into focus, and his gaze flickers between me and the ticket.

"Hey, is everything okay?" he asks, stepping inside the closet and lowering himself onto the stool beside me. His touch is soft as he rubs my back.

"Yeah, I was just, ummm—"

"Looking to make sure it's real, that you're not dreaming?"

"Uh-huh." My throat tightens.

Mark's fingers close gently around the slip of paper, drawing it from my grasp.

"I can't believe this is real either." He traces the numbers on the ticket with a thumb and his smile stretches.

Then he looks up from the ticket, his gaze meeting mine. "Drew Reynolds, you've just won nine hundred thousand dollars, and you don't look at all excited."

I force a grimace of a smile, injecting as much fake cheerfulness as I can muster into my voice. "I'm just a little shocked, that's all, just taking it all in."

He pulls me close, wrapping his arm around my shoulder. "This is amazing, Drew. Everything's going to change now."

He's right about that. If I claim it, everything will change and not how he thinks it will. The universe certainly has one twisted sense of humor, dangling the solution to all our problems just out of reach, reminding me of what I could have had if I wasn't hiding such a terrible secret.

"Mark..." My voice falters. My husband's name feels foreign on my tongue, a name tied to a life that was never truly mine. My entire body is begging me to confess, to tell him everything about my past. Maybe, just maybe he will understand. Everything I did was for love, it was all for the right reasons. I still don't see how I could in good conscience have played it any other way.

Not that this argument would stand up in court.

"Yes," he murmurs, pressing the ticket back in my hand, then pulling me close.

The tears in my eyes blur my vision as I lean into his embrace, breathing in the warm spices from his aftershave and the smell of clean laundry. Soon my tears spill over and soak the collar of his pajamas. If I go to prison, I'll never smell him again, never feel his arms around my body.

"I'm happy as we are, here with you." I suddenly feel a deep urge to enjoy every moment with him to the fullest, to hold on to every memory of him that I can. If there is a possibility of a life without him, then I want to savor every last fragment of this life we have built together.

"I know you are," he whispers in my ear, his voice soft and reassuring as he strokes my hair. "We're happy together. But this is our new beginning, Drew. We don't even have to stay in this house. We can get a place that's all ours, we could even build it from the ground up."

I swallow the tears in my throat and look up at him. "You would do that, move to a different house?"

He gives a nod, his eyes lighting up. "For you? In a heartbeat."

His words tangle around my heartstrings.

"I don't know what I've done to deserve you," I whisper into his chest.

This cursed piece of paper is about to blow up my life. I can't claim it, but I also can't find it in me to give it up. Jason might need it one day. But what can I possibly tell Mark?

SIX

Pulling my knees up to my chest, tears prickle at the corners of my eyes and I squeeze them shut. Thank God Mark is already out for his morning swim and can't see me struggling with this guilt.

What the hell am I going to do?

Pushing aside the covers, I slide out of bed. Inside the closet, I reach for a pair of black leggings and a white oversized t-shirt that hangs loosely over my frame. Then I head to the bathroom to brush my teeth and splash cold water on my face.

My hair is forced into its usual messy bun, strands escaping and framing my face. My friend and colleague, Tia Morris, who usually has a new hairstyle every day, is always making fun of my bun. She thinks that, as a hairstylist, I should experiment more with my hair, but I've always been a low-maintenance kind of person.

Before I leave the room, I find myself standing in front of my bedside table, staring at the drawer. Every couple of hours after I went back to bed last night, I reached inside to see if the ticket was still there. Now I open the drawer and pull it out again, taking in the numbers one by one before I head downstairs to the junk drawer in the kitchen for an envelope. Once I've found one, with a heavy heart I slide the ticket inside and seal it. Then I push it into one of the deep pockets of my running jacket.

At 7 a.m. I leave the house, blinking away the remnants of a sleepless night. Outside the air is already thick with humidity and the promise of a scorching day. The faint chirping of the birds is the only sound until I take off running, my feet pounding hard. Thankfully, my route doesn't take me past Sarah's townhouse because seeing her first thing in the morning again would send my day straight to hell.

As I pick up speed on my jog, the ticket feels like it's burning into my skin.

But there's something else I feel too. That feeling again, that someone is watching me.

Glancing around in the lazy morning light, there's just the usual early risers. Mr. Francis from three doors down, the retired police officer who is always tending to his roses; Mrs. Leonard, the widow living next door who never misses her early morning yoga sessions in her front yard next to her ginger cat; and Mr. George, who is standing on his porch, yawning, with his newspaper tucked under one arm and a steaming cup of coffee in the other.

Though some of them wave at me, they aren't really paying me any attention. They're all busy with their own lives and morning rituals. I keep running, my muscles warming, my lungs burning as I push forward harder and faster until houses blur into streaks of color.

Normally, I would stop by Sip & Snack first to see Jason, but I'm a little early. They don't open until 7:30. So, I head straight to the bench and crash onto it, feeling hot and breathless. Then, a sound causes my head to snap up, my eyes zooming in on the bushes nearby.

Time comes to a standstill as I hold my breath.

To my relief, a squirrel finally darts out of the bushes, its fluffy tail bouncing high as it darts toward a nearby tree, standing for a few seconds at the base. Before it has a chance to climb up, the photographer in me reaches into my pocket for my phone, opening the camera app as I try to steady my hands.

I've always loved taking photos of nature, the way it offers fleeting moments of beauty that feel almost sacred. A perfect sunrise, a delicate bloom. Capturing these scenes has always been my way of holding onto something pure, something untouched by the darkness in my life.

Ready for the perfect shot, I lean forward slowly, zooming in on the little creature until it fills the screen just right. The squirrel seems to sense that it's in the spotlight and it turns its head to gaze straight into the lens. My finger taps just before it springs up the tree. Then I sit for a while longer, until the doors of Sip & Snack open, and I get to my feet, ready to go and see my son.

But first I pull out the envelope and place it right where I found it yesterday. That ticket is not mine. Someone else forgot it here and the right thing to do is to give them a chance to find it.

As I start to walk away, feeling as if a huge weight has lifted from my shoulders, my phone rings. It's Mark. I usually wait for him to return from his swim before heading out, so he must have been surprised to find me gone.

"Hey, babe. You're out early," he says. "Are you already out for your jog?"

"Yeah, I'm just taking a break now," I respond, glancing back at the envelope.

"Great." He pauses. "I've been thinking—we should do something special today."

My heart sinks and I press my fingers against my left temple. "Special?"

"Definitely. Drew, what happened is huge. You won the

lottery! Let's go out for breakfast somewhere nice. We need to celebrate properly."

"That sounds really lovely, babe, but I'm sorry. I think I'll be out for a while longer. I need... I just need to clear my head."

"Are you sure?" There's a pause and I know he can sense something is not right. "Are you feeling okay?"

I force a strained laugh. "Yes, of course. Maybe I'm just a little overwhelmed, that's all."

There's a brief silence on the line and a duck flutters its wings and takes off over the water.

"I understand, my love. It is a lot to take in. But remember, we can use that money to change our lives for the better. Take your time and jog as much as you need. Maybe we could go out for dinner tonight instead? We can go to the Mariner's Catch and order one of those seafood towers."

He knows just how to get me. The seafood tower is the restaurant's specialty, a stack of locally caught seafood, served beautifully on a glass stand. It's absolutely delicious, such a treat. If I say no to that, he will know that something is very wrong.

"Yeah, tonight. That sounds good."

"Perfect! I'll make a reservation for seven."

I hang up and stumble back to the bench, my chest tight, a panic attack looming. The whole world tilts, and a black curtain creeps into my vision.

Before I know it, I've scooped up the envelope again and I shove it into my pocket. I can't let go, not yet.

I'll think of something. I always do.

## SEVEN

There's nothing I need more right now than the distracting noise and chaos of the Lounge. The buzz of hairdryers, the snip of scissors, and the constant chatter of my colleagues and clients. As my hands glide through Cora Henderson's thick locks, admiring my work, I hear one name standing out in the hum. Lori.

This particular nugget of gossip is coming from Maggie and Vanessa, Helen's twin daughters who are probably going to own this place one day. They often style their hair in the same way and today they are wearing goddess braids, their blonde hair glossy and perfectly set around their heads.

"Someone saw Lori yesterday with her ex-boyfriend," says Vanessa.

"You think they're going to get back together?" asks Maggie.

"I wouldn't be surprised, to be honest." Vanessa reaches for a brush and starts running it through her client's hair. "All I know is that they were seen at Honeywood yesterday having a coffee together."

My stomach churns. This is a small town and I'm pretty

sure Maggie and Vanessa both know that Lori is dating my son. They're talking about her openly knowing very well that I can hear everything.

"Which ex are we talking about here?" Maggie asks, lifting a lock of hair from her client's shoulder.

"Does it matter?" Vanessa scoffs. "That girl has been through half the guys in Stoneview. But I'm thinking it's the previous one, the one she dumped last Christmas."

Lori and Jason have only been in a relationship for seven months and I am devastated to think that she's already looking around for someone else. Jason is so smitten with her.

Removing the apron from Cora, I turn her around so she can admire her new look. Her brown eyes shine as she places both hands on her cheeks and squeals. "This is perfect. I love it, Drew. Thank you so much."

She had asked for the look that Rachel had in the *Friends* series, and I think I nailed it. Her hair looks glossy and flowy and the highlights complement her green eyes.

After she pays, I go to the staff room for a breather and find Tia there, getting ready for her shift. Her hair is tied into a beautiful bun at the back of her head leaving out curly ringlets that soften her slightly angular features.

Tia started at the salon a month after I did as a hairdresser in training. At the time, I found it odd that she'd leave a career in criminal law to become a hairdresser in the town she grew up in, especially after studying for all those years. But she explained that defending criminals was never her dream, it was her parents'. She'd come to a point where she just wasn't happy and decided to change direction. When she started at the salon, we became instant friends. It just clicked between us from day one.

"Are you okay, Drew?" she asks. "You look upset; is everything okay at home?"

"You mean in my marriage, right?" I say, immediately defensive.

Tia raises an eyebrow and I shake my head. "Why do you always assume that my problems have to do with my marriage? Tia, I know you don't like my husband for reasons I'll never understand, but he's really a good man and our marriage is perfect."

"Come on, Drew, nothing is ever perfect." She throws her hands up in the air in resignation. "But if you say so."

"What's that supposed to mean?" As far as I know, Mark and Tia have only been in the same room once. Not long after Tia and I became friends, I invited her over for dinner, but she looked uncomfortable and barely said a word to him. When I asked her about it later, she just shook her head and said she had a "feeling" about him.

Since then, she's only accepted a handful of invitations to my home and most of them were when Mark was not around. And lately, she's been asking a lot of questions about him and our relationship. Whenever I mention an argument we had, she looks at me with as much concern as if my entire world was falling apart. I know she's just being an overprotective friend, but it feels like she's reading too much into things and I desperately wish she accepted the love of my life.

"Drew, I didn't mean anything by it." She studies my face. "I care and I want what's best for you. And Mark—"

"—is good for me." I cut her off before she can finish, heat flooding my cheeks. "I really don't get what you have against him. You don't even make an effort to get to know him."

"I'm a good judge of character, Drew." Her voice is gentle, her eyes softening. "And there's something about Mark. I'm sure he's not the man you think he is."

"You know what, Tia, for the sake of our friendship, I think we should kill this conversation."

Tia opens her mouth, then closes it, nodding. "All right. We won't talk about it anymore." She puts a hand on my shoulder. "But I know there's something bothering you. Tell me about it."

"I just heard something that rubbed me the wrong way, that's all." I sink into a chair and grip my knees. "Lori might be going back to her ex-boyfriend. She was seen with him yesterday at Honeywood."

"Which of her ex-boyfriends?" she asks, and I feel like screaming. She too knows that Lori has been with a lot of guys in this town.

"No idea. But she's clearly about to hurt Jason and I—"

Tia strokes my arm. "I'm so sorry, lovely. I know you're worried about him. But whatever happens, I'm sure Jason can handle it. You're too protective of the boy. He's not even a boy, he's a grown man."

I know I am protective, maybe too much. But it's for good reason, and I can't explain why to her or anyone else. They will never understand the lengths I will go to for my son or the things we have been through.

"I just don't want to see him get hurt."

"You know what?" Tia runs her hand up and down my back. "The only thing you can do here is to be there for him when he needs you. Sometimes things just don't work out in a relationship."

As she speaks, she opens her locker to retrieve something, and an old newspaper falls out.

I draw in a sudden breath as the headline catches my eye. It's folded to an article about Melody's accident and death.

Tia quickly grabs the paper before I can react and shoves it back into the locker.

I find her reaction strange, but I don't say anything. I don't know *what* to say. There's nothing wrong with her keeping a newspaper in her locker. But why on earth is she keeping one about my husband's first wife's death?

Just as I'm starting to dwell on it, Helen calls out our names, and I'm almost relieved to have the distraction. Leaving the staff room, we find her standing in the middle of the salon floor, wearing a pair of Bermuda shorts and a white silk blouse tucked into them. Her hair is the same shade as her girls', but instead of being braided up, hers is glossy and straight as it flows down both her shoulders. Helen always looks both elegant and casual, not an easy thing to pull off.

She pushes her hands into her pockets and smiles at all of us in turn—me, Vanessa, Maggie, Tia, and Marlene, who works both as a receptionist and a hairstylist.

"Ladies, I'm pretty sure you know what today is. Any moment from now, the VIP clients will arrive, and I want you to make them feel as special as you did last time."

Sure enough, when I glance at the glass door, I see five figures huddled together outside, wearing a patchwork of worn coats despite the heat. One of the things I love about Helen is that she always prides herself on doing good in the community, and her latest initiative is giving the homeless regular free treatments.

I smile as my gaze lingers on Martin, who is in his late fifties. He is standing behind all of them, but his eyes are bright and I can see the white of his teeth peeking out from his bushy, graying beard.

"We're ready," Tia says, rubbing her hands together.

The doors open and the VIPs walk in, ready for a fresh look.

Martin comes straight to me, still grinning. "Hello there, Drew," he says, "I hope you're doing good today."

I wasn't, but seeing his excited face and thinking about what his life must be like and the problems he faces daily compared to me, I feel too ashamed to admit I'm struggling.

"I'm doing great." Straightening myself up, I focus my mind on Martin. This is his time, and this is my job. He came here today so I can make him feel special and that's what I have to do. "Can I get you something to drink? We have orange, apple, and grape juice." My eyes glance at one wall of the salon, where a small snack bar has been set up.

"I'm all right for now," he says, sitting down into the chair I point him to.

"Right. If you need anything, just let me know." I place my hands on his salt and pepper hair. "What do you want me to do for you today?"

"Just like last time, all I need is for you to tame the wilderness." A chuckle escapes him as he runs a hand through his shoulder-length hair.

Last time, I wanted to give Martin a complete makeover because when most of the homeless people walk into this place, they want to leave looking and feeling completely different. But he didn't want it. He said he wanted to still recognize himself in the mirror. I guess the person he used to be before he ended up on the street is not someone he considers himself to be anymore.

"A cleanup it is," I say, draping a cape around him before I get started on washing his hair.

Forcing myself to be here and nowhere else, I wet Martin's hair and listen to the running water and the soft jazz coming from the hidden speakers around the salon.

His locks are thick, stubborn, and tangled but they soften under my fingers. The water grows murky as I rinse out the first layer of grime, and I feel an odd sense of satisfaction when the strands beneath emerge softer and cleaner.

I gently massage the shampoo into his scalp, eucalyptus and peppermint drifting up into my nostrils. Martin closes his eyes and lets out a sigh.

As he relaxes, he gets started telling me about interesting things he's experienced on the streets, especially his favorite story of last Christmas when he went to sleep and woke up to find bags of groceries next to him.

"That's a day I'll never forget. And every time I find myself taking life for granted, I remember that there are angels everywhere and they show up when we least expect it." He opens his eyes again for a brief moment but before our eyes can meet, he closes them again.

Martin is not very different from many other homeless people I have come into contact with. Many of them find it very hard to make eye contact. But that's all right by me. I can understand not wanting to be seen.

I finish washing out the shampoo and begin conditioning his hair. He lets me work, his posture relaxing further as the tension seeps out of him. When I'm done, I gently towel-dry his hair, then begin carefully tidying it up along with his beard, using a fine-toothed comb to smooth out the edges of his beard and making sure his hair falls just right.

"Tell me how things are going with you, Drew," he says. "Did that sister-in-law of yours show up again to stir up trouble?"

I look to my side to see Tia staring at me with a cocked eyebrow. She is barely acknowledging her client, simply getting the job done with the least possible interaction.

"No," I say in a low voice. "I didn't see her today. I'm keeping my distance."

"Well, let's hope you don't lose the house and have to move in with her."

"Yes, I hope so as well."

I can feel Tia shooting daggers at me now.

Ignoring her, I towel-dry Martin's hair again, making sure to remove any excess moisture. Then, I grab the blow dryer and work through it with a gentle touch, giving his hair a soft, finished look.

"You're all set," I say finally, removing the cape with a flourish.

Martin stands up and examines himself in the mirror, smiling. "You did it again. Thank you, Drew."

"Anytime." My heart warms as I watch him heading to the snack bar.

While the others are still busy with their clients, I disappear to the staff room for a moment to myself.

Sitting down, I switch on my phone to find several messages from Mark, all of them about how excited he is about our big celebration. Switching off my phone again, I toss it back into my purse and lean my head back against my locker, my eyes closed. I don't know how long I've been there when Tia's voice startles me.

"That Martin sure knows a lot about you," she says, sitting down next to me and taking off her shoes, massaging her feet. "I have a feeling he knows more about you and your life than even I do."

After seeing that newspaper fall out of her locker, I can't help wondering the same about her. Why did she look so flustered? I push the thought to the back of my mind again. The last thing I want to talk about is my husband's dead wife.

"That's ridiculous, Tia. You know everything about me." My guess is she's upset because I won't discuss my marriage with her.

"That's not true, and you know it. For starters, I don't know about your life before you moved to Stoneview. You never talk about it even though you know everything about me and my messy life. That my parents don't talk to me because I ditched law, that I've been engaged for three years and still have not set a wedding date."

"Wait, last week you said you had finally set a date and were working on the invites?"

"Well, maybe the date doesn't feel right anymore." She stands up and starts digging inside her locker. Then she pulls out a can of hairspray and sprays it all over her hair, fixing it in place. She drops down next to me again and this time she takes both my hands into hers. "It just makes me sad, Drew. We are supposed to be best friends, but I feel like there's this large part of you I don't know, things that make up the real you."

"You know my sister-in-law gives me hell. And you know that Mark and I are having financial problems."

"I know, but we all have them, don't we? At least we're better off than homeless Martin. What's up with him anyway? He honestly seems a little obsessed with you."

"He's just a nice person and I like talking to him when I go for a walk in the park."

"It kind of feels like you enjoy his company more than mine."

Her tone is joking, but I can see she's actually offended. The thing is, I don't tell anyone else much about my past. Not Tia, not Martin, not even Mark.

"I know you probably went through some crap in your life, Drew. But you know you can tell me everything, right?"

I almost smile at that, because she just has no idea. Tia thinks that me telling her about myself would bring us closer, but I know it would be the end of our friendship.

"Tia, you know everything that's important about me. There's not much more to know, really." I squeeze her hands tight. I have no idea why she keeps pressing me so much to open up. She gets like this at least once a week and it's starting to bug me.

To my relief, Marlene pokes her head through the door to tell Tia that her next client is here. Tia's eyebrows furrow in a way that tells me this conversation isn't over, but she stands and straightens her bright-green pencil skirt.

The rest of my day goes by fast. I give a Locks Lounge special to Angela from Danny's Grocers, a wash and blowout to Roselle, a kindergarten teacher, and then a buzz cut to Jimmy, a high school senior. Finally, I step out of the Lounge, exhausted.

When I get into my car, I switch on my phone and I'm relieved to see a message from Mark apologizing that he won't be able to make dinner anymore.

But before I head home, I decide to make one stop that fills me with dread—a visit to the post office. One of the few places where locals play the lottery.

# EIGHT

I push open the door and step into the dim interior of the post office. It has exposed brick walls and rustic wooden beams overhead, and the scent of freshly brewed coffee blends with the faint smell of old paper. I make a conscious effort to stand tall and exude confidence, but I shiver as a cool blast of air from the AC hits my face.

Tucked away in the back corner is a section dedicated to the lottery, combining postal services with the excitement of gambling. Colorful, eye-catching signs hang above, boldly proclaiming slogans like "Dream Big, Play Smart!" and "Your Ticket to a Better Tomorrow!" One display case holds a multitude of multi-colored scratch tickets, each one offering the hope of life-changing prizes.

There's a man behind the counter sorting through a stack of mail. He has brown hair streaked with dull silver and a thin line for a mouth. Dressed in a simple button-up shirt with the sleeves rolled up to his elbows, he reveals a set of three heart tattoos in various sizes. He glances up and smiles, the corners of his eyes crinkling. "Can I help you with anything, ma'am?"

"Just some information," I start. I lick my dry lips and continue. "On the process for claiming a big prize."

Shoving my hands into the pockets of my jeans, I smile brightly.

If I thought the man was cheerful before, this time he almost knocks over his chair as he stands up and leans over the counter full of excitement. "Oh? You hit the jackpot?"

I swallow hard. "No... I just... I'm curious, that's all."

His smile fades. "Well, all wins over five hundred dollars need to be claimed in person because they require paperwork and sometimes publicity."

"Publicity?" I echo, my stomach dropping. I don't know what I expected coming here. All the information I'm asking him is right on the website. What's the point of torturing myself?

"Oh yes." The man rubs his chin. "In fact, someone recently hit it big. Nine hundred grand. Everyone's been dying to know who it is, and if it's someone from Stoneview."

"Wow," I say. My mouth feels like it's filled with cotton. "That's a lot of money."

"Yes, indeed." The man shakes his head. "A life-changing amount. That person will have their name up in lights." He looks up into space as though he's imagining it all happening to him.

"Sounds overwhelming, doesn't it?" I manage a chuckle.

"Sure does. But also exciting." He narrows his eyes at me. "You seem—"

"Curious?" I say quickly. "Yeah, but I don't play the lottery. Just asking for a friend, that's all."

"Of course." He doesn't seem completely convinced, but he lets it go. "Well, if your friend needs any help, she can come by or give us a call anytime."

"Thank you." I take a few steps back and walk out quickly.

Outside, I blink in the harsh sunlight before fumbling inside my purse for my keys. Back in my car, I slide behind the wheel and lean against the headrest.

*Publicity.* The thought of my name and face plastered across the papers, online and everywhere makes me feel suffocated. I roll down the window and take several deep breaths before I drive.

I really don't want to take this away from Mark, the opportunity to watch him come home without our debt weighing heavy on his shoulders. And I know one day this money could be desperately needed for Jason. It might even be lifesaving if for some reason he needs specialist help or treatment. But if I take it, I would be ripping apart the fabric of the life I have carefully stitched together. I would be revealing every scar, unveiling every secret I have fought so hard to hide. Most importantly, it could seriously harm my son.

I find driving quite soothing, so I meander around, listening to the hum of the engine. When I finally get home, I'm surprised to find Mark's car parked in the driveway when I expected him to be home much later. As I make my way to the front door, my stomach starts to twist. Now I have to feed him even more lies even though I hate myself for it.

The moment I enter the house, the smell of cooked food greets me.

"Hey, beautiful," he says appearing in the hall, his arms open for me to walk into.

"Hey, you." I lean into his body. "I didn't know you were going to come home so soon."

"It's a surprise, that's why I canceled our dinner plans. I wanted to make us something special myself. Come and sit down. Food will be ready soon."

When I enter the dining room, I notice that there are not only two plates on the table, but five. My heart sinks. I'm an introvert, and often prefer my own company, but Mark is the opposite and loves to host.

"Is someone joining us?"

He rests his hands on my shoulders and kisses me. "We were both so excited that we forgot today is Friday. Family dinner, remember? Since we didn't celebrate fourth of July as a family, we should make up for it, you know? Kind of our own belated celebration. Everyone should be here any moment."

When Jason moved out of our house, Mark was afraid we might drift apart as a family and implemented FFDs—Friday Family Dinners. As much as I love spending time with my husband and my son, Sarah is family too and she's always invited. Due to everyone's varied schedules, we're not always able to make our weekly tradition happen and while this may disappoint Mark, for me it's a relief when I don't have to pretend that I like Sarah just to keep the peace.

I force a smile. "You're right. That's lovely."

Mark doesn't notice my discomfort as he makes trips to and from the kitchen, bringing in plates of salads, meats, garlic breads and so much more food.

"Don't tell me you cooked all that. I mean, I know you can be quite the chef but—"

"No way," he chuckles. "I made a few things but I also ordered in. Now that our luck has changed, we might as well live a little, don't you think?"

There's another twist in my chest, but I hide pain well. I always have. "I guess so. Do you need help?" I desperately need something to do with my shaking hands.

"No, I've got it. You just sit there and relax." As he passes me, he plants a kiss on the top of my head.

Finally, all the food is on the table and Mark is sitting in the chair next to me. With a grin on his face, he reaches for my hand. "Have you told Sarah or Jason yet, about the money?"

I shake my head. "Not yet."

"I think tonight will be a good night to tell them, don't you think? They'll be so excited and happy for us."

"Excuse me," I murmur as I walk out of the dining room. In the bathroom, I slump against the wall tiles before I cool myself down with a hand towel drenched in water.

Then I open the door to find Mark standing in front of me. "Honey, you look upset. What's wrong? Did something happen?"

"Baby, I'm so sorry. I didn't know how to tell you." Instead of looking into his eyes, I focus on a spot past his shoulders. "I lost the lottery ticket."

## NINE

The winning lottery ticket, our escape route from financial ruin, is gone. At least that's what I made Mark believe, just to buy myself some more time.

He stands there, his mouth slightly open, unable to process what I've just told him. I watch as his eyes cloud with shock and disappointment. "It's okay," he finally says, his voice slightly husky. "After dinner, we'll look for it. If it's in the house, we'll find it together."

"There's no point, Mark," I say, my voice breaking. "I've already looked everywhere."

He steps closer, determination replacing the initial shock. "It has to be somewhere, right?"

I swallow hard, hating myself for what I'm about to say. "It might not be in the house," I admit, feeling a fresh wave of shame. "I took it to work."

Mark's face goes pale, his lips parting as if to say something, but he stops himself.

Tears well up in my eyes. "I'm so sorry."

He takes a deep breath and, noticing my distress, pulls me into a hug, his strong arms encircling me just as the doorbell rings, followed by the sound of a key turning in the lock. Sarah.

Mark pulls away and heads toward the front door, his shoulders slumped. I slip back into the restroom, needing a moment to compose myself, to wash away the tears. The woman loathes me, and I can't let her see me in this state.

I splash cold water on my face, willing myself to snap out of it. I think of Jason. He'll be here tonight, at least I can find some solace in that. I miss him so much since he moved out. Taking a deep breath, I leave the restroom and head into the dining room.

One of Sarah's hands is holding a bottle of red wine and the other is on Mark's arm.

"Are you okay, Mark? You look upset." I have never doubted for a moment that she loves her brother, just as I've never doubted that she hates me.

He nods. "I'm fine. Just excited for our dinner together as a family."

"So am I." She flashes him a smile before turning to me and handing over the bottle of wine.

"Thanks." I pass the wine to Mark without hesitation, because the sight of alcohol alone makes my stomach churn.

"Drew, how are you? You look a little... tired." Sarah steps forward and offers me a hug, the kind that might seem warm to anyone watching.

"No, I'm okay, Sarah. Thanks." I pull away before she does.

She continues to hold my gaze with a thin smile. Just yesterday, she made it clear that she thinks I'm not good enough for her brother. Now, in front of him, she's pretending to be happy to see me.

The sound of the front door opening again signals Jason's arrival. Relief washes over me until I see Lori trailing behind him and I remember the rumors I heard about her at the salon. But I greet her politely, then pull Jason into a long hug. When I finally let go, he goes to hug Mark, the interaction polite.

They've never been close, something I've always regretted but could never force. Jason never wanted me to marry Mark, and the underlying friction has lingered ever since.

We settle around the dinner table, the atmosphere strained. Lori and Jason have moved their chairs close to each other and he has his arm around her shoulders. As we start eating, Mark and Sarah discuss Shoreline and how it's struggling. Seeing the stress etched into his features, I hate myself even more.

"I'm so tired of fighting for the company to stay above water," Mark concludes with an exhausted sigh.

"You do look tired," Sarah says, concern creeping into her voice. "You need a break, Mark. When was the last time you even went on vacation?" Her eyes suddenly light up. "I'm planning a skiing trip around Christmas or New Year's. Maybe you should come." She turns to look at me. "Have you ever skied before, Drew?"

I open my mouth, then I sense Jason's eyes on me. "No, I haven't," I manage.

Jason drops his fork onto his plate with a loud clatter. My heart pounds, and I feel my face flush as I glance at him nervously. His jaw is tight, his expression strained. Panic rises in my chest and I feel something blocking my throat.

Sarah's eyes flick between me and Jason.

"I'm... I'm just not a fan of snow," I stammer, forcing a small smile to cover my discomfort.

"That's a shame." Sarah twirls her wine glass. "You never took Jason as a small child to the snow? It's such a beautiful sport. He would've loved it."

Before I can respond, Lori jumps in. "Maybe you and I should go skiing sometime, Jason. I could teach you. It's really fun."

Jason glances at me before muttering, "Maybe." He pushes his chair back abruptly, the legs scraping. "Excuse me, I'll be right back."

As he walks away, I struggle to keep my emotions under control and my hands grip my napkin.

I'm relieved when Mark shifts the conversation, asking Sarah about her work at the *Gazette*. "Finding any big stories lately, sis?"

Sarah takes a sip of wine and shrugs. "The paper's also struggling, but I'm hoping to find a story that will turn things around."

Lori's eyes light up. "I was offered a job at the *Gazette*. I start next week."

Jason, walking back into the room, beams with pride and kisses her on the cheek before he sits back down, but Sarah's expression darkens. "Who gave you the job?" she asks.

"Sam Marino," Lori replies, grinning like a little girl.

Sarah takes another gulp of wine, draining her glass before refilling it again. "I'm a little surprised. You need education and experience to be a reporter."

Lori's smile falters, then she lifts her chin up. "It's an admin job, but I hope to work my way up."

"Sure, but it's not that simple, love." Sarah's tone is icy as she pierces a piece of lettuce as if it did something to upset her.

Mark changes the subject again, asking Jason about his job. As usual, Jason's answers are vague, his responses clipped, and I can see Mark's frustration growing. Sarah just sits there with a sour expression on her face.

The stilted conversations continue as we eat, and the clinking of cutlery fills the awkward silences.

When the plates are finally empty, I get up quickly, needing an excuse to escape the table. "Jason, sweetheart, can you help me with the dishes?"

He nods, and we retreat to the kitchen. When we're alone, I broach the topic that's been gnawing at me. "I heard something today, about Lori. Someone saw her with her ex-boyfriend at Honeywood."

Jason's face hardens. "Mom, I know you don't like her, and you keep finding every reason for us not to be together. But I'm tired of you trying to control my life. Just stop."

I inhale sharply. Where's all this coming from? I'm not used to him speaking to me that way.

"I'm just worried about you, baby. I don't want you to get hurt."

He slams a dish into the sink. "You need to trust me."

"I'm sorry," I whisper, but he's already walking out of the kitchen.

I follow him back into the dining room, where he grabs Lori's hand. "We need to go."

Mark looks up, concern etched on his face. "What happened?" he asks, but Jason and Lori have already left the room.

"Nothing," I say and return to the kitchen, resuming my task.

The dishes clatter in the sink and a few minutes later, Mark and Sarah appear in the doorway, offering to help.

"No, thank you," I say, my voice tight. "I can handle it."

They exchange a look but leave me to my thoughts. When they're gone, I clutch the edge of the sink and bite my lower lip.

I am honestly terrified of losing my son over this girl, terrified of him losing himself again. The tears I've been holding back spill over and I let them fall, hoping no one walks in.

When I finally compose myself, I continue with the washing-up. Then I dry my hands and go back to check if there are more dishes to bring in. As I approach the door, I overhear Mark and Sarah.

"The ticket is gone," Mark says heavily. "She said she lost it."

"You've got to be kidding me," Sarah exclaims. "You're telling me she won nine hundred thousand dollars, and she immediately lost the ticket? How is that even possible?" She lowers her voice. "Mark, I know you trust your wife, but are you sure she really lost it?"

"What are you talking about?" Mark sounds incredulous. "Of course she did."

"It just seems so unlikely, Mark. What if she didn't lose it? What if she kept it for herself and her son?"

# TEN

What do I do now? I can hardly just go in and sit with them at the dining table as if nothing happened. I open the door wider, walk in, and grab my phone. Then I meet Mark's gaze. "I'm not feeling well. I hope you don't mind me going to bed early."

"What's wrong, babe?" he asks.

"Oh, it's nothing, just a headache. I need to lie down."

Mark's eyes soften, but I notice something different in them. Something has shifted. "All right. Get some rest. I'll be right up."

After saying goodnight, I walk away, feeling Sarah's eyes on my back. Inside the bedroom, I close the door and lean against it, pulling in deep breaths.

All I really want to do is drop into bed, but first I lift the mattress and pull out the lottery ticket. Then I head to the library, which needs to be organized; books are still in piles on the floor.

My eyes scan the room until they land on a framed photo of a beautiful beach at sunset. After making sure the door is locked, I remove the frame from the wall and pry open the back before slipping the ticket inside. I secure the frame back in place, praying with all my heart that no one will find it there.

Back in the bedroom, I lie in bed for what feels like an eternity before I hear the front door close, and soon after, Mark comes in, his expression distracted. He moves around the room in silence, changing into his boxer shorts and t-shirt.

"Why did you tell her?" I ask, rolling over to face him as he settles into bed beside me.

"Tell who what?" He fluffs his pillow and plops back onto it.

"Why did you tell Sarah about the ticket?"

He falls silent for a long while, then reaches under the covers to take my hand. "Honey, Sarah is family. Maybe try getting to know her better?"

I move my hand away from his. "You know she doesn't like me."

"You always say that. But it's not true, she's just missing Melody. You know they were best friends."

"Exactly. That's why she'll never accept me."

Sarah made it very clear from day one that she doesn't want me here. A few days after our wedding, she whispered in my ear:

*"He will never love you as much as he loved her."*

Those words haunt me every single day, cutting deeply into my heart.

"I still don't understand why you had to tell her about the ticket," I say. "It's already lost, so what's the point?"

"I don't know," he replies with a sigh and pulls away from me. "It just came out, I guess. If I hurt your feelings, I'm sorry. Let's just get some sleep."

He leans over and kisses my forehead before turning away. He does this when he's upset, instead of kissing me on the lips.

Mark is completely blind and trusting when it comes to Sarah, always making excuses for her behavior because she was deeply affected by their parents' death when she was still in high school. As the older brother, he feels responsible and will do anything to support her. But this is not just about Sarah. He's understandably struggling to forgive me for losing a ticket that could have changed our lives forever.

I lie in bed with my eyes open, staring at the dark ceiling while listening to Mark snoring softly beside me. Suddenly I pull myself out of bed. If Sarah suspects I'm hiding the ticket, I need to hide it more carefully.

I go and fetch it then make my way to the garage, facing another mountain of boxes that have not been unpacked. One of them is labeled "Jason's Childhood Stuff." I bring it down and open it. There are all kinds of things in there, things I never want to forget, that remind me of when my grown-up son was a little boy with chubby cheeks and rolls on his legs. Toys, favorite blankets, and so many more sentimental items. These are the things I lean on when I don't recognize the boy I gave birth to.

I reach all the way to the bottom until I find what I'm looking for: a cream and brown teddy bear that Dean gave Jason the day he was born. Jason refused to part with it until the age of eleven, when he thought of himself as too grown-up for stuffed animals.

I unzip the little blue and white striped coat. Then I turn it on its back, where there is a zip that starts at the nape of the neck and ends just below the middle of the back. Jason used to hide little things in here, sweets and coins, shells he found at the beach. I slip the ticket inside, burying it deep within the fluff before zipping the bear back up. There's no way anyone will think to look there, I tell myself as I dress the bear back in its little coat before returning it to the box.

The soft light barely illuminates the cluttered space filled with the boxes we haven't unpacked since moving in. My eyes land on a stack of Melody's boxes in the corner. I've never gone through her things before, except to pack away the ones that were inside my office. But tonight, something pulls me toward them.

I walk over to the stack and pull down one of the boxes. Inside are various keepsakes, pieces of her life with Mark. Photos, letters, little trinkets from their life together. I dig deeper, unable to stop myself even though it feels wrong. Then, at the bottom, something catches my eye—a high school yearbook. I pause for a moment, my hand hovering over it. I hadn't expected that. I open it up and flip through the pages.

And that's when I see it.

On the page showing Melody's graduating class, there's a group photo. I blink in surprise. Melody is there, smiling next to someone else who makes me take a sharp inhale. It's Tia, with her hair in thin braids, leaning into Melody like they were close friends.

What the hell?

I stare at the photo, my mind spinning. Tia has never mentioned she knew Melody. Not once.

I quickly close the yearbook and shove it back into the box. My heart pounds in my chest as I try to process what I just saw. Why didn't she ever tell me?

Suddenly, the garage door opens, and I nearly jump out of my skin. Mark is standing in the doorway, rubbing his eyes. He frowns as he comes closer. "It's the middle of the night, Drew. What are you doing in the garage?" He smooths my hair back gently.

"I couldn't sleep. Thought I'd go through some old memory boxes of Jason's things as a distraction. I feel so awful about the ticket."

"Come on, sweetheart," he says softly. "I'll make us some tea."

I follow him inside, leaving the boxes—and the photo of Melody and Tia—behind. I watch Mark boil water and prepare our peppermint tea. The normalcy of it all feels surreal. As he sets the cups down on the kitchen table, I can't hold back any longer.

"Mark," I ask casually, "did Tia and Melody know each other?"

He looks up, surprised, but not overly so. "Yeah, they were friends in high school. Why?"

I swallow hard. "No reason, I just heard something today and it made me curious. Why didn't you tell me that they were friends?"

Mark shrugs. "It's not important, and I try not to bring Melody up around you. I don't want to upset you."

I nod slowly, but my mind is racing. Why didn't *Tia* ever tell me about Melody?

# ELEVEN

As I sip my coffee on Monday morning—four days since I found the ticket—I go through the pile of mail that has been sitting on the kitchen counter for days. The usual bills, a couple of grocery store flyers, and something from the bank that I can't be bothered with right now.

I pick up an envelope from the pile. There's no return address, but it looks like the sort of thing that could be from the water company or the electric, probably something overdue. I tear it open without a second thought, already preparing myself for another reminder that we're skating on thin ice.

But instead of a bill, my eyes land on something that doesn't make sense, a note from St. Michael's Parish—which is a few blocks from where we live—thanking Mark for a one-thousand-dollar donation.

I blink and the paper flutters in my hand as I scan it again, my mind scrambling to connect the dots. Mark donated one thousand dollars? To a *church*?

I set my coffee down. Mark has never been religious. Not once in our time together has he even mentioned anything about a church, let alone wanting to make a massive donation like this.

And one thousand dollars? We just don't have that kind of money to spare, not with all the bills we have hanging over us.

It's not like Melody had any connection to a church, either. From what I know, her ashes were scattered over the ocean.

Nothing about this makes any sense.

I flip the note over, hoping there's some explanation. But there's nothing. Just a thank you note for a major donation to a place he's never mentioned, with money we don't have.

I should ask him. I should confront him, right now. He's already left for work, but I could call him. My throat tightens, and I just... I can't. Not yet. It's too much on top of everything else. The lie I told him about the lottery ticket is still fresh on my lips, my guilt simmering inside me. It would be a bit rich of me to accuse him, given all the secrets I'm hiding.

I tuck the note back into the envelope and file it away in my mind, to be dealt with later. Gulping down my coffee, and ignoring my regular breakfast of granola and fruit with Greek yogurt, I get ready to go for my jog and hope it will bring me some clarity.

As usual, I stop by Sip & Snack to see Jason. The café is busy, so he just hands me my coffee, kisses me on the cheek, and tells me he doesn't have time to chat, just like he did the past few days. I wait a few more minutes, hoping he'll take a short break, and our eyes meet occasionally across the room.

I know he's avoiding me, after what I said about his girl-friend. Finally, feeling defeated, I leave the café and head back outside. I jog for another thirty minutes and before returning home, I make my usual stop at the memorial, where I kneel down and start tidying up, removing wilted flowers and straight-ening the ones that are still fresh.

It's always messy here, with the wind constantly shifting the offerings left by visitors. But I can't stand to see it like that; it feels disrespectful. As I gather the scattered petals and arrange them neatly in a pile, something cool and smooth touches my fingers. Looking down, I see it, a white ski helmet nestled among the floral tributes. It's covered in signatures and handwritten messages in colorful markers.

One message, written in bright-red ink, catches the light and draws my eye. The words, all in small caps, stand out against the white surface.

*I'M SO SORRY FOR WHAT HAPPENED. I WISH I COULD*
*TURN BACK TIME AND YOU'D STILL BE HERE.*

I scan the words, searching for a name, an initial, anything that might tell me who wrote it. But there's nothing.

Other notes surround it, written in cheerful pinks, greens, and purples:

*You'll always be our shining star! Miss you forever! Life won't*
*be the same without you.*

Out of habit, I take a photo of the memorial, and another with the helmet zoomed in.

Then I stand, my knees suddenly weak, and stumble back a few steps. My eyes are glued to the helmet as if it might come to life and drag me back to the past.

The longer I stare at it, the more my pulse quickens, a cold sweat breaking out across my forehead. My breath becomes shallow, and before I know it, I'm running. I run from the memorial, from the helmet, from the memories.

The wind roars in my ears, but it's overpowered by the thumping of my heart and the rushing of blood in my head.

It feels as though I'm being hunted. Like someone is coming for me. Someone who knows what I did.

# TWELVE



I walk through the front door, the heating a relief after the chilly breeze this late December afternoon. Our house is modest but welcoming, tucked at the end of a quiet street in a suburban neighborhood in Mapleford, Colorado. It's the kind of house we dreamed of before we moved in, with white shutters and a brick facade that catches the evening light just right. Inside, it's always been warm and inviting.

I throw off my shoes and walk in the direction of the living room, already visualizing myself sinking into the beige over-stuffed couch, with its quilted throw draped casually over the back. But as I step into the room, my breath catches in my throat.

Dean, who should be at work now, is sitting on the couch, his broad shoulders hunched forward, hands clasped tightly together. His sandy-blond hair is messy, like he's run his hands through it a thousand times, and his face—God, his face. When he looks up at me, his blue eyes are hollow, vacant, staring back at me. His normally cheerful expression has been replaced by an unfamiliar, hard mask.

But it's the bottle on the coffee table that steals my attention. A bottle of gin. My eyes lock onto it, and suddenly, my entire body freezes. I can't look away. It's like the air has been sucked out of the room, and all that's left is me and that damn bottle. The label glints under the low lamplight.

My pulse thunders in my ears, my knees weaken, and for a second, I think I might collapse. In my mind there's a jumble of images—years of watching my father, his shaking hands as he poured drink after drink, his glassy eyes, the shouting, the smell of liquor. That same bottle, night after night, destroying everything.

No. Not again.

I step forward, trying to drag my gaze away, but it's glued there, fixed on the unopened gin. Every nerve in my body is screaming to get rid of it, to throw it across the room, but I can't move.

Why is it here?

I force myself to sit next to Dean on the couch. I'm grateful Jason isn't home. He's out bowling with friends, and for that, I silently thank God. He shouldn't see this. Not Dean like this. Not the bottle and certainly not me, barely holding it together.

The silence between us feels heavy, like something has shattered, and the pieces are spread out across the room. My gaze drifts to the mantel, where Jason's soccer trophies are scattered, and family photos from our trips to the mountains hang on the wall above it.

I glance at Dean again. Something is terribly wrong.

Finally, he speaks, his voice hoarse. "I've been suspended."

The words drop like stones, sinking deep into my chest. He keeps his gaze down, not looking at me, his fingers tightening into fists on his lap. "There's an investigation. Internal Affairs. I

—" He stops, clenching his jaw, his body rigid like he's holding himself together by sheer force of will.

I frown at him. "What happened?"

Dean's lips press into a thin line. "I shot someone... by mistake." His voice cracks. "A criminal. He'd raped a woman. I thought he was reaching for a weapon, but—" He stops again, his words faltering as if he can't bear to say the rest out loud.

My mouth goes dry. The air around us feels heavy, suffocating. "Was it really a mistake?" I ask, even though I already know the answer. I can see it in his eyes. There's something raw and unspoken there.

Three years ago, someone raped Dean's sister and got away with it. Dean has never let it go.

He rakes a hand through his hair again, eyes darting toward the bottle, then away. "I don't want to go to prison," he says softly, his voice breaking. "I can't."

I don't know what to say. My mind is torn between the man I love sitting next to me and the horrifying realization of what he's done. What it means. And yet, I can't let myself fall apart. Not now. Not when he's looking at me like I'm the only thing keeping him from sinking into the abyss.

"You won't," I manage to say. "They'll clear your name. They'll see it was self-defense." My voice wavers, but I cling to the hope that maybe, just maybe, I'm right.

He doesn't respond. He just stares at the floor.

My eyes flicker back to the bottle on the table, and I reach for it. "This isn't the answer," I say, my voice firmer now. "We're not doing this, Dean. You're not doing this."

Dean doesn't move as I stand, carrying the bottle with me. I don't know what else to do. I want to cry, but the tears won't come. I walk to the kitchen, feeling his eyes follow me, but I don't turn around. I set it on the counter and stare at it for a long time, my heart pounding in my chest, my breaths shallow.

I won't let it happen again.

Maybe I can fix this. Maybe if we just get away from here, from everything, he'll realize there are other ways to cope. "Let's go to the cabin," I say when I return to the living room, where I find my husband staring at the space where the bottle was only a moment ago. "Christmas is in a week. We'll spend it there. Just the three of us. Jason loves it. The mountains, the skiing... it'll give us some peace." I try to sound hopeful, but the words feel fragile, like they might break apart in the air before reaching his ears.

Dean nods slowly, staring down at his knees.

The cabin is only an hour's drive away, nestled high in the Colorado Rockies, surrounded by towering pines and endless snow. It's where we've spent so many winters, skiing down the slopes and sipping cocoa by the fire, Jason laughing as he made snow angels.

But now... now, I'm not sure if even the mountains can save us.

When I get back to the kitchen to get dinner started, my eyes fall on the bottle of alcohol again, and the memories crash over me like a wave. The smell of alcohol, the shouting, the fear. The years I spent watching it tear my family apart.

Not again.

I won't let alcohol destroy my life. Not this time. I'll do whatever it takes to keep it out.

# THIRTEEN

Present Day

I jump into the shower, telling myself over and over again that the helmet I saw at the memorial meant nothing. The woman who died must have been passionate about skiing. That must be it. This has nothing to do with me.

As I dry myself off, I glance out the bedroom window toward the street.

There's someone there. They're leaving our driveway and heading down the street, dressed in a beige and black mini dress with black stilettos, slicked-back dark hair glistening in the light. It's Sarah.

She was in the house while I was in the shower, must have been here when I got back from my jog, and I didn't even know it.

Anger scorches through my veins, and I get dressed quickly and leave the house. When I arrive at Sarah's white townhouse, surrounded by cream roses, I ring the bell and then follow up with knocking on the door so hard my knuckles ache.

After the fifth knock, the door swings open and she's standing there, looking all innocent.

"What are you doing here?"

I fold my arms across my chest. "I came to ask what you were doing at our house just now."

Her tinkling laughter topples my confidence. "Your house?" She raises an eyebrow and shakes her head. "That's Mark's house. Mark and Melody bought it together."

"Mark and I are married now. You can't just show up whenever you like just because you have a key, Sarah."

"Melody gave me that key before you were even in the picture. She told me I could come and go whenever I like. If you think you're going to keep me from coming to my brother's house, you're wrong."

"Sarah, that's not what I'm saying. I'm just... What were you doing there?"

I think I know very well what she was doing there.

"There were a few things I needed from the garage that belonged to Melody, since you threw out all her personal belongings."

"What things?"

"Just a few memories." She leans against the doorframe. "Now if you would excuse me, I have a lot to do." With that, she closes the door, leaving me standing outside.


I'm fuming the entire morning at work. Tia notices my distress and asks—no, forces—me to have coffee with her during our lunchbreak so we can talk about it.

As we settle at a table in Honeywood, she goes right out and asks me what's going on.

"You are not yourself today. What happened?"

I shrug. "Sarah happened."

"What did she do this time?" she asks, but before we

continue our conversation, Judy, the waitress, comes over to take our orders.

As usual, Tia has a hard time choosing what hot beverage to order, and it doesn't help that Honeywood has quite a selection of teas, coffees, hot chocolates, and more unusual drinks like lavender lattes and turmeric tonics. Tia has to be the most indecisive person I've ever met, and her parents most likely played a role in that. The fact that she dropped her law career greatly disappointed them. They are both successful lawyers, and so is her brother. Even though she's a grown woman and can make her own decisions, they went so far as to cut ties with her following her decision. It's clear to me that she now lives her life afraid to make mistakes and avoids making decisions altogether.

Now, she keeps going back and forth between a turmeric tonic and a simple chai latte, with Judy waiting patiently, holding her little notepad.

"Oh, I don't know," Tia says finally, chewing her lower lip. "What's the best one?" she asks Judy.

"Well," Judy replies, a knowing smile on her lips because we come here often enough for her to know about Tia's little game of indecision, "both are quite popular, but the chai latte is my favorite."

"All right, I'll take your word for it."

"And how about you?" Judy turns to me, her pen poised over the notepad.

"A cappuccino with an extra shot of espresso, thanks," I say, not even bothering to look at the menu.

Judy nods, jots it down, and shuffles away. As soon as she's gone, I rest both hands on the table, one on top of the other. "Back to Sarah. Well, she came over again uninvited and didn't even bother to let me know she was there. I just saw her leaving."

"And where were you?"

"I was in the shower."

"Did she tell you why she came?"

"Does she need a reason? Apparently, she needed something of Melody's." I press the palm of my hand to my aching forehead briefly. "I'm so tired of that woman."

"Then you need to stand your ground." Tia grips both my hands and looks me straight in the eyes. "You let her walk all over you."

"I know. It's just that Mark is so protective of her."

"Try talking to him again. Make him understand."

"I really don't want to be the person standing between him and his sister." Holding Tia's gaze, I decide to bring up the elephant in the room. "Hey, there's something I've been meaning to ask you, about Melody. I came across an old yearbook in the garage and I saw a photo of you and her together."

Tia blinks in surprise. "Oh, that." She rubs the back of her neck. "Yeah, we went to high school together. We were friends for a while."

I raise an eyebrow. "You never mentioned it."

She shrugs. "I didn't want to make you feel uncomfortable or like you were less than her, Drew. I became your friend because I like you, that's all."

Despite her reassurance, I can't help but feel uneasy. "I appreciate that. But it's a little strange, you know? Sharing a friend with Mark's late wife."

Tia reaches across the table and squeezes my hand. "I get that. And I'm sorry I didn't tell you sooner. It just felt complicated."

"I understand. And I'm really sorry for your loss. Even if you were only friends in school, it must have been hard to lose Melody."

Tia's expression darkens. "Thanks. I just wish justice could be done, you know? That they could find the person that killed her." She frowns, then glances away. "I'm surprised Mark was never a suspect, honestly. I know he's your husband, but sometimes I wonder if—"

"Mark had nothing to do with it!" I snap. "Why do you even think he would do something like that to his wife? He loved her so much."

Tia murmurs something under her breath.

"Sorry, I didn't catch that. What did you just say?" A bitter taste touches the back of my throat.

"Nothing. It doesn't matter. Mark is your husband, and I promised not to meddle, so I'm sorry for bringing it up." She quickly averts her eyes. "But I'm just wondering if there's something he kept from the police, if he has secrets."

"No, he doesn't." I take a deep breath, wishing there wasn't a tiny part of me that doubts my words. I remember the donation Mark made to that church, and my shoulders tense up.

"So, how are things with the house?" Tia asks, changing the subject as she nods to thank Judy for placing our drinks on the table. "Are you still worried you are about to lose it?"

I stare into my cappuccino. It's a little hard to have a normal conversation after what she's just insinuated, but I pretend to be fine. "It doesn't look good, honestly. We really might end up moving in with Sarah, and that would be torture for me."

"You know what? Maybe a miracle will happen, and you won't need to. Let's think positively!"

She has no idea how much I know that to be true, that miracles can happen. Finding that lottery ticket on the bench was one of them. But why would God send that to me if He knew there was no way I could claim the prize? It must have been meant for somebody else, and I robbed them of it. We talk about other things and when it comes time to pay and Tia opens her wallet, my eyes are immediately drawn to something familiar.

There's a red slip of paper sticking out from between the notes and receipts—a lottery ticket, or several actually judging from the thickness.

"I didn't know you play the lottery, Tia?" I say.

She shrugs, sliding out a crisp note to settle our bill. "Yeah, it's a habit I picked up recently. Someone inspired me to try my luck, and it's actually kind of fun." She zips her wallet shut again and tucks it into her purse.

We spend a little more time chatting, then she asks if I can come over to her apartment this coming Saturday to water her plants while she's away for a few days with Edward, her fiancé of three whole years.

"Eddy is a judge at a dance competition in Boca Raton, and until this morning I wasn't sure whether I'd be accompanying him."

One of Tia's passions is dancing, and she and Edward met when she attended one of his salsa classes, four years ago. He's the owner of Echo Dance, a studio here in Stoneview.

I drain my cup. "No problem, I'd be happy to take care of your babies." Tia loves her plants and her apartment almost resembles an indoor forest. "But I refuse to talk to them like you do."

She chuckles. "Thank you. You're the best." She gets to her feet, gives me a kiss on the cheek and says goodbye. She's done for the day at the salon and she and Edward are already heading out of town within the hour.

Before I return to work, I stop by Cedar Park and spot Martin on his usual worn-out bench, playing his harmonica. The good thing about him is that we can be around each other in silence and not have to speak, yet somehow it feels like we've had the best conversation. I put some coins into his bowl, but he refuses them, handing them back to me. Perhaps noticing that I need something to soothe me, he invites me to sit down next to him, and he just plays music.

After a while, he stops playing and looks over at me with a gentle smile. "You seem troubled today, Drew. What's on your mind?"

My shoulders start relaxing from just being near him. "It's Sarah, my sister-in-law. She was at the house this morning while I was in the shower. She let herself in without saying a word to me. She keeps acting like it's her house, not ours. It's driving me crazy."

Martin places his harmonica on his lap and leans back on the bench. "Family can be tough, especially when there's unresolved grief. Sounds like she hasn't moved on from Melody's passing. Losing someone close changes people. They hold on to anything that reminds them of the person they lost. The house, the memories, even the people."

I consider his words, my anger softening slightly. "I know. But she's really pushing boundaries, trying to make me feel like an outsider in my own home."

Martin's eyes scan the park thoughtfully. "Sometimes, people act out when they feel threatened or displaced. It's not always about you. It's about their own sense of loss and confusion."

"That's true," I admit, rubbing my temples. "But it's so hard to deal with her when she keeps coming into our space like that. It makes me feel powerless." I pat Martin's arm and get to my feet. "I should get back to work."

As I start to walk away, Martin's voice stops me. "Oh, and Drew..."

I turn back, eyebrows raised.

"Just before you got here, I saw someone who looked a lot like her, your sister-in-law. I remember the face from that article she wrote, the one you showed me in the paper once. There was something a bit strange about her."

"What do you mean?"

Martin looks uncertain, rubbing the back of his neck. "She was walking along that path, talking on the phone, and she seemed pretty agitated, you know? She was begging someone, telling them not to tell anyone. That she'd send them the money as soon as she can. I couldn't be sure, but I thought it was her. Anyway, maybe she's been giving you a hard time because she's dealing with some issues of her own. Sometimes people take out their frustrations on those who are closest to them. That doesn't make it right, but it could be a reason."

I head back to the salon, wondering what could be going on with Sarah, and exchange a few words with my colleagues. It's when I walk to the back to check the schedule that Marlene calls out my name.

"You just missed your sister-in-law, making an appointment for later in the month. Weird that she didn't just call."

I cut hair, chat, smile, doing my best to push Sarah out of my mind. When I return to my station after grabbing a coffee for my latest client, I find him holding up a photo.

"This fell from your apron pocket."

I take the photo from him and my heart stops. It's a picture of me, Jason, and Dean, standing in the snow, dressed in ski gear, beaming at the camera.

How did this get here? I haven't seen it since Dean died.

"Thanks." I stuff the photo into my apron pocket. Now I know why Sarah was here. My apron was hanging on the back of my station while I was out, and Sarah would have known it was mine. What has she found out about me?

I excuse myself hurriedly, practically sprinting toward the ladies' room. Once inside, I lock the door behind me and lean against the sink, gasping for air.

I pull the photo out again, staring at the faces in the picture. Dean's smile, my own, the bright sun reflecting off the snow. It was such a perfect day, one of those rare, precious moments. We had no idea what was about to happen, that life would never be the same again.

I'm scrambling for another explanation. I've been

unpacking old things recently and my mind has been all over the place. It's possible that it slipped out and got mixed up with the things I carry around with me, and I didn't notice. That has to be it, right?

I can't bear the alternative, that Sarah knows I have a secret.

Although, given what Martin overheard, it sounds like I am not the only one.

# FOURTEEN



The cabin is nestled deep in the woods of Aspen Ridge, our little haven in the Colorado mountains. It's the kind of place you'd see on a postcard, a small mountain village where the outside world slips away.

With its charming, snow-covered streets and twinkling Christmas lights, Aspen Ridge feels magical this time of year. Every house, every shop is draped in holiday decorations, with wreaths on doors, strings of lights twinkling in the snow, and garlands hanging from windowsills. The air smells of pine, cold, and chimney smoke. It's everything I love about winter, my favorite season.

When we walked into our cabin yesterday, it was like stepping into a Christmas movie. Roger and Lily, the couple we rent it from every year—for peanuts because they're friends of Dean —had lined the mantel with LED candles, sprigs of holly and pinecones. There's a tree in the corner, decorated with red and gold baubles and glowing white lights. Now the fire is crackling gently in the hearth, spitting out sparks and sending shadows dancing along the wood-paneled walls. Everything about this place is perfect, as it always is.

Everything except us.

I stand by the large kitchen window, staring out at the view I love so much. The snow-covered peaks of the Silvercrest Mountains stand tall in the distance, their jagged edges softened by the last light of the day. The sky is painted with hues of pink, orange, and purple as the sun dips below the horizon. I'm busy taking photos of it, like I did last year before I sold a sunset shot for more than I ever imagined. The cold air seeps in through the open window, biting at my skin as the camera clicks again, and again, and finally I stop and shut the window.

Dean's out for a walk, clearing his head, or at least that's what he told me, and Jason is upstairs in his room, absorbed in the world of his video games. The cabin is small enough for me to hear the distant sounds of gunfire and explosions, the rhythmic clicking of buttons, and his exclamations and mutters when something doesn't go as planned. The occasional burst of laughter tugs at something inside me. Jason loves it here. We all do. It's why I suggested we spend Christmas here, away from everything.

I walk to the kettle and brew myself a cup of chamomile tea. The warmth feels good as I wrap my cold fingers around the mug and carry it back to the living room, where the fire is roaring now, filling the space with its heat.

I sink into the couch, pulling one of the thick blankets over me, trying to let the warmth of the cabin soothe me. But I can't stop thinking about Dean.

The investigation is weighing on him. I can see it in everything he does, or doesn't do. He's barely been eating, barely sleeping, and every time I ask him about it, he shuts me out. I know he's terrified that the investigation will find him guilty, that they'll decide he really did kill that man in cold blood. I'm terrified too.

I take a sip of tea, letting myself begin to relax for just a moment. When the front door finally creaks open, cold air rushes in, sending a shiver down my spine, but it's not the cold that makes my heart race.

Dean steps inside, snow clinging to his boots, his coat dusted with it, his face flushed—not from the cold, but from something else. He sways slightly as he kicks off his boots and shrugs off his coat, and when his eyes meet mine, I feel like the ground has just dropped out from under me.

The smell hits me next. Alcohol. Faint, but unmistakable. My chest tightens. I set my tea down, afraid I might drop it, as I watch him stumble over to me, his eyes heavy. He's not drunk, but on the verge of it. And that's enough to terrify me. All these years my husband has never touched a drop of alcohol—not once. Not after he heard what it did to my family, what it did to me.

"Have you been drinking?"

He drops onto the couch beside me, his weight sinking the cushions as he leans in and kisses me clumsily. "Stopped at the bar in town," he mumbles, his voice thick. "Just had a few beers with Roger."

I pull back from him, my pulse slamming against my temples. "You went to a bar?" I repeat quietly, trying to keep my voice low so Jason won't hear. But even at that volume, there's anger in my voice, sharp and cutting. "Since when do you go to bars?"

Dean's expression shifts and irritation flickers in his eyes. He straightens up, his voice hardening as he snaps back at me, "I'm a grown man. I'm allowed to have a drink if I want to. Don't worry, I can control myself." His words are blunt, casual.

*I can control myself.*

I remember my father saying exactly that before he transformed into a monster.

FIFTEEN

It's Saturday, and I've decided to clean the house from top to bottom while Mark is busy at the gym. Anything to keep my thoughts from spiraling.

Putting on my headphones, I blast some classical music and start in the living room, where I dust the shelves, feeling the smooth wood beneath my fingers, the heady scent of lemon polish filling the air. The kitchen is the last place I scrub until my fingers and palms feel raw, and every surface is glinting. I wipe down the counters with a clean cloth, then move on to the stainless-steel appliances, polishing them until they shine. By the time I'm done, it's already after lunch, but I can't bring myself to eat. Instead, I head to my library and tackle some of the boxes that still haven't been unpacked.

I roll up my sleeves and begin arranging the books on the shelves, organizing them by color and genre. Classics with their rich leather bindings, modern novels with their bright, bold covers, and the muted tones of historical non-fiction—all find their places. I run my fingers over the titles because I love how the embossed letters feel beneath them.

As I work, I catch the occasional whiff of old paper, a scent that evokes memories of late nights spent reading under the covers or in the living room with my grandma.

This is it. This is my feel-good place, the space I can come to when things get too much. I'm about to believe that too, but then I remember the conversation I had with Sarah in this room, how she reminded me that I don't belong here with Mark. Suddenly, I feel weak at the knees and find myself sinking onto one of the boxes.

She was here again yesterday evening and spent a lot of time talking to him in a hushed voice. Before she left, she put on her usual act, gave me a hug, and wished me a good night. Mark stood by, smiling at both of us, thinking we had made up, and he said as much when we went to bed. Knowing there's nothing I can say to make him see his sister in another light, I said nothing.

Later, as I got ready for bed, I noticed that some items in my closet were out of place. She had been in there, going through my things.

Now, sitting here and looking at all my books, some in piles on the floor and others still in boxes, I find it hard to breathe. I've always suffered from claustrophobia and now my whole life feels like one small box.

Instead of forcing myself to tackle the rest of the boxes, I grab a random self-help book and take it with me to the bedroom, climbing under the covers in the middle of the day.

Forty minutes later, I'm still staring at the same page, the words blurring in front of me, failing to make sense. Soon, my eyes start to grow heavy, and I let my eyelids shut.

When I wake up, it's to the sound of a door slamming somewhere in the house. I sit up in bed, my head pounding, disoriented from the deep nap I hadn't planned on having.

Wondering which door or window had slammed, I drag myself out of bed and tour the house.

In the kitchen, I notice something on the counter I had scrubbed earlier. It glints in the light spilling in from the windows. My eyes narrow and as I move closer, I see it's an earring. I pick it up and stare at it in my palm. After a moment, my breath catches in my throat.

It's a pearl earring with tiny diamonds around it, and it's identical to the ones Melody wore when she married Mark. I scrubbed this counter, and when I left, there was nothing there.

I glance at the back door, and sure enough, it's open. I know I closed it before I went upstairs because Mrs. Leonard's cat tends to sneak in occasionally, and it's hard to find her. Someone opened it, and I can guess who.

This whole thing with Sarah is really getting out of hand. Fuming, I charge out of the house and head straight to her place. But even though her Honda is parked in the drive, and I hear a sound on the other side of the door, she doesn't open it.

"Sarah, I know you're in there," I call, knocking again and shouting her name.

I turn around and notice that one of the neighbors is staring, and I wonder how many people know about the animosity between me and Sarah. This is a small town, and people love to gossip.

Left with no other choice, I turn away, my cheeks burning. I know exactly what she's trying to do. She's trying to push me so far that I'll just pack up and leave. Telling Mark I lied about losing the ticket is just another way for her to drive a wedge between us. She wants us to break up, so that Mark can move in with her, for them to be one happy family without me. Seething but forcing myself to stay calm, I get into the car and drive to Sip & Snack.

When I arrive, Jason is cracking jokes with customers and

sharing trivia as usual. This time, they're quizzing him on the capital cities of the world, and he's getting every single one right.

Even as a child he was obsessed with trivia and his intelligence and curiosity always amazed me. I can't help wondering what he would have become if he hadn't ended up on that dark path. As a mother, it's hard not to blame myself.

I don't try to force him to talk to me. Instead, I sit at a table by the window overlooking the pond where I found the lottery ticket and allow myself to be served by another barista. I order a cappuccino and a toasted bagel with cream cheese, and try not to stare at my son. If he doesn't come over for a chat, I will leave as quietly as I came. The more you try to force Jason to talk or open up, the more he closes off.

Laughter rings out in the café as he says something to a group of kids who seem to be about his age. Looking at him, it's hard to think he's carrying so much weight, that he's tormented by so much. That smile on his face, which reminds me so much of his father's, is such a great camouflage.

I'm about ready to leave when, to my surprise, he comes to my table.

"Afternoon, Mom," he says and my heart lifts inside my chest, just like it did the first time he called me mommy while I was giving him a bath.

"Hey, baby." I pause. "Don't worry, I'm not here to disturb you at work. I just needed something to eat." Although honestly, I really need to talk to someone.

He sits down opposite me and folds his arms on the table. "You look upset. So, what did she do this time? I'm guessing it's about Sarah, again."

"She's been going through my things, and today, she left one of Melody's earrings on the kitchen counter."

Jason is quiet for a long time. My son and I are used to

having conversations without words, because there are things that are too risky to talk about.

"She was going through your stuff? What was she looking for?" He leans forward. "Mom, do you think—"

I quickly take his hand and shake my head. "Don't say it. I think she was just prying, and the earring was one of her little reminders that I don't belong there."

"Did you talk to Mark about it?"

I sigh. "You know how Mark is when it comes to her."

Jason's Adam's apple rises and then falls. "You need to be careful, Mom. Sarah is good at finding things out. It's her job. She could destroy everything, not just your marriage."

"She's not going to find out anything, don't worry," I say, wishing I believed my own words. I glance back through the café window, half-expecting to see Sarah standing out there.

Jason gives me a long, searching look, then stands, folding the conversation away as neatly as he does his apron when his shift ends.

"I'll see you later," he says with a tired smile and gives me a peck on the cheek.

I leave the café not long after, and as I walk toward my car, I dig inside my pocket for my keys. When I look up again, I see it. A small, folded piece of paper tucked under my windshield wiper.

Holding my breath, I reach for it.

The message is written in rushed, messy handwriting.

*Freedom comes only with facing the truth and confronting your past.*

My heart thuds as my gaze scans my surroundings, every shadow and parked car a potential threat.

But the small parking lot is deserted except for a handful of cars, none of which I recognize. I'm certain it was Sarah. She really must know something, or at least she suspects it. But I won't be rattled, I'll hold my nerve.

There's nothing else I can do, is there?

# SIXTEEN

Tia's apartment is in the heart of Stoneview, right above a bustling street lined with antique stores and busy cafés. I step inside, letting the door close softly behind me. The apartment is quiet, except for the soft hum of the fridge. Plants are everywhere, just as I remember, but it still takes me a moment to adjust to the sheer number of them. They line the windowsills, hang from the ceiling, and crowd every available surface.

I set my bag down on the entryway table, the crumpled note from the car still inside. I don't take it out. I've spent the whole drive here trying to shove it from my mind. Sarah wants to see me anxious, making mistakes, exposing my secrets. She *can't* know everything, because if she did, I'd have already lost everything.

I head to the kitchen, where Tia keeps the watering can. Her kitchen is an eclectic space with soft, buttery-yellow walls that make the room feel warm and inviting. A small wooden table sits in the corner by the window, just big enough for two, and it's cluttered with a few things—a vase filled with white roses, a ceramic bowl of lemons and limes, and a stack of unopened mail. A drying rack stands next to the sink, filled with multi-colored dishes and Tia's favorite mug with a slogan that reads, "Dance Through Life's Twists and Turns."

I fill the watering can and start with the plants by the window. The afternoon light filters through the leaves, causing shadows to form on the floor. I pour the water slowly, making sure each plant gets just enough. As I do so, I notice the little things that make this space so undeniably Tia. The mismatched cushions on the couch—one a vibrant red, the other a soft pastel blue. She told me that she could not choose between the two, so she bought both. The same goes for the throw blankets draped over the armchair in the corner; one is a deep, rich burgundy, and the other a soft, muted gray.

I move to the coffee table, where a stack of magazines catches my eye. Wedding magazines. The top one is brand new, glossy and bright, but as I pick it up, I notice the ones underneath are older, their covers faded and dog-eared. I flip through them, seeing page after page marked with sticky notes, corners folded down on articles about venues, dresses, and floral arrangements.

Tia has been engaged for three years, and she's been collecting these magazines for just as long, planning a wedding that never seems to get any closer. I'm sure she keeps revisiting these magazines over and over again, unable to commit to any one idea.

The words from the note flash in my mind again, sharper this time, daring me. *Confront your past.* I force myself to focus on the magazines instead, flipping through them to distract myself, but the pressure builds in my chest.

*Pull yourself together, Drew.*

Drawing in a deep breath, I set the magazines aside and water the ferns hanging from the ceiling, then move to the small succulent garden on the coffee table. The bookshelf catches my eye next. It's packed, not just with novels, but with remnants of a life Tia left behind.

Her law books take up an entire shelf, their spines barely touched. Although I admire her for having the courage to walk away from her lucrative career in law, the fact that she kept the books means that the decision still haunts her. The books are a reminder of the path she veered from but never truly let go of.

I continue to water the plants as I make my way to the bathroom. Hair products—countless bottles and tubes—are neatly arranged on the counter and in the cabinets. Tia loves experimenting with hair, always trying out new styles and colors, both on herself and on the clients who come into the salon. I smile as I water the small potted plant she keeps on the bathroom windowsill before popping into her bedroom to tend to the plant babies she keeps in there. Her collection of dancing shoes is lined up against the wall, in every color and style imaginable —heels, flats, sneakers—all well-worn from countless dance classes.

On my way back to the living room, I spot another stack of papers on the coffee table, tucked under the wedding magazines.

I hesitate, then reach for them, flipping through the yellowed pages. They are all *Gazette* issues dated years ago, some as far back as five years, but many of them are from two years ago. I pull one of those out because there's a piece of paper sticking out from it.

I open to the place Tia bookmarked to find an article on Melody's death.

The piece of paper falls to the floor and when I pick it up, my chest tightens to the point of pain.

It's a list of dates and questions, scribbled in Tia's handwriting. There are several dates circled in red, and next to them are questions like "What happened here?" and "Who was involved?" Below the questions are names, but all are crossed out with thick, bold lines. Except one. Mark.

## SEVENTEEN

I go downstairs to find Mark in the kitchen, standing in front of the junk drawer.

"Morning, baby. Are you looking for something?"

He swivels around as though I've caught him doing something he shouldn't. But then his face clears up and he puts on a small smile.

He crosses the distance between us and gives me a kiss. "I was just looking for... Okay, I was looking for the ticket, to be honest."

I swallow hard. "I told you that I already searched everywhere. And I think I lost it at work or somewhere out of the house."

Mark lowers himself into one of the chairs at the kitchen table and buries his hands into his hair. "I know. I thought maybe... I was just trying my luck. It's hard to accept that we lost so much money that could have helped us out of this mess." He looks up, then drops his gaze to the table. That's when I notice the large stack of envelopes. Without looking at them closely, I know they're bills.

"We didn't lose it, Mark. *I* did and I'm really sorry."

He stands up again and goes to the window, his back to me. "I know, and I'm sorry too, for getting so worked up. It's just that we're buried in debt and... the thought of losing this house—"

"We'll find a solution." Trying not to think about the ticket, I stand up and go to my husband, wrapping my arms around him. "It's going to be all right, honey."

"I can't see how." His voice is a croak. "We are completely tapped out." Given that Mark is usually a look-on-the-bright-side kind of person, seeing him this worried must mean things are really bad.

I rest my head in the space between his shoulder blades. "I'm really sorry, baby. I should have been more careful."

He simply nods, then detaches himself from me.

"I'm going for a swim," he says, stepping out of the kitchen. He does not need to tell me in words just how upset he is with me. It's vibrating off him.

After he leaves, I drop into a chair at the table and just stare into space. When I start spiraling, I get up, get dressed, and head out the door, jogging to the nearby woods. I just need to forget my troubles for a moment.

The woods are silent, except for the occasional birdsong and rustle of leaves. Removing my phone from my pocket, I open the camera app and direct the lens toward the canopy, catching the sunlight through the quivering leaves. As I trek farther into the woods, I see a fox darting through the underbrush, its fiery red tail standing out against the muted greens and browns. I manage to take a quick shot before it disappears into the thicket. Breathing easier, I move farther in. There's a small creek that runs through the heart of these woods and I soon find it. The water is clear and it glistens under the sun's rays that manage to pierce through the thick foliage above.

Photography used to be a huge part of my old life, but I *needed* to start over. So, I chose to leave behind some of my old passions. Now, as I crouch by the side of the creek, angling my phone for a shot of the water's reflection, I realize how much I've missed this, missed me. The thrill of capturing a moment in time, the mindful serenity it offers.

When I straighten up, the phone still raised to my face, I notice a flash of blue. There is something, someone, standing in the distance, hidden by the trunk of a large tree. I snap a photo and lower my phone. But they're too far away for me to make out their face.

My heart beating fast inside my chest, I walk in that direction, but before I can make it halfway, the figure turns and disappears. My heart pounding even louder now, I quicken my pace, my determination replacing fear. By the time I reach the tree, I see the person, whoever they are, fleeing in the distance.

I pull up the photo I took of them and zoom in, but only their body is visible, revealing a pair of jeans and a hooded sweater. I stare at the image for a moment longer, but there's nothing else to glean from it.

Shaking my head, I scroll through my camera roll absent-mindedly, flipping through the recent photos of the woods, the creek, the fox. And then, something makes me stop. I stare at a new image of a beautiful mountain, my eyes zooming in. The mountain in Aspen Ridge that was visible from the kitchen of our little cabin. It's a photo of another photograph, that had been placed on a wooden surface. My heart stutters. I took that photo the day Dean walked into the cabin with the stench of alcohol on his breath.

There is an enlarged and framed version of this photo that hangs in Jason's apartment, that he begged me to give him as the only reminder of our old life.

But how is it here? On my phone? My copy was in the garage, inside a box I haven't opened in quite some time, one filled with my personal memories.

Suddenly, the trees feel like they're closing in and there's a pressure in my chest that won't let me breathe. I stuff my phone back into my pocket and continue my walk. I don't understand this, but I can't think about that place right now. I can't.

A knot tightening in my stomach, I go deeper into the woods, and the rustling leaves and chirping birds start to drown out my thoughts. I take a few more photos of a beautiful bird perched on a high branch, its feathers a vibrant sapphire in the morning sunlight; a curious squirrel poking its head out from behind an old tree stump, and the flowers blooming by the creek's edge, their fragile petals and leaves kissed by dew drops.

When I finally check the time on my phone, an hour has passed, so I trek back home. Normally, Mark would already have left the house half an hour ago, but I find him dressed and drinking coffee while reading a fitness magazine as he leans against the counter. Thankfully, he no longer looks upset, or he's just hiding it very well.

"How about I come with you to the gym today?" I desperately want the distraction.

"But you hate going to the gym and I'll be working all day, anyway." Mark tries to keep Sundays free for us as much as he can, but since he had to let go of some employees to keep costs low, all hands are needed on deck.

"Doesn't matter. I'm thinking I might join a Pilates class. It's been a while."

"Sounds like a plan," he replies, smiling at me before taking a last sip of his coffee.

On our drive to the gym, my brain is on high alert. It flicks between the stranger in the woods, the skiing photo in my apron pocket, the newspapers in Tia's apartment, and now that mountain photo on my phone. I crank up the music on the radio, hoping it will drown out my rising panic.


Coming to the gym with Mark was the best decision I made today. As I stretch in my Pilates class, I feel the tension melt away. The instructor, a petite woman named Andrea with biceps that I can only dream of, moves around the room correcting postures and encouraging everyone to engage their core. As she adjusts my pose slightly, stretching me further than I thought was possible, I feel both physical and mental relief.

Then I spot a woman smiling at me from across the room. It's Hannah Howard, the owner of the Bliss & Twine flower shop, the woman who did my wedding flowers. I've always found her to be very beautiful. She has almond-shaped eyes that sparkle with warmth and glowing skin that looks like it has been kissed by the sun, and her tight brown curls are pulled back into a youthful ponytail.

Even though it's a small town, I have not seen her in a while, but I know she and her husband Nathan Howard—a well-known criminal lawyer—travel a lot with their daughter, Lennie.

I smile back at her, memories of my wedding day flooding back as I recall the stunning arrangements she created for me. The bouquet she crafted was nothing short of breathtaking. Elegant creamy white roses were the focal point and among them were blush-pink peonies. Hannah had also included sprigs of eucalyptus and trailing tendrils of ivy. The burst of colors and scents of the flowers come alive again in my mind, just as vivid as they were on our special day.

Back then, I was so hopeful my plan would work, that my secrets would always stay safe. Now I'm not so sure.

Once finished with the session, Hannah and I find each other in the changing rooms.

"Great class, wasn't it?" She dabs a towel to her forehead. "Andrea really knows how to make us work. I don't know what I would do if your husband ever closes this gym down."

I pause while redoing my ponytail. "Who said that it's closing down?"

"Just word on the street. Mark told me it's not true and I really hope he's right."

"He is right," I say quickly. I don't care much about the house, but this is Mark's life and I love him too much to see it crumble. It doesn't even matter that a portion of it belongs to Sarah too.

"I'm so happy to hear that." She lays her hand on her belly and sighs. "I'm trying to stay as fit as I can before baby number two comes. I heard it helps a person bounce back quicker."

I raise an eyebrow. "You're pregnant? That's great. How far along are you?"

"Just twelve weeks. But time flies." She pauses. "Anyway, have a great day, Drew. One of these days I'm going to make an appointment at the salon. I think it's time for a new look." She raises a hand to twirl a thick lock of hair around her index finger.

"Absolutely. I can't wait." My gaze flicks to her curly hair, now cascading down her back. I can't wait to get my hands on it. Most of our clients just want the same old styles or a touch-up, so a complete hair transformation is always thrilling.

After Hannah walks away, I turn to leave and that's when I see her.

Lori is holding a bright-pink yoga mat and a black and white gym bag. I didn't realize she was a member here, and Mark did not mention it. She hesitantly lifts her hand to wave at me and I smile, but I don't have the energy to go and make small talk with her today. I wave back at her before I walk away.

As I reach the door, I glance over my shoulder and find her staring at me. This time, she's not smiling—in fact, her eyes are narrowed, her lips pressed into a tight line.

## EIGHTEEN

After dinner, when Mark heads upstairs to take a call, I go into the garage and scan the shelves, looking for the one box I haven't opened in almost a year. It's clearly labeled with the words "Drew's Memories" from when I first packed it.

I had been unable to part with its contents even though I was sure I would never want to revisit the painful reminders inside. Memories of Dean and the life we created together. I pull down a few of the boxes and lift the lids to check inside. Clothes. Kitchenware. Random trinkets. I check the next shelf, then the next. Where is it?

Anxiety curls tight in my chest as I move faster, pulling more boxes down, searching every shelf, every corner of the garage. It's not here. It's gone. I step back, heart slamming against my ribs. Although I didn't look inside, I remember seeing the box a couple of days ago. Or was it weeks? It was definitely here. I know it was.

Later that night, as we settle into bed, I turn to Mark, trying to sound casual, but I can't hide the edge in my voice.

"Have you seen the box from the garage with my old memories?" I ask, hoping maybe—just maybe—he moved it for some reason.

Mark frowns, glancing at me briefly. "No, why?"

I try to smile. "Just wondering."

He shrugs and gives me a goodnight kiss, but I lay back against the pillows, staring at the ceiling. Am I imagining it, or was he avoiding looking in my eyes just now?

The sheets are cool next to me when I wake up in the morning. Mark has already left for his swim. I stretch, thinking about my usual jog, but the idea of running feels exhausting. I lie there a moment longer before an idea pops into my head.

Maybe I could surprise Mark by greeting him at the beach with coffee and a picnic breakfast. This energizes me and I slip out of bed, throw on a pair of gray sweatpants, and head downstairs. A thermos of coffee, a few sandwiches, and some fruit—nothing fancy, but enough to show him I'm thinking about him, about us. I pack it all into a small basket and leave the house.

When I get to the beach, though, something's off. The shoreline stretches out in front of me, empty. No Mark. The usual spot where he leaves his towel and clothes is empty too. I scan the horizon. Maybe he's further out, swimming in deeper waters, but there's nothing. No sign of him at all. I check my phone, thinking maybe I missed a message. Nothing.

My fingers move almost on instinct as I open the tracking app on my phone, the one we both have for emergencies. I know this is not an emergency, but I am curious where he is. Then I stare at the screen in confusion. St. Michael's Parish, the same church he made that massive donation to. Why would he be there?

I walk back to the house and put the basket down on the counter. There's something going on with Mark, something he hasn't told me, and I need to know what. I grab my car keys and hurry to the car.

A few minutes later, I pull up in front of the church.

Whatever is going on, it's something Mark kept hidden from me and he clearly doesn't want me to see him. I step out of the car and walk up the narrow pathway, noticing the ivy clinging to the old stone walls, creeping around the edges of the stained-glass windows.

Inside, the air is cool and almost damp, carrying the faint scent of incense and old wood. I scan the empty pews before I hear voices, low and hushed. The confessional booth. I shouldn't be here. This is wrong. But before I can convince myself to turn around and walk away, I hear Mark's voice coming from the other side of the wooden wall.

"That night, Melody told me about something she did and I didn't take it well," he says slowly. "She's dead because of me. I shouldn't have reacted the way I did. Now she's gone and I'll never forgive myself."

My breath catches as I press myself against the wall of the confessional. The priest murmurs something in response, but I don't hear it. Sweat prickling at the back of my neck, I back away slowly and slip out of the church as quietly as I can and hurry to my car, sliding into the driver's seat and closing my eyes.

It seems Mark has been donating to this church as a way to clear his conscience. I don't understand what's going on, but one thing is clear: my husband has secrets too.

Could they be as dark as mine?

## NINETEEN

By 11 o'clock, I've already had three clients, two trims and a touch-up of the pesky grays. There's something about getting your hair done that just makes you feel like a whole new person, ready to conquer the world. I don't do much to my own hair, but I love to see my clients' eyes light up when they look at themselves in the mirror.

I run my fingers through Mrs. Palmer's hair, sectioning it off as I prepare to trim her split ends. She's one of my regulars, sweet and chatty as ever. But today, I can barely focus on our conversation. My mind keeps slipping back to St. Michael's Parish and Mark's words echo in my head like they've taken up residence there.

Is he feeling guilty because he and Melody had some kind of argument before her accident, so he thinks she wouldn't have died if it wasn't for him? That must be it. Right?

I switch to thinning shears, creating soft layers in Mrs. Palmer's fine hair.

"You always work magic with my hair, Drew," Mrs. Palmer says, her voice full of appreciation as she looks in the mirror.

I smile. "It's all you, Mrs. Palmer. I just help bring it out."

After my fifth client, I'm about to start on the next when I glance up at the small TV on the wall, just as the room seems to have gone quiet. Tia and everyone else have their eyes transfixed on it. It's set to one of the local channels and the flashing headline reads:

$900,000 PRIZE STILL UNCLAIMED AFTER TWO
WEEKS

The reporter on the local news is Molly Winters, a thirty-something with chestnut hair and a perfect porcelain smile. She's standing outside Luxor Lottery, her purple blazer fluttering in the wind. She talks with her usual calm demeanor, but there's a flicker of excitement in her dark eyes.

"It's been two weeks since the winning lottery ticket numbers were drawn," she says, "and the winner has yet to come forward. The winning numbers were twelve, twenty-three, twenty-seven, thirty-two, forty-three and... hold on... let me check my notes... yes, and fifty-one. You heard it right, folks! If you haven't checked your ticket yet, now is the time to do it. If the winner doesn't claim the prize within six months, the jackpot goes back into the pool. The clock is ticking, people, and someone out there is sitting on a fortune."

I still have a few months, enough time to come up with a plan.

A murmur of excitement and disbelief echoes through the salon. I watch one of the clients, Mrs. Dorothy, a sweet, frail woman in her late seventies, whose hair Tia is currently styling, rummage through her purse to produce a crumpled lottery ticket.

Mrs. Dorothy comes in every two weeks for a perm and touch-up and always talks about her grandchildren. Her face crumples when she checks the numbers on her ticket, a sigh of resignation passing her lips. Tia pats her shoulder in silent comfort just as the salon falls back into its usual chatter. Everyone is discussing what they would do if they won such a large amount of money. Everyone except me.

"You think it's somebody from out of town?" Helen asks as she passes through to get to her office at the back of the main salon floor.

"Could be." Vanessa twirls a lock of her hair around her finger, forgetting that she's giving a client a trim. "Whoever it is, maybe they don't even know they won."

"Or maybe they lost it." Helen enters her office and closes the door behind her, leaving us to continue the conversation.

"Yes," Tia jumps in. "Or maybe, they are just too scared to claim it. Imagine the attention it would draw. Not everyone is prepared for that. What do you think, Drew?" She stares at me.

I open my mouth to reply but find no words coming out.

My client, an elderly gentleman named Mr. Robinson, noticing my silence, chuckles. "Maybe she's the one who won. Look at her, speechless." There's a round of laughter and I know I have to say something and quick.

"That's ridiculous... I wish." Running a comb through Mr. Robinson's thinning hair, I laugh along, although it sounds more like a strangled gasp. "Maybe the winner doesn't need the money."

The sound of more laughter fills the salon.

"Who wouldn't want nearly a million dollars?" another client chimes in. "Even if you don't need it, you could give it to family or charity."

"Or travel the world," adds Leah Ranger, a bank teller, whose permanent curls bounce slightly as she nods to herself just as Maggie finishes drying her hair. "Imagine, Paris, Rome..."

As my stomach curls with anxiety, I listen to my colleagues discussing the lottery ticket I have hidden away in a teddy bear at my house.

What if the original owner of the ticket saw the numbers

before they lost it? Would they remember them, and might they have any proof they bought it?

And even if I do ever claim the money, would they come forward to reveal that the ticket was never mine to begin with?

Luckily for me, the conversation shifts to other topics and I move on to the next client, a woman named Lorelei with a thick mane of red hair.

After I'm done, Helen comes over.

"Go ahead and have your lunch break, hon. You look like you could use a rest." Helen is not only our boss, but she has become a mother figure to all of us.

I glance at the clock. "I still have fifteen minutes before my break." But Helen insists, and so I leave my station, pulling the apron off.

Making my way to the park, I find Martin sitting at his usual spot, and when he sees me approach him, he stops playing and gives me one of the brightest smiles.

"Hey there, pretty lady." He pushes aside his dirty coat to make room for me on the rickety, old bench. "Busy day?"

"You can say that again. I brought you a sandwich." He accepts it and we eat while he tells me that he's looking for a job.

I wish him luck and when it's time for me to get back to the salon, he reaches into his pocket and pulls out a twenty. "Get yourself a little treat."

I shake my head and blink away the tears. "Martin, you don't have to do that. *You* get yourself a little treat."

When he sees that I won't take no for an answer, he looks a little embarrassed as he shrugs. "All right then, have yourself a nice day."

I find my next client waiting. But it's not just anyone. It's Lori. She smiles, and I muster a fake one in return.

"This young lady wanted you to do her hair," Tia says, giving my shoulder a squeeze.

"Hi Drew, I only have a thirty-minute lunch break. Just a simple wash and trim, nothing fancy."

I get to work, and after a while to break the awkward silence, I ask her a question. "How are things with you and Jason?" I want to gauge how much she cares about my son, or if she's planning to ditch him for her ex.

"Great." She meets my gaze in the mirror. "Drew, I know you don't seem to like me very much, but I really care about your son."

"So, you are serious about him, honestly?" I decide to be direct.

"Look, if things don't work out, people move on. But right now, things are going well with us."

There's a pause, and then she continues trying to make conversation.

"I know you haven't been living in Stoneview for very long, but how do you like it compared to your hometown in Colorado? Jason mentioned the name, but I can't seem to remember it."

I really hope Jason didn't tell her too much about where we came from.

"Every town has its positives and negatives." I wet her hair and begin massaging shampoo into it.

"That's true. My mother is originally from New York, and although she likes living in a small town now, she doesn't like that people get into each other's business," she continues as I rinse her hair.

"How is your mother doing these days, Lori?" a client I don't know interrupts. She's a petite, elderly woman with greenish hair. She had tried to dye her hair at home and it hadn't worked out in her favor, so Tia is doing what she can to fix it.

I feel Lori stiffen a little under my fingers. "She's fine," she mumbles.

I know Lori's mother is sick and I do feel sorry for the girl. Having to care for her mother at such a young age must be tough.

The other woman tries to pry further, but Lori only gives one-word answers until the woman gives up and turns her attention back to Tia. There is a silence between Lori and me that's filled with the sounds of hairdryers, scissors snipping, and muted conversations.

"Drew," Lori asks, "I've always wanted to know more about Jason's childhood, but he doesn't talk much about it at all. Can you maybe tell me a little about your life together when he was growing up?"

"It was just like any other childhood. There's really not much to say except that he was an adorable little boy."

I find myself thinking back to the past, past the dark times, focusing on when he was a toddler, chasing me around the house. How his high-pitched belly laugh echoed through the halls, how his bright eyes widened in delight when he discovered something new. The days when I would wake up early in the morning to make him his favorite chocolate chip pancakes and his face lit up with a toothy grin smeared with syrup.

"And how was life after his father passed away? I know it affected him a lot. He mentioned falling into some bad habits."

The entire salon falls silent again and I feel Tia's eyes on me. She has tried many times to get me to talk to her about that part of our lives and never really got anywhere.

"Forgive me, Lori," I say with a forced smile. "That's not something I wish to discuss. I hope you understand."

"Yeah, of course"

She asks a few more personal questions as I continue working on her hair, but when she doesn't get answers, she starts talking about her new job at the *Gazette*.

"I've been given a new project that I'm hoping will prove my worth as more than just an admin."

"That's fantastic news for you," Marlene comments. "Maybe one day we will see your name in the paper."

As they continue discussing Lori's future at the newspaper, I turn my attention back to my work, and when she finally leaves, I retreat to the staff room and pull out my phone.

I quickly dial Jason's number.

"Hey, Mom," he answers on the second ring, sounding cheerful. "What's up?"

I take a deep breath and try to keep my voice steady. "Jason, I was wondering... Did you come by the house recently? I can't seem to find that old box of my memories. We packed it together when we were moving, remember?" Please let him say yes, that he needed something from it. I squeeze my eyes shut and blow out a breath. "You know what? It doesn't matter."

I'm being ridiculous, grasping at straws. Why am I even asking him instead of going straight to Sarah—the person I suspect took the photo I found on my phone to creep me out, and who surely still has the box and is digging around in my past? Jason has nothing to do with any of this. But the truth is, I don't have the courage to confront Sarah. It's like poking a hornet's nest. What if she retaliates and does something even worse?

"No, I haven't seen that box in ages," Jason says, curiosity seeping into his voice. "Why?"

"I just can't find it, that's all. But... Never mind, I'll keep looking." I try my best to sound casual. "Maybe I moved it somewhere else."

"Yeah. I doubt anyone would just take it, Mom. It's not like there's anything valuable in it—just sentimental stuff, right?"

"You're right. I was just wondering." I swallow down my anxiety but clutch the phone tighter. "By the way, Lori came by for a hair appointment today. She was asking a lot of questions about your childhood. I hope you didn't reveal anything... about Aspen Ridge?"

"No, Mom. Of course not." Jason lowers his voice. "We promised each other we would never tell anyone."

At the end of the day, I change my mind and stop by Sarah's place to confront her after all because not doing so is driving me insane.

All guns blazing, I point out, without beating around the bush, that I know she took my box. It must have been the time she pretended to be looking for some memories of Melody's. But I don't mention the mountain photo that was in there, that she photographed with my phone.

As I had expected, she folds her arms across her chest and denies it point blank. "Drew, why would I take your little box of memories?" Before I can respond, she continues, "You probably misplaced it. There's been a lot on your mind lately, wouldn't you say?" She narrows her eyes. "Wait a minute. Why do you look so upset about it anyway? Are you keeping some secrets in there you're afraid I might discover?"

My heart stutters. "That's not it, Sarah," I protest weakly. "It's just that those are personal memories. Private things."

She studies me for a long moment. "Right," she drawls out, her tone sickeningly sweet. "I could come and help you look if you like? We wouldn't want you to lose the precious memories of your *dead husband*, would we?"

"No, thank you, Sarah," I respond firmly. "That won't be necessary."

As I walk away, I pray that whatever she finds next in the box won't help her put all the pieces of my secret together.

# TWENTY



Two days have passed since we arrived in Aspen Ridge, and the air between Dean and me feels electric, charged with unspoken words. But today, the day before Christmas, is different. We're going skiing, and I can't shake the excitement that buzzes beneath my skin. The thought of gliding down the slopes, the wind whipping past me, fills me with a sense of freedom I haven't felt in weeks. I crave it, that release from the weight of worry that has settled on my chest recently.

The drive up the mountain is stunning, the road winding and steep, flanked by towering pine trees heavy with snow. The sun is bright, casting a dazzling light that dances off the glistening white landscape. I can see the outline of the ski resort coming into view, its colorful buildings standing out against the stark white drifts.

Jason's excitement is palpable too as he glances out the window, taking in the breathtaking scenery. He's always loved skiing, and the thought of hitting the slopes fills him with a childlike joy. But Dean remains somber. I steal glances at him, the image of him stumbling into the cabin replaying in my mind.

When we arrive at the resort, I'm surprised by how quiet it is. Last year, it was bustling with families, laughter ringing in the air, but today there are only a few people and it feels almost deserted. The trails are inviting and vast, with untouched powder glistening under the sun. As we step out of the car, the bitter cold bites and I wrap my arms around myself. Jason races ahead, his laughter echoing through the crisp air, while Dean trudges behind us.

Before we hit the slopes, we make our way to the only restaurant at the base of the mountain for a drink. The inside is warm and cozy with wooden beams overhead and the smell of hearty meals wafting through the air.

We head to the bar area, which is separated from the dining space. It's quieter here, with a few skiers perched on stools, nursing drinks. Jason, already distracted by the familiar faces of kids his age sitting at a nearby table, leaves Dean and me at the bar to greet them.

I order a lemonade, and Dean, leaning casually against the counter, orders a beer. His voice is low and unbothered as he asks the bartender for it. The weight of his choice settles over me.

"Dean," I say in a low voice, stepping closer, "you can't drink now, right before skiing. It's dangerous."

He turns to me, a flash of annoyance crossing his face. "What's your problem? It's just a beer," he replies, his tone dismissive.

Worried that Dean might not stop at just one beer, I shoot a glance at Jason, who's chatting with his friends, laughing, and completely unaware. I can't bear the thought of him seeing his father drunk or even tipsy. I don't want my son to be the kid I was.

"Dean, please," I press, urgency creeping into my voice. "I

don't want him to see you like this. I don't want him to think it's okay to drink to handle difficulties."

His expression hardens. "You've become quite controlling lately, haven't you?" he shoots back, raising an eyebrow. "I can handle myself. It's not like I'm drinking to get drunk." He downs the beer, his eyes never leaving mine.

I'm furious now. "It's not just about you! It's about us. We're a family. How do you think Jason will feel?" I glance at our son again, hoping he won't notice the growing rift between us.

Dean dismisses me, downing the last of his beer before paying the bill. "Let's go, Jason! Time to hit the slopes!" he calls, his voice cheerful, but I can hear the edge beneath it.

When we reach the skiing area, Jason looks back at Dean, confusion written on his face. "Dad, are you okay? You seem a bit... off." The question hangs in the air and the silence deepens until Jason asks again.

"Don't worry about it, Jason. I'm fine!" Dean snaps, his tone harsh.

I jolt at the sound, my heart jumping to my throat as I watch Jason's expression shift from concern to irritation. He grabs his ski gear, muttering under his breath that he'll go join his friends instead.

"Great," I say, feeling my frustration boil over as soon as Jason is out of earshot. I turn to Dean, who is still standing there, his brow furrowed. "Can't you see what you're doing?"

Dean backs away from me, his arms crossed defensively over his chest. "I'm a grown man. I can do what I want."

In that moment, I'm no longer standing in Aspen Ridge. I'm a little girl again, trapped in the nightmare of my father's drunken nights.

I feel the anger boiling inside me, hot and visceral, and I can't hold it back.

# TWENTY-ONE



"Mark, I really think I should stay home." Standing in front of the closet mirror, fully dressed in jeans and a wine-red satin blouse, I don't feel ready for our dinner at Sarah's house.

We usually have our Friday family dinners at our place, and I prefer it that way. It's easier to deal with Sarah's jabs at me when I'm in my own home, but this time, she insisted we do something different.

On Tuesday, the day after I confronted her about taking my box, I found it inside the garage again, unsealed. So yes, it was definitely her.

I immediately removed some of my most personal items—like some photobooks filled with pictures I took when I was still a photographer—and placed them inside a smaller box, which I tucked away on the top shelf in my library. As for the ski photos, I destroyed them, as painful as it was, but it was necessary to erase that part of my past.

"Honey," Mark says from the bedroom. "Sarah is trying to reach out, to get close to you. In fact I'm pretty sure this dinner is all about you. She's making an effort. I really think you should do the same."

I spritz on some perfume and step out of the closet. "You think she's doing this for me? I doubt it." If it wouldn't hurt his feelings, I'd laugh.

"You know what I really think, Drew?" Mark says, sinking onto the bed in his white t-shirt and faded jeans. "Since we got married, it feels like you've been intentionally keeping your distance from her. I know you two didn't hit it off initially, but I feel like you're keeping her from getting close to you. She really wants to get to know you."

"Mark, I'm sorry, I wish it wasn't this way. But your sister doesn't like me and she never will. I'm surprised you don't see that."

"I think you're wrong." He stands up again. "Either way, we should get going. Maybe tonight will change things for you two."

I stay silent because there's no point in arguing.

My legs feel shaky as we walk to Sarah's place, and when we arrive, the door swings open. Sarah stands there in a flowing, floral dress, her hair slicked back and glossy. With the light behind her, she looks like a fairy. If only her inside matched her exterior.

"Mark, Drew, I'm so glad you could come. I know it's last minute." She hugs her brother, then gives me a peck on the cheek that makes my skin crawl.

"You didn't have to do this, Sarah," I say, following her into the kitchen with a tuna noodle casserole I made after work.

"Oh, don't be ridiculous. I don't mind doing the hosting this time." She takes the casserole but places it on the kitchen counter instead of with the other dishes. I doubt it'll make it to the table.

The kitchen is a mess. There are pots and pans hanging from a rack above the island, but they all look like they haven't been touched in ages. The sink is filled with dirty dishes, and a faint smell of dust permeates the air.

"Did you invite Jason?" I ask.

"Oh, no!" She presses a hand to her chest. "Silly me. I totally forgot. I'm so sorry, Drew."

"Wait, Jason wasn't invited?" Mark says from the doorway. "But it's family night."

"I know, I feel so terrible about it. But he's young, I'm sure he has something else to do tonight."

That's true, I know he's on a date with Lori. She came into the salon again today for a wash and blowout. To be honest, stopping by twice in one week—when she never used to—made me a bit suspicious, especially since she was badgering me with more questions about Jason's childhood. She said she had a date tonight and wanted to look good. Unable to stop myself, I asked if it was with Jason, and she confirmed it was.

Even though I know Jason would never choose this dinner over a date with his girlfriend, it still stings to know my son is not wanted.

"Excuse me." Desperate for a moment alone, I walk out of the kitchen.

In the living room, I walk past Sarah's white grand piano and step outside on the porch, then I pull out my phone and call Jason. The view is stunning, with the waves crashing against the shore. It's close enough for me to smell the salt in the air.

"Sweetheart, we're having a family dinner at Sarah's. Do you want to come over?" I know he won't, but I don't want him finding out later and being upset he wasn't invited.

"At Sarah's?" He scoffs. "Hell no. I'll miss that one."

"Thought so. So, what are you doing tonight? Anything fun?"

"Not really. Just staying home, playing video games."

"You're not doing something with Lori?"

He pauses. "No. She's out with a friend."

I take a deep breath. "Okay. I just didn't want you to be alone tonight. Or to feel unwanted."

"I'm not coming to Sarah's, Mom. But thanks, you have a good time." He chuckles and we hang up.

When I return to the kitchen, my heart is heavy. Could Lori be with the ex that Maggie and Vanessa mentioned? I need to prepare for the fallout if she breaks Jason's heart. He doesn't handle rejection well. I've seen it, and it was ugly.

"Dinner is ready," Sarah calls. "Let's head to the dining room."

The dining room, unlike the kitchen, shows signs of recent effort, and the large wooden table—that sits under a large turquoise pendant light—is set for three. The walls are lined with family photos, mostly of Mark and Sarah growing up, and a few of Mark with Melody, which I try not to look at.

As we sit down, I wish I were anywhere but here.

"This all looks delicious, Sarah, though I doubt you cooked it." Mark points to the chicken curry, rice, and salads.

Sarah laughs, reaching for a napkin. "You know I'm not much of a cook. I ordered from Sears."

"Sears?" Mark's face pales.

"It was Melody's favorite restaurant, remember? Since it's her birthday, I thought it fitting to order from there."

Mark glances at me, and I shift uneasily. It's Melody's birthday, and I forgot. I know how painful these anniversaries can be, and I should have been there for Mark. I should have remembered and let him know I care.

Anyway, here it is, the real reason Sarah invited us. I can't believe she's using Melody's birthday to find a way to hurt me. Melody's memory deserves better.

"They have delicious food at Sears." Mark squeezes my hand.

But Sarah isn't done.

"Drew, did Mark ever tell you he met Melody at Sears?" she

asks, serving food like it's a normal conversation. "And after they got married, they celebrated every anniversary there."

"Sarah!" Mark throws her a warning look.

"No, Sarah, he never said." I pick up a fork and start eating. "But this food is delicious."

I suggested going to Sears with Mark a couple of times, but he always had an excuse. Then a few months ago, I found a photo of him and Melody eating at that restaurant, and I never mentioned it again. It was an important place to them, and I completely understand Mark wanting to keep it sacred.

I have always respected and valued his memories of her. But Sarah is riding roughshod over Mark's grief in her bid to make Melody the third person in our marriage.

Almost as if Melody isn't really dead.

# TWENTY-TWO

"I'm sorry but Jason didn't come in today. He called in sick," Sandra Lopez tells me the next morning as I stand before her, breathless after my jog.

Sandra is the owner of Sip & Snack, a woman in her mid-twenties with wheat-colored hair that falls in an untamed cascade of loose curls.

"Oh, did he say what's wrong with him?"

Sandra lifts her eyes from the coffee machine and fixes me with a sympathetic gaze. "No, he didn't specify." She pours frothed milk into a cup and continues, "He sounded kind of out of it and just said he wasn't feeling well. I didn't want to pry. He said he'll be here tomorrow."

I thank Sandra, then leave and call Jason. The phone doesn't even ring.

Has he relapsed?

No. I won't even allow myself to think that thought, not now. Not ever.

But I need to see my son, to confirm that my fears are not real.

Hurrying home, I barge into the house to get my car keys and I'm met by the smell of bacon frying even though Mark left for work before I did. Entering the kitchen, I see Sarah standing at the stove flipping a strip of bacon. On the counter is a plate with an omelet and toast.

"What are you doing here?" There's really no point in pretending to be nice, not today.

"Oh, Drew!" She dries her hands on a towel as she takes a few steps toward me. "Funny thing happened. I was about to head to the office when I saw Jason dropped off here by a taxi. Since he didn't look too well, I decided to come and check on him."

"What do you mean? Where's Jason?"

"His place, I guess. He came here, but you weren't around so he asked me to call him another cab as his phone was out of battery. I thought I'd stay here for a little bit and tell you when you got home. He looked really rough. Like he had quite the night. You know."

My heart stutters as she turns back to her bacon. "You want to join me for breakfast? I can make you another plate."

"No, thanks. I need to go to Jason."

I turn on my heel and as I flee the kitchen I hear her last words. "I'm really trying here, Drew, but you keep pushing me away."

I don't have the headspace or energy to respond to her right now. Grabbing my purse and car keys, I slip out the door and run to my car.

Jason's apartment is in a building on the east side of town, and it takes me twenty-five agonizing minutes to get there, weaving through the early morning traffic. I have a spare key, so when I arrive, I rush into the lobby and press the elevator button with unsteady fingers.

When I get to the third floor and run to his door, I'm just

inserting the key when the door is thrown open and suddenly, Lori is standing there.

"Hi, Lori," I say through gritted teeth. "Where's Jason?"

Without saying a word, she leads me to the living room.

Jason's living room is small, with mismatched furniture that looks like it was gathered from garage sales and hand-me-downs. A worn-out couch with faded cushions sits against one wall, the fabric fraying at the edges. When he moved in, the furniture was already there and when we offered to buy him some new pieces, he refused, saying that he was fine with what he had. I know he really just wanted to prove that he could stand on his own two feet.

But among the disarray, one thing stands out: a beautiful photograph of the Silvercrest Mountains on the wall above the couch, identical to the one Sarah used to torture me. As panic rises in my chest, I quickly look away to see Jason sprawled on the sofa, his lanky frame barely fitting on the cushions.

His face is pale, with dark circles under his eyes, and his hair is pasted to his forehead by sweat.

The TV is blaring a violent car chase, but he seems oblivious to it.

This is it. The moment I have been fearing ever since he became sober. The bottles of whiskey scattered around him confirm my worst nightmare.

"Oh, baby," I drop to my knees next to the moss green sofa and brush a lock of hair from his damp forehead. "What happened?"

The stench of liquor and vomit on him is nauseating, but he's my boy and nothing will ever make me leave his side.

I look up at Lori, her face full of worry, her hands wringing the fabric of her pastel blouse.

"Would you mind if I speak to Jason alone?"

"Sure. Of course." She walks to the kitchen and shuts the door.

I lean close to Jason's ear and whisper, "Jason, you're really drunk. When you came to the house looking for me, did you say anything to anyone about—"

He glances up at me. "I didn't tell anyone anything," he mumbles. "I'm not stupid."

But for a moment I think I see a flicker of fear in his eyes.

# TWENTY-THREE

Not long after I arrive at Jason's place, Lori leaves to go home to take care of her mom. But I stay to look after my son, guiding him into the bathroom to get himself cleaned up. Then I head to the kitchen.

The mess there is impossible to ignore: empty alcohol bottles scattered on the floor, half-eaten pizza slices tossed haphazardly on the counter. I clean it up, throwing away the bottles and wiping down the counter, trying to restore some order to the chaos.

Before moving to the living room to make sure there are no more bottles lying around, I brew some coffee, and its potent scent immediately fills the small apartment.

"Mom?" I suddenly hear Jason's voice just as I pour him a large mug of coffee. His voice is clearer now, less drenched in alcohol. He's wearing a blue and white striped morning robe I remember getting him one Christmas, but I can't remember which. It must be a while back because it looks a little tight on him now. His hair is still damp, and there's a look of abject remorse on his face that breaks my heart.

"Yes, love?" I say gently.

"I'm sorry," he says, sounding like a little boy. "Mom, I... I messed up."

"Shh..." I murmur, placing the coffee on the table before pulling him into a hug. He's much taller than me now, and his head rests on top of mine instead of the other way around. But right now, he feels like my little boy again, a boy desperate for his mother's understanding.

When we pull apart, I guide him into a chair and shift the coffee closer to him.

I pour myself a cup as well and sit down opposite him. "Talk to me, Jason. Why did you relapse?"

He shrugs and then when his eyes meet mine, I see tears swimming in them. "I thought Lori was with some other guy last night." He rubs the side of his stubbled face and he looks away, ashamed. "She didn't answer my calls."

"Jason, look at me." I wait until those gray eyes, so like my own, meet mine again. "You're stronger than this. You have to be. You know what's at stake." I take a sip of coffee. "So, did Lori go out with another guy?"

He shakes his head. "No, we were going to go on a date but then she went out with her best friend who was having a rough time. She said her phone was dead. That's why she didn't answer my calls or return them."

It's all I can do not to let the relief flood through me. Maybe Jason will still be okay.

"Jason, remember what I said. You have to be stronger than this." I cannot afford to be gentle now. Not when there's so much that could go wrong, so much to lose. "You cannot let a girl or anyone else have so much power over you." I inhale sharply. "You didn't even make it to work today. Do you remember how hard it was for you to get that job?"

He nods, almost as if he's moving through water. However, I can see a glimmer of the son I know in his bloodshot eyes, a flash of the fighter inside him.

"Promise me, Jason. No more drinking."

"Yeah... I promise." He takes a huge gulp of his coffee. "It won't happen again."

"Good. And we'll get through this. I know you'll come back from this, and you're not alone. I'm here."

Soon Jason heads to his room to sleep off the hangover and I finish cleaning up. On the way out the door, I give Mark a call. I would have preferred to keep this between me and Jason, but Sarah knows and there's no way in hell she's going to keep quiet about it.

"Is there anything I can do?" Mark asks, his voice heavy with concern.

"I think all he needs is for us to be there for him."

When I arrive home, I head straight to my library, my sanctuary. But I freeze in the doorway, my eyes scanning the room.

Something's off. The shelves are wrong. Books that should nestle together in familiar sequence are out of place. I always keep a very specific order, a system known only to me. But now it's in chaos. Different genres are all mixed together, self-help books lodged between fantasy novels and crime thrillers. The historical fiction section is a mess of classics and contemporary fiction.

What is Sarah playing at?

When Mark comes home after work, I reassure him that Jason is all right and doesn't need to attend AA meetings after this one slip-up. Then while I'm cooking dinner, a chicken stew with dumplings and salad on the side, I ask about his day.

"It was busy non-stop." He leans against the kitchen counter and reaches for a cherry tomato. He pops it into his mouth, savors it for a moment, then continues speaking. "Meetings all day, then I had to cover for Rick. He called in sick last minute."

Rick is one of the personal trainers at the gym and Mark has been having issues with him for weeks. His constant unreliability has placed unnecessary stress on Mark.

"That must be the third time he's called in sick this month. Maybe it's time to have a serious talk," I suggest while chopping a cucumber.

"Did everything else go okay?"

"Actually, we had a bit of an emergency this morning." His brow creases with concern. "The sauna overheated—some sort of electrical fault. Could've been bad if someone hadn't noticed the smell of burning."

"Oh my God! Was anyone hurt?"

"Thankfully, no. We cleared everyone out and shut down the power. But we'll have to close off the sauna until it's fixed."

"Is that going to be expensive?"

"Insurance should cover most of it, but yeah, it'll set us back a bit." He runs a hand through his hair.

I reach for his hand. "We'll manage. We always do." I turn back to the cooking.

"Love, you don't look well," he says when he notices that I've gone quiet. Turning me to face him, his eyes scan my face and his fingers trace along the tense lines of my jaw before brushing back a few strands of hair from my forehead. "You're worried about your son and that's understandable."

"Yes," I confess and glance back at the stew. "It's Jason, but it's more than just that."

He stands quietly next to me, his presence providing a comforting warmth.

I take a deep breath. "When I got home, the library was a mess. You know how much I like to keep it organized. But today, when I came back from seeing Jason, my books were all over the place. Someone has been in there, Mark."

"And let me guess, you think it was Sarah."

"I just can't imagine who else it would be," I say, feeling

defensive. "She has a key, and she was here making breakfast when I left this morning."

"Well, it wasn't Sarah. It was me. I was there before leaving for work."

"Wait, what? Why? Did you need something in particular?" I ask.

He hesitates. "I wanted to find a book to read."

But Mark rarely reads, and when he does, it's usually business or fitness magazines.

Why is he lying to me?

My best guess is, he heard about the deadline to claim the money and went looking for the ticket again. So, he still doesn't believe me. He believes Sarah, that I'm hiding it away, biding my time before I claim it for myself and leave him.

Even worse than Mark losing faith in me is that he's right to doubt me. I am lying to him, I have hidden it, but he could never imagine the reason why I can't afford the public attention of a lottery win.

If he finds out the secret I hope to take to my deathbed, what will he do? That question haunts me for the rest of the weekend.

## TWENTY-FOUR

Instead of going for my jog on Monday morning, I gather some flowers from the garden for later, then hop into my car and drive straight to Sip & Snack.

The first thing I hear when I step inside is my son's voice.

"Eighty percent of the Earth's surface is covered by water," he announces to a middle-aged woman in a bright-purple scarf.

"Really? I had no idea." A man nearby wearing a leather jacket lowers his steaming cup. "So that means we're more water than land!"

"Yep, but even more fascinating is that only a portion of that water has been explored."

I feel relieved as I watch Jason standing tall and confident again, back in his element, and I go to sit by the window.

The morning sunlight pours through, forming patterns on the white table. In the center sits a large broken mug, expertly glued and filled with white hydrangeas. What a great way to turn a broken thing into something beautiful, I think to myself. It reminds me of Jason, who continually puts himself back together in a way that's different, but also beautiful.

"I'll ask Jason to bring over your usual, Drew," Sandra says with a smile, then she leans over and whispers, "He's doing very well today, as you can see." She glances over to Jason, who is now deep in conversation about the Mariana Trench with the leather jacket man. "The customers love him. When he wasn't here last weekend, this place was like a tomb."

"Thanks, Sandra." At her words, a swell of pride rolls through my chest. "He has that effect on people. And he loves this place."

Sandra returns to work, serving customers and pouring coffee with an easy grace.

The air in the small café is alive with the warmth of the morning sun and the warm scents of coffee and freshly baked cinnamon pastries. The jazz music coming from the speakers is soothing and I find myself forgetting all the things that happened yesterday.

But then my mind begins to whir again. That lady in the corner with oversized sunglasses and a red beret. The couple by the counter, who seem to be looking in my direction. The old man sitting near the entrance, reading a newspaper with a magnifying glass, who occasionally looks in my direction. Is the real winner of that lottery money among them? It feels like they are watching me, as though they know what I did. Every shadow seems to whisper an accusation, every glance holds a threat.

"Here you go, Mom." Jason is suddenly standing in front of me with my mug of steaming mocha and whipped cream. I was so engrossed in my paranoia that I didn't see or hear him approach.

"Thanks, baby," I say, keeping my voice level. "You look great today. How are you feeling?"

"Every day's a new beginning, right?" He picks up my hand and squeezes it. "You don't have to worry, Mom." He lowers his voice and leans in. "It won't happen again. But you really should stop coming here to check up on me. I can handle myself and this is my place of work. You know what? If you want to know if I'm okay, I'll give you a call every morning." He kisses me on the cheek and disappears, weaving his way through the tables, dropping a greeting, a fact or a joke as he goes.

I wrap my hands around the warm ceramic and consider what he just told me. As much as I want to protect him, I just can't. Maybe I should let go a little, stop coming to the café for a while. I know this place is good for him. I could just come to the pond and steal a glance through the windows. But he needs to know I trust him with his recovery, just like I trusted him with my secret for so many years.

After a while, I pay and stand up to leave, but before going home, I stop by the memorial on my street and walk over to it with the bouquet of yellow tulips that I picked from my garden earlier.

I'm tucking them closer to the base of the trunk when I see it. A torn corner of a newspaper article with a photo.

Only half of the image is visible along the tattered edge. But I'd know that face anywhere.

## TWENTY-FIVE

When I arrive at the Lounge, I'm not even close to ready to cut or do anything else to anyone's hair. Unlike me, everyone seems to be in a great mood. Marlene can't stop talking about a stockbroker she met at the grocery store who called to ask her out on a date.

When I spot Tia across the room, prepping her station, I think back to her hints that Mark had something to do with Melody's death. I brushed them off, but now I feel like I need to know more.

At eleven, when Tia and I both have some free time before our next clients, I approach her. "Hey, do you want to go for a quick walk in the park?" I ask. "I need some fresh air."

She raises an eyebrow but nods. "Sure, let's go."

We walk in silence at first, the sounds of birds chirping and the distant chatter of other park-goers filling the gaps between us. After a few minutes, I clear my throat.

"Tia, I needed to ask you about what you said the other day," I begin, my voice low. "That you think Mark did something to Melody."

Tia's expression shifts, her face growing serious. She stops walking and glances around as if to make sure no one can overhear us. "You sure you want to go there?"

I nod. "Yes. Why do you suspect him?"

She takes a deep breath. "Melody told me something before she died. We had reconnected shortly before everything happened, and she confided in me." Her voice drops even lower, almost a whisper. "She was having an affair. And the day she died, she called me and said she had finally told Mark the truth. That she had never seen him that angry. She honestly sounded terrified on the phone, like she didn't know what he might do next."

My pulse races, a chill creeping up my spine. "I can't believe Mark never told me any of this," I say, my voice shaking now. My chest feels tight. "I mean, it's not my business, but still..."

Tia bites her lip. "I know this is not something you want to hear, but what if he somehow caused that accident? You need to be careful."

"He's not dangerous, Tia. I know my husband."

"You are his wife, you would believe that. But it's not just me who thinks this, there is a reason why Melody's parents distanced themselves from him after Mel died. They left town a few months after her funeral, but I've been in touch with them, and they have the same suspicions as me."

I think back to that donation Mark made to the church, and the confession I overheard, and shiver. No, it can't be true. Not Mark. "We should get back to work."

Tia nods, and we head back to the salon in silence.

As we enter the staff room, I try to steady my hands, but I'm unable to rid myself of the nervous energy that's coursing through me.

·   ·   ·

Pretending everything is normal, I return to the salon floor to start working on my first client—a woman called Josephine. I'm really not in the mood for her constant complaining.

"Sorry, doll," Marlene whispers as she points me her way. "Vanessa is off today, so you'll have to do the honors."

"Perfect," I mutter under my breath. Pasting a smile on my face, I march toward a fidgety Josephine. I'm not really sure why she comes in every week; her Barbie hair is always in the same pristine condition.

"Hi, Josephine," I greet her warmly, hoping my forced cheerfulness isn't too obvious.

"Finally!" she snaps. Her icy-blue eyes glare at me. "I've been waiting ages, darling."

"It's only been five minutes." I point to the clock. "But I'm sorry to keep you waiting. Let's not waste any more time," I say, ushering her toward my station while gritting my teeth.

She huffs and puffs, but obediently sits in the plush seat.

"So, what can I do for you? The usual?" The usual is a wash, a blow-dry, and a curl. "Or do you want to try something new today?" I ask, hoping to distract her from being so snippy.

"Umm, let's see," she says with a twist of her silicone-filled lips. "I'm thinking today maybe we will go for something a bit different. Change my hair in a way that it still screams glamor, but with a twist of something exciting."

I raise my eyebrows at her reflection. "Oh, Josephine! That's a fun idea!" My hands have already started to navigate through her silky tresses. "How about we try some loose waves with a side part? It'll give you more body and it's sophisticated. What do you think?" I propose.

She tilts her head from side to side. "Fine. But don't be too drastic. I still want to recognize myself."

"Understood," I say and once I've begun, Josephine doesn't make any more fuss. She sits quietly, her eyes closing occasionally while I wash, condition, and brush through her hair. This makes my job much easier, and when I'm done, she shocks me by leaning forward, her eyes lighting up.

"I... I really like it," she murmurs. She then turns to me, a genuine smile softening her usually stiff features. "No, I love it. It's different but it's still me. I want you to be my new hairstylist."

At that moment, Helen happens to pass by—dressed in a cream pantsuit and heels—as she sweeps loose strands of hair from the marble floors and overhears Josephine's declaration. She freezes in her tracks, broom still in hand, her eyes wide with shock.

She turns to look at me, then at Josephine, before breaking into a wide grin that gets even wider when Josephine hands me the largest tip anyone has ever given me, and immediately makes an appointment for the next week. All the coins and crisp bills are stuffed hastily into my apron pocket and it feels like a small fortune. I wish I could share it with my other shocked colleagues, but Helen has a rule that tips belong solely to the recipient.

After Josephine leaves, Helen walks over to congratulate me.

"I'm not sure whether Vanessa will be overjoyed she won't have to deal with Josephine's complaining or upset to lose the tips," I say.

"I'll handle Vanessa. A customer has made her choice and that's final. You did fantastic work today. Maybe Josephine's complaining days are over, and that's a relief for all of us." Helen's words, full of sincere pride, warm me from the inside out.

But when I look at my colleagues, from Marlene, to Maggie, to Tia, they don't look very happy. In fact, Tia looks downright crestfallen.

She's been my support ever since we became friends, always cheering me on whenever I felt I was failing at something. To see her usually vibrant eyes clouded over with disappointment pierces me. What is going on with her?

The rest of the day unfurls with an undercurrent of unease. As I wash hair, trim split ends, and sweep up, I feel eyes burn into my back. The salon is filled with the familiar hum of hairdryers and the murmur of conversation, but to me it all sounds like an overwhelming mess of noise. I'm so relieved when I can finally leave. But Tia stops me seconds before I step through the door.

"I'm sorry about earlier, if I upset you. Are we still on for a girls' night in at your place?" When I don't respond, she adds, "Don't tell me you forgot. We set it for seven last week, but I can only be there at eight. Edward's not feeling well, and I want to check on him before I come over. But if it's too late—"

"No, eight is fine. See you later." I'll do my best to make sure we have a lovely evening, but if we are going to remain friends, there will be no more talk of my husband being a suspect in his first wife's death.


It's five minutes after six when I pull up to our street, and Sarah's townhouse looms into view. But it's not the well-tended flower beds or the crisp white picket fence that draws my gaze. It's the two figures on the porch.

One of them is Lori. There's no mistaking the sleek pony-tail, the way she tilts her head as she listens.

My breath catches in my throat, and I slow the car almost to a crawl. Since when do they...? What could they possibly be discussing? I can't hear their words, but they look so chummy.

It's none of your business, Drew. Keep driving.

With a conscious effort, I press down on the accelerator, forcing the car forward. They work together, so it's completely logical they might become friends. But surely Lori knows that

Sarah and Jason don't get along? Not to mention that family dinner when Sarah was openly rude to Lori.

I look back once more, seeing them in a deep conversation.

My mind whirling, I step inside our house and within minutes, I see it.

Our wedding photo, which stands on the living room mantel, has been replaced by Mark and Melody's.

# TWENTY-SIX

A few minutes after I get home, Mark arrives too, but he leaves again shortly after for a fitness expo in Atlanta. He won't be back until Wednesday. I can't tell if I am relieved or lonely, but I'm looking forward to a girls' night in with Tia.

I send him a quick message.

*Thinking of you. Good luck at the expo. Love you, Babe.*

Then I call Jason to check up on him.

"On my way home, Mom. Stop worrying all the time."

"I'm not worrying." I let out a breath. "Just wanted to wish my son a good evening."

Jason chuckles because he knows me too well, but at least he's no longer upset with me.

Before I go to the kitchen, I check the rooms upstairs for any more of Sarah's twisted little surprises. I'm relieved to find nothing, but I can still taste the anger I felt when I found Mark and Melody's wedding photo on the living room mantel.

I removed it swiftly, and when Mark arrived home, I brought it up. To my outrage he refused to believe Sarah did it.

"Don't be ridiculous. Mel gave her the key for emergencies." His voice was a mix of frustration and disbelief. "She wouldn't do something like that."

I clenched my teeth as I took a deep breath.

"Okay, but Mark, if she didn't do it, then who did?" At this point, I'm wondering whether he thinks I'm setting her up, and I feel like I'm being gaslit. "Look, she's clearly hell-bent on torturing me. And she doesn't use that key for emergencies. She walks into our home like she owns it."

By the time he walked out the door, we were two strangers, barely saying a word to each other. Now, scanning the library, I'm hit by a wave of frustration so intense it leaves me breathless. How many times will I have to prove myself before he believes me over her?

With a shake of my head, I check the last few rooms. But everything is in order and undisturbed. I force myself to let go of my paranoia and try to enjoy the evening ahead with Tia.

Inside the kitchen, I pull out the ingredients for my signature spinach, avocado, and artichoke dip, and I find the chopping and stirring quite soothing.

When all the snacks are prepped and ready to be enjoyed, I head upstairs. I still have an hour before she arrives, so I decide to have a bath. Steam envelops me as I sink into the tub, the warmth seeping into my bones. I close my eyes and try to lose myself in the tranquility, and soon the heat makes me drowsy. Before I know it, I can no longer fight sleep.

Then a sound jolts me awake. Did the bell ring? My heart hammers as I sit up, the water sloshing. I grab my phone from the white table next to the tub. Thirty minutes before Tia is due to arrive. Tia is never early.

I pad down the stairs in my bathrobe and open the front door. There's no one there.

But my handbag is lying on its side on the console table, and its contents are no longer organized inside, the way I like them to be, separated in their pockets. No, they are all inside the largest pocket in a chaotic mess.

I fish out my wallet, and my fingers skim over the soft satin lining. Receipts that were meant to be nestled together in one pocket are all scattered. One flutters to the ground, and I snatch it up, fuming.

"Sarah," I hiss as my anger bubbles up.

All this time I've played nice, kept my mouth shut, danced around her like a moth around a flame.

"Enough," I murmur and run back upstairs to get dressed. I'm going to confront her and this time I won't be polite about it.

I shove open the closet door with more force than necessary. And then I freeze as my stomach drops.

Melody's wedding dress is hanging in our closet over the long mirror.

The pearls of the mermaid-style gown glint in the dim light, sewn into the ivory fabric in beautiful clusters. It's stunning and ethereal, but it's completely out of place here.

It's also swaying slightly, as though moved by a gentle breeze that I can't feel.

Then I notice a piece of paper pinned to its hem and I stumble back. The black and white photo stares up at me from a torn newspaper article, just like the one I had found at the memorial site. Melody.

My heart thunders and, with each shallow breath, I feel the walls of the closet close in. I want to run, but instead I find myself snatching the article from the dress and sinking to the floor.

It's a *Stoneview Gazette* article, dated two years ago, and its headline screams at me, burning itself into my brain:

LOCAL WOMAN KILLED IN HIT-AND-RUN TRAGEDY: DRIVER STILL AT LARGE

The words blur before my eyes, the black ink merging with the white paper, and I'm taken right back there to the night that altered the entire course of my life.

Even though I'd rather be doing anything else and even though I feel like I'm dying inside, I force myself to read the article:

*Melody Reynolds (32) was struck down in the prime of her life last Thursday evening when she fell victim to a hit-and-run driver on Elm Grove, only a few blocks from her home. Mrs. Reynolds is currently in a coma at Stoneview General Hospital, fighting for her life.*

*Authorities are seeking any information regarding the incident. The vehicle in question has not been identified and the driver fled without a trace.*

*Mark Reynolds, husband of the victim, has issued a plea for anyone with knowledge of the crime to come forward.*

Beneath the text is Melody's photo, the same one displayed at the memorial site. Her hair cascades in soft waves down her shoulders, framing a face that radiates kindness and peace.

"Melody," I whisper and trace the outline of her face in the photograph, a face that once brought so much joy to the man I love. A man who doesn't know the truth. My vision blurs with unshed tears. "Please forgive me."

It's obvious Sarah knows what I did. And now she is taunting me with the very secret I've gone to such lengths to hide.

The desire I had earlier to go and confront her dies within me. She has too much on me now and the thought of facing her and seeing the triumph in her eyes sends nausea bubbling through me. She might even be waiting for me with the cops, I think wildly.

Whatever happens next, I know one thing for certain: It's over, and soon Mark will find out what I did. That's if he doesn't already know…

# TWENTY-SEVEN

## SARAH

Two Days Ago

On Saturday morning, I'm walking to my blue Honda Civic, planning to stop by the bakery for breakfast before driving to the office to grab some important files I left behind yesterday, when I spot a taxi cruising by my house. There's a familiar person sitting inside it.

Through the back window, I spot Jason's face leaning against the window. His mouth is open, and his eyes look vague and unfocussed.

"Good morning, Sarah?" Mrs. Leonard takes a short break from her garden yoga to wave, and I wave back absentmindedly, my feet already carrying me in the direction of Mark's house because that's where the taxi must be headed.

What is Jason doing here when he should be at work? I heard from Drew that he works every Saturday because it's the busiest time at the café.

A curious nature is what makes me a good reporter, I tell myself as I near the house just as the taxi comes to a halt and

Jason's door swings open. To my surprise, he literally stumbles out.

The way he leans on the cab for support, the way his hands fumble, and the way his hair is as rumpled as his gray t-shirt tells me everything I need to know.

I rush as quickly as I can on my four-inch heels toward him.

"Jason!" My voice slices through the morning stillness. But I get no response from him; he's too caught up in trying not to fall flat on his face.

When I reach him, I smell it immediately, the stench of cheap liquor. As soon as the door slams shut, the taxi peels away from the curb and I'm left alone with him, Drew's drunk son.

Mark once told me that after his father died, Jason had a drinking problem, but he's been sober for quite some time. I've never seen him drunk until now.

"Jason," I call out when I catch up with him at the front door. "What happened? What are you doing here?"

He doesn't answer, just fumbles with his key, trying to open the door and failing, even dropping the key a couple of times.

"Do you need help?" I offer, but Jason flinches, turning to look at me with bloodshot eyes. He blinks a few times, as though trying to place me, before recognition dawns. Despite his clearly inebriated state, I see something resembling relief flicker across his face briefly.

"Mom?" he slurs, the single word coming out husky, then blinks several more times before focusing on my face. "Sarah... I thought—I need..." He trails off and turns away.

To my horror, I watch as he lurches to the side, retching into the well-tended rose bushes that Melody used to so lovingly care for.

I take a step back, but despite my disgust, I can't leave him. I've never cared much for him or his mother, understandably, but nonetheless I feel a sense of responsibility toward him.

Reaching for his arm, I try to steady him, but he sways

dangerously, nearly causing both of us to tumble into the roses. I feel his weight against me as his knees buckle.

"Jason!" I snap and grab the hand holding the key, gripping it tightly as I attempt to pry it from his grasp. "Let me open the door."

Finally, he lets go and I manage to insert the key into the lock, swinging the door wide open. Then I half drag, half carry him inside, depositing him unceremoniously on the sleek leather couch in the living room.

"My mom... Need to talk to her about."

I call out for Drew, but I'm pretty sure she went out for her run because her jogging sneakers that she always keeps by the front door are missing. I sigh, rubbing my temples.

"All right, Jason," I say. "I'm going to get you some water. You stay here."

"No," he slurs as he turns over on the couch, propping himself up on an elbow. "Need to talk to Mom... now..."

"She's not at home. What do you want to talk to her about so urgently?"

"About what she did." Unable to hold himself up on his elbow any longer, he drops back onto the couch, sprawling out and closing his eyes. His lips move as he struggles to form words, his speech slurred by whatever substance he's on. "It's important... I can't do this anymore. I'm tired of keeping her secret."

Despite the smell coming from him, I move closer, my heart thumping. "Secret? What did she do?" I take his hand and squeeze gently. "Jason, you need to tell me. What secret are you talking about?"

He groans and rolls his head to the side, eyes still closed as he pulls his hand away from mine. "The car accident."

# TWENTY-EIGHT

"My mom…" Jason continues while I hold my breath and try not to move so he doesn't spook and stop talking. "She's a good person. Didn't mean to hit her." He starts sobbing now, his shoulders shaking vigorously. I freeze as seconds tick by, filled only with the sound of his heart-wrenching cries.

"Hit who, Jason?" I lean closer, my pulse thrumming in my ears. The room is starting to shrink around me now and the air in my lungs feels thin, as if I'm trying to breathe underwater.

"Melody," he chokes out, and my world tilts on its axis.

"Melody?" My best friend, whose loss carved a hole in my brother's heart. Ice spreads through my stomach and freezes the mess of questions before they spill out of me.

"Mom did it. But she is sorry," he murmurs as he stares into space. "She's really so sorry. No cops."

"Sorry won't bring her back," I murmur but I don't think he even hears me as he continues to mutter things that don't make sense.

When I get to my feet, I can barely hold myself upright.

From the moment Drew entered Mark's life, something about her made me uncomfortable. That's why I looked through her things when I got the chance, searching for clues to prove me right. Mark wouldn't listen to me; he thought I was just unable to accept her because of my grief. But we are like two opposite poles of a magnet that repel each other.

Even so, of all the things I thought she could be, all the secrets I suspected she could be hiding, like for some weird reason lying to our faces that she and Jason have never skied before even though I found lots of skiing photos in that precious box of hers, I never for a moment expected this.

When I told Mark about the lie about skiing, he brushed it off and wouldn't discuss it all, saying I'm just looking for anything to discredit his wife. But now this he can't ignore.

Drew is a killer, who is now married to my brother. Living in Melody, her victim's house.

For two years, the police have been trying to find the driver of the car that hit Melody and drove off without looking back. Two long years of anguish, fear, and uncertainty. How could I have known that the culprit is right here under our very noses, weaving herself so seamlessly into the fabric of our lives, masquerading as a loving wife to my brother?

The thought alone makes my blood boil with an anger so raw and so pure that it sears through my veins.

How does that woman sleep at night, next to the husband of the woman she killed? Only someone so evil and ruthless could pull that off.

"Jason," I whisper, finally finding my voice even though it sounds different to my own ears. "Are you absolutely sure?"

"I need to go home." He pushes himself to a sitting position. "I need to get out of here."

I'm tempted to ask him to stay and wait for his mother, but when Drew comes home, I want us to be alone. Although I don't want her to know that I know, not yet. I need time to think about what to do. Jason will probably not remember in a few hours what he told me.

I watch as he pulls out his phone and tries to turn it on, perhaps to call a taxi, but the screen remains black. Cursing, he drops it on the couch.

"I'll call you an Uber," I tell him and quickly input his address into the app on my phone. Jason's eyes, misty from alcohol, barely register what I'm doing. As the confirmation pops up, I guide him to the front door.

"Thank you," he slurs as he stumbles out the door.

When the Uber arrives, I help him inside, like a good aunt should. I even call his girlfriend to let her know what happened and that it might be a good idea for her to meet him at his apartment. My job is done.

I'm grateful to him for unveiling the truth that's been lurking in the shadows all these years. But very soon, he and his mother will be out of our lives for good.

As I watch the car drive away, I make a silent vow. I will make Drew pay. For Melody. For Mark. For me.

Drew Reynolds, your days of hiding are over.

Instead of going out to eat my breakfast as planned, I stay in the house. I want Drew to find me here, making myself at home in the kitchen that will always belong to Melody.

But I don't want her to suspect a thing, so I need to pull myself together, to be a better actress than she has been all this time.

I could pick up the phone right now and get her arrested, but that would be too easy. Drew needs to feel her world crumble in the worst possible way, right before she loses everything. Just like Melody.

# TWENTY-NINE

## DREW



I'm sitting on the closet floor, and each word of the newspaper headline echoes in my brain as the paper crinkles in my palm. Every inhale feels like a gasp and each exhale a shudder. It's happening, a full-blown panic attack that's clawing its way up from the depths of my darkest memory.

"Sarah knows," I whisper to the empty room, the words slicing through the silence.

Another shudder escapes my lips and I drop the crumpled article onto the floor.

Jason must have told her. He's the only one who knows what happened, the truth of that horrific night. And he saw her when he was drunk and liable to say anything.

"Melody..." The name is a strangled sob. In my mind's eye, I see everything, and I hear the sounds—the headlights, the impact, the dreadful stillness that followed it. Those images have haunted me every day in the last two years.

I form fists with both hands and thump them against my

temples, forcing myself to focus and think. If Sarah knows I'm responsible for Melody's death, there's no telling what she'll do.

I feel the walls closing in on me, the handcuffs clicking on my wrists.

Finally, I manage to pull myself to my feet. My eyes land on the crumpled article, and I snatch it off the floor. Staggering to the bathroom, my movements are jerky and uncoordinated as though someone else is pulling the strings. I splash cold water on my face and, still dripping wet, I fling open the window to allow more air to flood the room.

My trembling hands tear the article into small pieces before I flush them down the toilet just as a terrible thought hits me and I drop to the edge of the tub, clutching the lip tight.

What if it's not Sarah? What if it's Mark?

He has been so strange these last few days. Then there was that day he was looking for something in my library. Maybe it wasn't the lottery ticket as I thought. Was he searching for evidence? A diary, a scrawled note or a confession hidden among my books, somewhere I'd never think he'd look?

But no, it can't be him, he's miles away and I was in the closet before taking a bath. Whoever snuck in to hang up the dress and pin the article to it was close by.

Anyway, touching Melody's wedding dress and seeing her face in that article would have torn him apart. He wouldn't use Melody's memory to torment me; his heart is too saturated with grief. And if he knew, as much as he loves me, wouldn't he call the cops right away?

"It's not him," I breathe out. "It can't be."

Sarah is the one person who would relish watching me squirm until I shatter completely.

Her hate for me is a living thing that's just waiting to strike.

Jason told her the truth a few days ago and now she is tormenting me, waiting for me to confess. I have to get a grip, to be strong. Right now, it's still her word against mine.

Clutching at the little shred of courage I have left, I steel myself for what comes next. Whatever Sarah has planned, I'll face it.

I grab Melody's wedding dress and take it to the garage, but just as I fold it and put it inside its garment bag that has been left discarded on top of a box, the doorbell inside the house shrills. Tia. I totally forgot she was coming over.

"Damn it," I mutter, wiping my moist palms on my jeans.

"Coming!" I call as I rush through the door connecting the garage to the house.

I quickly go into the downstairs bathroom, and a glance in the mirror confirms my fears. I look terrible. My eyes are red-rimmed and haunted, and my skin is as pale as a sheet. The panic is carved into every line on my face.

"I can do this," I whisper to my reflection, dabbing at my swollen eyes with a cloth dipped in cold water. Then I stride to the front door, taking deep breaths and preparing my lips for a smile.

"Hey, you," I say as I open the door. Surprisingly, the words come out steadier than I feel. "Sorry, I was just in the back."

Tia's eyes widen. "Drew, are you okay?" She moves the bag of snacks she's holding to her other arm.

"Yeah, I'm fine." I manage to choke out a forced laugh. "It's just been a long day. Come in." I open the door wider for her to enter as I glance past her shoulders to see if Sarah is out there, watching my breakdown.

"You really don't look well," Tia insists when we walk into the kitchen, and she puts down the bag she's carrying. "Come on, sweetie, sit down."

Leaving no room for argument, she steers me to the kitchen table and pulls out a chair and guides me into it.

"Drew, what happened? Did you tell Mark what I said? Did he hurt you?" There's an edge to Tia's voice.

I shake my head, pressing my lips together, but before I know it, tears are running down my cheeks.

Tia pulls out a chair for herself and takes both my hands in hers. "What's going on, sweetheart? I know you don't like to bother people with your problems, but we're friends. Come on, talk to me. You can tell me anything. If he touched you, I swear—"

"Mark did nothing to me. Like I said before, he's a good man, Tia." Wiping my eyes, I know I need to give her something, anything, to redirect her attention from my husband. "An old friend passed away. I just found out." The lie tumbles from my lips before I can stop it.

"Oh." She looks almost disappointed. "God, I'm so sorry." Her brow creases with genuine sympathy and she draws me into a hug.

After a while, she gets up to get me a glass of water and tissues. "Was your friend ill or was it an accident?" She drops back into her seat.

I hesitate for a moment, ready to fabricate details as I go. "A short illness."

"I'm so sorry, Drew. If you need anything..."

"I'm sorry to ruin tonight, but I really just want to be alone." I blow my nose loudly. "To process everything. I hope you understand."

"Of course I understand, honey." Tia pushes out of her chair and makes me comfortable on the couch, putting all the snacks she brought on the coffee table.

When she finally steps out the door, the relief is palpable. I watch through the window as she walks to her car. Then she turns around, frowning as she looks back at the house, and it seems as if she looks over at someone or something else, out of my vision. She nods briefly, then gets in her car and drives off.

## THIRTY

Half an hour after Tia is gone, Sarah still hasn't come over to confront me, so I get into my car. The steering wheel feels slick under my palms.

"Focus," I mutter to myself as the streetlamps blur past and I fix my thoughts on the roads and the rhythm of the traffic lights changing from red, to orange, to green. I also crank up the volume of the radio, even though none of the songs register in my mind. The music is simply white noise, merging with the hum of the engine and the whisper of tires against the tarmac.

Finally, Jason's apartment building looms into view, a concrete structure against the darkening skyline, which somehow seems more menacing now. I find a parking spot near the entrance and turn off the car, still debating with myself whether it was actually a good idea to come here.

My hands are between my knees and I'm taking deep, measured breaths to calm myself, and then after a few more seconds of silent pep talk, I finally push open the car door and step out.

The short walk to Jason's door feels like an eternity. Could this be the last day I get to speak to my son before I'm thrown behind bars? That brief kiss Mark gave me before he left for his trip, was it the last time I will ever feel his lips on mine?

I don't use my emergency key to enter Jason's apartment because in my rush out of the house, I forgot it. So, I buzz the intercom, and the sound jolts me. As I wait for him to buzz me up, I notice the fabric of my blouse sticking to my back. The air is thick and humid.

A few moments pass in silence. I press the intercom again, my heartbeat thundering in my ears.

Finally, I hear a crackle and Jason's voice filters through the static. "Who is it?" he asks, sounding a little annoyed.

"Hi, honey. It's me, Mom," I answer, trying to make my voice sound as normal as possible.

His response is immediate. The door buzzes open and I'm welcomed into the sterile gray hallway that leads to his apartment.

I find him standing in the doorway and when he sees me, his eyes flicker over my rumpled state, widening with alarm. "Mom, are you okay?"

I force a fleeting smile. "I'm fine, Jason." Stepping into his apartment, I notice Lori in tight, dark jeans and a white cropped top standing in the kitchen doorway, a rag in her hand. I give her a small smile and a wave, breathing in the smell of tomato sauce, pungent garlic, and heady oregano.

"You're cooking dinner." I look back at Jason. "I'm sorry if I'm disturbing."

"Mom, what are you doing here?" His features have taken on a worried expression, his eyes piercing into mine with questions.

"We need to talk... alone." My eyes flicker to Lori, then back to him.

Jason's lips press into a thin line, and he nods slightly, motioning for me to wait while he whispers something into Lori's ear.

She nods quietly and, with evident hesitation, she backs away toward the bedroom, stealing one final glance back at me before disappearing.

"I think we should go and talk in my car," I say. This is a small apartment, and I can't run the risk of us being overheard.

Jason follows me to the parking lot without protest, the concern etched deep into his features. "Mom, what's wrong?" His voice is laced with anxiety.

I don't say a thing until we're safely inside my car with the door locked.

"Say something," he urges. "You're scaring me. What's going on?"

Swallowing hard, I turn to him and get straight to the point. "Jason," I start. "That day when you showed up drunk at the house. Did you tell Sarah anything?"

At first, Jason is quiet, then he starts scratching his palm vigorously, something he used to do as a little boy when he was nervous. "No, I didn't, I already told you last time. Look, I need to go. Night, Mom." Before I can press him further, he pushes the door open and steps out.

"Night," I whisper to his retreating form.

I'll let him go and have his dinner before his world is shattered by watching his mother thrown behind bars, just like his grandfather.

I've lied to Mark about a lot of things, including my family. To him, my family is just a distant, painful memory, estranged parents who neglected me so much that I ended up in care.

Mark doesn't know about my father, the alcoholic. The man who resorted to violence when drunk.

He doesn't know about the night that ended with flashing blue lights and a body bag with my mother inside it.

And he doesn't know what I did.

## THIRTY-ONE

## SARAH

Working for a local newspaper in a small town like Stoneview is far from the glamorous career I imagined while studying for my bachelor's in journalism at the University of Tampa. But it pays the bills, and it means I get to be close to Mark, which I'm especially grateful for, knowing he'll soon be needing me more than ever.

Sitting down at my desk in my small office that's more like a closet than anything else, I dig my fingernails into my palms.

Seeing Sarah every day in my brother's house, putting on the facade of the ideal wife, is pure agony. She may try to deceive everyone else, but I know the truth. She is a manipulative, cold-hearted killer.

She should be in prison right now, but that feels like too easy a punishment. She's a murderer and a liar and I want her out of my brother's life, but it will be on my terms.

Thoughts of revenge fill my every waking moment, and even my dreams. It's as if a flame has been ignited within me and the desire for justice is the fuel driving me forward.

Somehow I need concrete evidence to show Mark that she

killed Melody. If there's one thing I know about my brother, it's that he can be trusting to a fault, and it would take him seeing the cruel truth in all its stark reality to believe that his wife is not the woman he thinks she is. I know how deeply he feels for her, and his love for her is so blinding that it would shut out any possibility of her guilt.

If I'm too blunt with my suspicions, he'll protect her. I hate that every time I criticize her, he comes to her defense as if his survival depends on it. It's maddening, especially now that I am aware of the truth.

Trying to collect myself, I bury my hands into my short black hair, sighing heavily as I stare at a calendar on the wall across from me. Getting back to my feet, I grab a pen and approach it. Then I put a red cross on Tuesday, July 31st—my birthday—and get back to my desk just as my boss, Sam Marino, knocks softly on my open door then walks in for our one-on-one meeting.

Sam has a beer belly that enters the room before the rest of him does, and a booming voice that echoes through the halls even when he whispers. He's balding, with tufts of gray hair scattered on the sides, and his thick glasses always seem to sit on the tip of his nose. He's not smiling as he steps into the room, and I know why.

He's not been pleased with anything I've been doing for the past few weeks, or months, for that matter. To be fair, I've definitely dropped the ball the past two weeks and it's all Drew's fault. She's constantly in my head. Of course, it doesn't help my case that the *Gazette* is not performing well due to the lack of groundbreaking stories. And for that, I have been under scrutiny. In Sam's eyes, I must either pull out a significant story or go down with the sinking ship.

"Sarah," he starts, leaning against my desk with a stern look on his face, "we need to talk about your performance lately."

"I know, Sam, I've been off my game," I admit before he spells it out for me.

"Damn right." He tugs at his tie that's a disgusting shade of magenta. He's a man of questionable taste, but he's also the man who signs my paychecks, so I grit my teeth and nod. "You're one of the best we've got, Reynolds, but we both know you've been slipping lately. You haven't brought me any fresh news for weeks. It's like you're not even trying." His words sting more than usual because they ring true. I've been too wrapped up in my personal life to focus on my work. "If this keeps up—"

"I know," I cut him off, unwilling to hear the rest of his sentence. "I'll get it together. I promise."

"See that you do." He straightens up, smoothing his light blue tweed jacket and adjusting his glasses, a serious glint in his eyes. "The *Gazette*'s reputation is at stake here, Sarah, and as our top reporter, we need you at your best."

Meetings with Sam never last more than ten minutes, and they always end with him reminding me that I am his best reporter, the one who always gets the scoop. He's trying to be encouraging, but it feels like a lot of pressure to me.

I earned the title of best reporter because I'm usually the first to bring in the stories that nobody else dared to touch, like the story of former Mayor McCall's illicit affairs which rocked our small town to its core. Or the corruption within the city council that created waves that resulted in a complete administration overhaul.

But now, all that seems like a faraway memory, as if I'd used up all my luck on those stories, and now I'm scraping the bottom of the barrel. I can't even remember the last time I had a lead on anything remotely significant. I really need to snap out of it before I lose my job.

Suddenly, my gaze moves back to the calendar and the red cross.

Until this moment, I had not planned on bringing the

family drama to work, and the last thing I want is to have my brother's life splashed across the paper. But if unveiling the truth about Drew means sacrificing a slice of our privacy, then it's a sacrifice I'm prepared to make. Why not kill two birds with one stone?

I swallow hard and taste a bitter and metallic taste at the back of my throat, as fear and desperation dance inside me. The thing is, if I'm not the one to drop the bomb, someone else will.

"And tidy up that desk. It's a pigsty," Sam snaps, a last jab before he leaves my office. The door clicks shut behind him, leaving me alone with the silence and the chaos of my desk. Papers are scattered across the wooden surface, a couple of empty coffee cups from this morning's (and yesterday's) caffeine fix, a stack of unopened envelopes I had been avoiding, and so much more. I run a hand through my tousled hair.

I'm about to dig in and start cleaning when I decide to do something else first, something much more important. I pick up the phone and dial.

"Lori," I say when she answers, "can you come to my office for a sec?"

Even though I was initially miffed when I found out that Sam had hired Lori to be one of the three office admins, since she started, I began to get on with her quite well. And then I had a brainwave; I tasked her with spying on Drew, to see if she was doing anything unusual, as I suspect she's squirreled that lottery ticket away somewhere.

Lori is so desperate to please that she agreed, without asking questions. Now I need her even more than ever. I need evidence and she is my best bet.

"Hey, Sarah," she chirps when she enters, her shiny ponytail swinging from side to side. "Need some more coffee or—"

"I need information, Lori." I motion for her to close the door, and she does as she's told.

"Information?" Her gaze flickers to the newspapers scattered across my messy desk. "About what?"

"Drew." I lean back in my chair. "I gave you this special project five days ago, and you still haven't delivered anything useful."

Lori's eyes widen, her cheeks flushing a pale pink. "I—I'm trying my best, Sarah, to see if Drew has any secrets. Drew doesn't share much and she sticks to her usual routine. I even went to her salon twice to get my hair done and chat with her, but she wouldn't tell me anything personal. It doesn't help that I don't know what I'm supposed to be looking for."

I sigh and clasp my hands on my desk. "Listen, like I said last time, I think Drew might be hiding something, and I'm worried about the impact it could have on her son, my nephew. I can't go into more detail than that, but you love Jason, don't you?"

"Yeah... of course, I do," she says. "He's my boyfriend."

"Then help me protect him, Lori." I motion for her to lean in, and whisper, "This is also a great way for you to hone your skills as a reporter and prove yourself as more than just an admin. It's a win-win. I really think you have talent."

She bobs her head, and a bright smile curls her lips. I do feel a little sorry for the kid. She's eighteen, a high-school dropout just like her boyfriend, with a father who died before she was born and a mother who's battling multiple sclerosis, and she's working this dead-end job for peanuts. She's a popular girl in town but she's had more than her share of hardships.

"I'll do my best, Sarah," Lori says, determination settling on her pretty face. "You'll have what you need soon. If there's anything to find out about Drew, I'll find it."

I offer her a tight smile. "Thank you, Lori. Just remember to stay discreet."

"Absolutely," she reassures me. "But I still think Jason deserves to know about this. I hate doing this behind his back."

"I understand, but not yet. We don't have all the facts, just a hunch. And besides, Jason is too close to his mother to see things clearly. He'll only get defensive and close up if he senses that we suspect her of anything. We need concrete evidence. Think like a journalist here, Lori."

"I understand." Lori's voice is firmer now.

# THIRTY-TWO

Late in the afternoon, my desk is still overflowing with documents, folders, and scattered papers. The computer screen flickers in the dim office light and my neck is stiff from hours of tense work. I hunch over the latest report from our private investigator, squinting to read the tiny, almost illegible handwriting.

I press my fists into my eyes, rubbing away the exhaustion and frustration. Today was supposed to be simple: cover the local bake sale for the *Gazette*, interview Mrs. Whitaker about her prize-winning rhubarb pie. The bake sale story is a fluff piece, but in Stoneview, it's as scandalous as it gets with Mrs. Whitaker accusing a rival baker of using store-bought crust. Front-page material. Small-town life, small-town news.

But I didn't get to any of that because I couldn't focus on anyone or anything else but Drew. I spent countless hours working out the perfect plan to bring her down. Everything else got postponed.

Looking at my desk again, I decide that maybe I don't need to tackle it all. I could do a bit today before leaving the office and get to the rest tomorrow, or more realistically, in the next two days.

Or I'll just start tomorrow. Before I know it, I'm grabbing my oversized leather bag, and stepping out into the quiet office hallway. It's only four, but I'm ready to call it a day. If Sam calls to ask where I am, I'll just tell him I'm on my way to interview someone for an article.

Outside, I shuffle across the parking lot, but the click-clack of my heels on the asphalt is giving me a headache. Sliding into the driver's seat of my car, I drop my bag onto the passenger seat and let out a long, slow exhale.

I turn the key in the ignition, the engine purring to life, and for a moment, I just sit there, staring blankly at the illuminated dashboard. What I need right now is to go home and jump under a hot shower before crawling under my Egyptian cotton sheets that Reed, the ex I broke up with two months ago, bought me. I'm obsessed with bed sheets. I absolutely love the feel of high-thread-count fabric against my skin. After a long, tiring day, it's my personal slice of heaven. There's nothing quite like the sensation of crisp, cool cotton on a hot day, or warm, comforting flannel in the dead of winter. But the sheets will have to wait.

As if moving with a will of their own, my hands steer the car toward Stoneview Senior Living Center, right on the edge of town. As the town shrinks behind me, I think of how Mark unwinds by lifting weights or swimming laps before dawn. Several times, he encouraged me to do the same, to find joy, peace, and calm through exercise, but that's not me. To me, every squat and every mile on the treadmill feels like punishment, a reminder of a past life I'd rather forget.

Growing up, our parents were also fitness fanatics, and it was from that shared passion that Shoreline Fitness was born. They practically lived in that place, both working on the business and working out. Their obsession infiltrated every corner of our lives. Mealtimes were peppered with discussions about protein intake and optimal muscle recovery. Bedtime stories were replaced by motivational speeches from famous athletes.

The only vacations we ever had were to fitness retreats, in the middle of nowhere, where the fun activities included morning jogs and sunset yoga. To Mark, they were a paradise. While he seemed to thrive on it all, soaking up the knowledge and growing stronger both physically and mentally, I was left feeling drained and exhausted. I felt like I was being forced to become someone I wasn't, to fit the family mold.

Unlike my brother, I decided to do something completely different. I wanted to become a journalist, so I studied it and modeled on the side. Fortunately, my parents were not alive to see that. At least, if they were alive, they would have been proud of Mark, who took over Shoreline Fitness, transforming it into a local empire. He even branched out into creating health products and food supplements, all while following our parents' original vision.

He was completely dedicated until Melody, the love of his life, died, and the business took a backseat while he grieved. Everything crashed and burned. Our parents' legacy is now on the brink of bankruptcy and soon it might not exist anymore.

When Mark told me that Drew had won a large sum of money in the lottery, money that could save Shoreline Fitness, I was so relieved because that business is Mark's life. But then he told me that she lost the ticket, and I didn't believe it for one second. A grand prize, gone just like that? Yeah, right.

Knowing what I now know, that she's a hardened liar—a murderer—I'm even more certain she hid that ticket and eventually she will claim the money and keep it for herself and her son. Maybe she's even thinking she can use it to make a run for it, start a new life under a new identity in case she one day gets discovered. It makes me physically sick to think she shares a bed with the man whose wife she killed. What exactly is she playing at?

I have to find that ticket and it has to be in the house somewhere. After the pain she caused Mark, he deserves that money, and so do I. In fact, I desperately need a cash injection right now.

When I finally see the Stoneview Senior Living Center appear on the horizon, I forget about Drew for the moment. The building is a massive complex with a red-brick facade, surrounded by stretches of well-kept lawns and vibrant flower gardens. Elderly residents are seated under large shade trees, engaged in happy discussions and laughter to end the day right.

The center is organized like a tight-knit community with neatly laid out pastel-colored bungalows spread around a sparkling lake at the heart of the property. A soft breeze floats in from the water, carrying with it the fragrance of fresh earth and blooming flowers.

As I pull into the parking lot next to a gleaming silver sedan, in front of a sky-blue bungalow that houses the administrative offices, I take a deep breath. I've made it through another day, and for now, this is my sanctuary. Perhaps it's strange to seek refuge among people who are living out their twilight years, but this place is filled with a sense of peace that I never found anywhere else. Things seem to move slower here, gentler.

Walking toward the main entrance that leads into the lobby, I briefly smile at Edna, who's sitting comfortably on her porch swing, engrossed as usual in a crossword puzzle. The woman never tires of them. She lifts her head to return my greeting, the fringes of her curly white hair dancing in the breeze.

"How's the crossword treating you today?" I ask as a free dose of energy floods me.

"It's like a stubborn mule, this one." She chuckles and gestures for me to come over and sit with her.

I shake my head gently. "I'd love to, but I can't stay long."

"Young people of nowadays, always rushing," she tuts, but there's kindness in her eyes. "You remind me of..."

"Your daughter?" I finish for her, knowing the story well. Apparently, her daughter is a big surgeon in New York, always caught up in the fast-paced life and barely having time to visit. At one point, she even suffered a heart attack due to stress. It was a wake-up call for her, but she had not been able to slow down much despite the scare.

"Ah, yes. Macy is always chasing the next big thing. Never finding it." She pauses. "Stay for dinner at least. It's only in fifteen minutes."

"Maybe I will," I call over my shoulder. As much as I do appreciate a fast-paced life most days, I don't want to end up like Macy.

I do stay for dinner, not to eat but to help out. I really enjoy spending time with the residents, including Edna, who are now shuffling toward the dining hall. I love the sense of community.

"Will you play piano for us tonight, Sarah?" Mr. Jacobs asks as he maneuvers his wheelchair closer, his pipe dangling from a corner of his lips.

"Sorry, not tonight," I say, feeling a pang of guilt. "Maybe next time."

When dinner is over and I've helped with the cleaning up, I escort eighty-five-year-old Mrs. Henderson, or Mrs. H. as she likes to be called, to her bungalow. I've been coming here for two years now, and Mrs. Henderson has been like a grandmother to me. My maternal and paternal grandparents died when I was too young to remember them.

"Sarah, dear, it's so good to see you. I feel like I haven't seen you in ages."

"I was just here two days ago, Mrs. H." I help her into her favorite recliner, the worn leather one by the window. From her seat, she has a perfect view of the garden and the water.

"Look what I brought you." I reach into my bag and pull out

a beautiful miniature birdhouse that's just the same shade of pink as Mrs. H's bungalow and the details are exquisite, from the texture of the wooden planks to the individual shingles on the roof. In her youth, Mrs. H. owned a store that sold handmade crafts, birdhouses being their specialty.

"Oh, Sarah…" she gasps, her fingertips gliding over the delicate structure. "Where in the world did you get this?"

"I found it yesterday in a small antique shop downtown. I saw it and instantly thought of you. Do you like it?"

"Of course I do, sweet child." Her eyes well up with tears as she brings it to her chest. "You're such a sweet girl." She reaches out to squeeze my hand. "But you look tired, dear."

"It's just been one of those days," I deflect.

She nods and doesn't dig deeper, but as she starts recounting stories of her youth, and how excited she is that one of her long-lost nephews will be visiting her tomorrow, my phone buzzes inside my bag.

"Excuse me," I whisper, stepping away to check the missed calls. There are three in total and a message from Lori.

"Sarah, I found something about Drew. It could be big. We need to talk. Can I come over to your place at six?"

I quickly send a text back agreeing to meet. But before I leave, there's something else I need to do, another resident I need to see.

On my way, I stop by the front desk and hand an envelope to Lucy, the receptionist. "For Mrs. Grayson's account."

"You have a heart of gold, Sarah," Lucy says, tucking the envelope into a folder. "Helping out your friend with her mother's expenses and all. It's hard to believe friendships like that exist."

"Well, they do. Trina and I are very close." Needing this conversation to end, I wave at her as I head to Mrs. Grayson's bungalow. When I knock, her weak voice calls out, "Come in."

She's slumped in a recliner, a shawl draped over her shoulders, her complexion paler than usual. "Sarah, you came." Her voice is raspy but full of warmth.

"Of course, Mrs. Grayson." I walk over to adjust the blanket covering her legs. "I heard you weren't feeling well today, and that's why you didn't come to dinner with the others. Did the nurse come by to check on you?"

"Oh yes, dear," she replies. "Just a touch of dizziness and fatigue. The nurse gave me something and told me to rest. I'll be fine tomorrow." She clasps my hand. "I've been thinking about my Trina a lot today. She's such a blessing, you know? Working so hard to keep me here. I don't know how she does it." Her voice cracks. "I just wish she didn't have to take on so much for me."

"I'm sure she's happy to do it. It's clear how much she loves you."

She nods, her watery eyes fixed on the television. "She tells me not to worry, but I know how expensive this place is, taking most of her nursing salary. She's a saint, my Trina is."

"You're right. She's incredible. It's a good thing she has you to inspire her."

Mrs. Grayson chuckles. "Oh, don't be silly. I'm just grateful God gave me a daughter like her."

As she continues talking about her daughter's sacrifices, I nod along, my mind wandering.

Finally, I squeeze her shoulder. "Mrs. Grayson, I'll come back again soon, okay? And if you need anything, just let me know."

"Thank you, Sarah," she whispers, her head already lolling to the side in exhaustion.

I leave the bungalow and take a deep breath of the cool evening air. The sweet scent of flowers lingers in the background, overshadowed by something heavier as I think of Mrs. Grayson and how she came to be in this place.

But she can never know. No one can.

# THIRTY-THREE

I find Lori on my doorstep and, as soon as she sees me, her eyes light up and she starts rummaging through her bag, then she pulls out a hardcover book.

"Here," she says, glancing behind her.

It's a book with a cover of a seascape bathed in moonlight. I've seen it before—it was in that box I took from Drew—but I flip the cover open anyway to the photos, each more stunning than the last. Remote beaches, a forest with the sun peeking through the leaves, a desert stretching under a star-studded sky.

It's hardly the smoking gun I need to blow Drew's life apart.

"This is supposed to be important?" My voice is flat and exhausted.

Lori takes it and leans in, her breath warm against my cheek. "Let's go inside and I'll show you."

Simply too tired to disagree and desperately needing to sit, I open the door and we both step into the living room that's almost as messy as my office, but I can't find it inside me to care.

When I drop onto the couch, Lori lowers herself down next to me.

"I found it in a box in Drew and Mark's library on the top

shelf, buried under some stuff," she whispers with a self-satisfied grin. "There were three copies so she might not notice immediately that one is missing."

"You broke into their house?"

"No, I had Jason's key. He doesn't know I took it." Looking sheepish, she hugs the book to her body. "You said I should do whatever it takes. Don't worry, no one saw me."

I find myself a little impressed. I guess I underestimated this girl and the lengths she would go to for her career.

"Show me what you found, Lori. Quickly." This book must hold something significant, if she's this excited about it, something I missed. And it must be important to Drew if she took it out of the garage and hid it inside Melody's studio.

Lori nods, then she starts flipping through the pages until she stops close to the middle. "Here."

The photograph takes up an entire page. It's of a snow-covered mountain, its white peaks blending seamlessly with the clouds and glistening under the sun like diamonds. The entire landscape is framed by a brilliant blue sky, and it's breathtaking.

"What am I supposed to be seeing? It's just a mountain, Lori." I need facts, evidence, not beautifully shot landscapes.

Lori points to the photograph. "Jason has this same image in his apartment and he told me his mother is the one who took it. She used to be some big-shot photographer and traveled the country taking pictures of places like this. I recognize others too. They are all hers."

I blink, digesting this new information. It's not new to me that Drew is a hobby photographer. But I had no idea she had once done it professionally.

Lori turns to the final page of the book and her finger stabs at where the artist is credited.

"Look," she says, her voice low and insistent. "The photographer's name."

My pulse roars in my ears as I read the name—Cassey Bell.

Cassey, not Drew. A mix of anger and triumph surges through me.

"Unbelievable," I manage to push out through gritted teeth and get up from the couch.

"Are you okay?" Lori asks.

"I'm fine." I keep my voice level. Lori doesn't know the full extent of what this woman is capable of, and it has to stay that way for now. The last thing I need is her tripping over her own ambition and jeopardizing everything. She's too impulsive and exposing Drew has to come at the right time.

"You did well, Lori. This is a good find. But don't tell anyone, especially Jason, about it."

Lori's lips curl into a hopeful smile, her eyes lighting up as she clasps her hands together like a little girl. "So, will you talk to Sam about letting me write something for the *Gazette* one day?"

"Listen," I say in a measured tone, "this is just a small piece of the puzzle. We're far from a full story." I stand up and lead her to the door. "I'll keep the book, but if you find anything else, let me know."

Once Lori leaves, I sit back down on the couch, the book heavy in my hands. My heart pounds as I flip through the pages again, stopping at the name *Cassey Bell*. I trace it with my finger, the letters practically burning into my skin.

I grab my laptop from the coffee table and open it, typing *Cassey Bell photographer* into the search bar. At first, nothing significant comes up, just scattered mentions of amateur competitions and a few scenic prints on sale through obscure sites. My frustration mounts, but I keep going, clicking through pages of results.

It's on the sixth page that I finally find something—a grainy article from nearly a decade ago. The headline reads:

TALENTED PHOTOGRAPHER HONORED AT NATIONAL
LANDSCAPE EXHIBITION

My breath catches as I scroll down and see a small, blurry photo of the honoree. She's a little younger, but there's no mistaking the face. It's Drew—or rather, Cassey Bell—with a shy smile, holding a framed photograph of the very mountain scene in the book.

I sit back, staring at the screen. Drew is Cassey Bell, and she's been hiding it all along. But why? Why bury a successful career? What else has she hidden?

The web of lies Drew has spun is starting to unravel, and I intend to pull every loose thread until it all falls apart.

After Lori leaves, I walk over to Mark and Melody's home. Then I just stand out there, watching Drew through the kitchen window, moving around from fridge to sink and to stove as if she belongs there.

My hands clench into fists at my sides. How dare she stand in Melody's kitchen, touching her kitchen utensils and dishware like they are hers.

I am desperate to confront her. But not yet. Not until the trap is set and the evidence is irrefutable. For now, I can only watch, wait, and plan. But tonight, she needs to know that someone knows. Then she can stew in her own fear. It's a slight opening of the curtain to give her a glimpse of the hurricane that's about to hit.

I know that Mark is not home because he told me yesterday he'd be driving to Atlanta for a last-minute fitness expo. I saw his car drive away not too long ago.

Tonight, alone in the house she stole, Drew won't be doing much sleeping knowing that someone knows and is coming for her.

When she finally leaves the kitchen, I wait a while before sneaking into the garage to get Melody's wedding dress. No more leaving little mementos of Melody around the house, like that wedding photo I sneaked in this morning for Drew to find. This time I'm going big, and when Mark returns, I'll show him the truth about the woman he married.

# THIRTY-FOUR

## DREW



It's Thursday morning, three days since I found the article and Melody's wedding dress, and I'm about to head out jogging. I'm trying not to show my fear, to stay calm while I figure out what is going on, but obviously I'm freaking out. When Mark came home from his trip last night, I broke down in tears and was crying so much that I had to tell him the same lie I told Tia, that a friend of mine died and that I will be taking today and tomorrow off work.

It's not like me, but I was going to stay in bed all day until Mark called me half an hour ago, urging me to go for my jog, promising that it would do me good.

Every second, I'm on edge, waiting for Sarah to make her next move, to tell Mark what she knows, but it has not happened yet. The anxiety is killing me.

I go straight for a full-blown sprint, pushing myself harder and harder, my lungs burning. Finally, I find myself returning to the memorial site. Like a masochist, I just can't help myself.

It feels like walking into a trap. But as usual, I kneel down and get to work. I remove the decaying petals, some of them from the flowers I brought last time I came.

When I'm done, I look up and my eyes lock onto the photo attached to the tree trunk, looking straight into those of the smiling woman, a woman frozen in time.

"Forgive me. I'm so sorry, Melody. I'm so sorry," I choke out and not for the first time, then I push to my feet and continue running without looking back. This time, I don't snap a photo. And I don't think I'll be coming back here. I could already be behind bars by tomorrow morning.

As my feet pound the pavement, my breath comes in sharp gasps and a damp chill clings to my back. I'm so desperate to run to Sip & Snack to see Jason, desperate for another hug from my son before we are torn apart. But I know he doesn't want me there.

Finally, back at the house, I'm about to jump into the shower when my phone rings and it's Mark checking up on me.

"Honey, I hope you did go out for that jog," he says, his gruff voice heavy with concern. "And you should really eat breakfast."

"Yes, I just got home. And I will eat, promise," I say automatically, even though the thought of food makes my stomach churn.

"Good. I'll check up on you again later." He pauses. "By the way, I know you might not feel up to it, but Sarah reminded me of the family dinner tomorrow night. I think it might also be good for you. You don't have to worry about a thing, I'll cook or we'll order in again."

My heart stumbles over a beat. Tomorrow? How did I forget?

What if this is the chance Sarah has been waiting for, the perfect time to expose me to Mark?

"Are you there?" Mark asks.

"Yes, yes." I shut my eyes tight. "Look, babe, can we cancel this time? I just really don't feel up to it."

He sighs. "Baby, I really think you need this, to be surrounded by family. I told Sarah about your friend, and she's really worried about you. We should do this. I think you'll feel better afterward. Just show your face for a bit, that's all I ask."

"I can't, Mark. I'm sorry, but we need to postpone to next Friday."

He finally gives in, but not without a sigh of exasperation first. "All right, all right. Next Friday it is." His voice is laced with disappointment. "You promise?"

"I promise," I say, swallowing hard. But I know by next Friday, I could be sitting in a dingy jail cell, and Mark will never want to see or talk to me again.

# THIRTY-FIVE

## SARAH



It's a busy Friday at the *Gazette* and my desk is strewn with papers and notebooks, pink, cream, and yellow sticky notes plastered all over my monitor. A half-empty coffee cup is creeping to the edge of the desk.

I stare at many open tabs on my screen, all the uninspiring small-town stories I'm struggling to care about but don't. Bake sales, gardening contests, another city council meeting—it all bores me to death.

I reach for a notepad and flip through old notes I made, scribbles, reminders of interviews, and facts that need verifying. The story in front of me is about a new playground being built near the elementary school. The council members were thrilled about it, but it's hardly front-page news. I can already hear the yawns from our readers.

Trying to stay awake after a sleepless night, I sip the coffee I brought into my office an hour ago and grimace at the acrid taste. I should get up and reheat it, but I can't muster up the energy. As I reach for my mouse to click aimlessly between tabs, my phone vibrates, the buzz cutting through the hum of fluorescent lights. Trina's name flashes on the screen, and I groan before I force a smile onto my face.

"Hi, Trina," I say, keeping my tone breezy.

"Hey there, Sarah!" Her voice is chipper, and the sound of waves in the background adds a cheerful note. "Hope I'm not interrupting anything. I just got a call from the home. They mentioned you stopped by to pay Mom's bill and even spent some time with her."

"Oh, yeah. I promised I would, and your mom's a sweetheart."

"Well, it means a lot," Trina says warmly. "You've been such a good friend."

"You're welcome." I glance at the clock on my desk. "But I'm kind of swamped right now, so—"

"Wait, Sarah. Before you go, there's one more thing. The nurse just called to tell me Mom's dizziness is getting worse again. They've prescribed new medication, and it's ready for pickup at the pharmacy downtown. I hate to ask, but could you...?"

"Of course," I say quickly. "I'm so sorry to hear that. Your mom must be feeling awful."

"Yeah," Trina sighs. "I hate being so far away when she needs me, but this trip was planned months ago. And honestly, I don't think she'd want me hovering over her anyway."

"Don't worry about it. I'll grab the medication and drop it off at the center as soon as I can."

"You're a lifesaver. Seriously, *I owe you*."

"It's nothing, really," I say, fiddling with a pen on my desk.

"Well, Sarah, let's plan to catch up properly when I'm back. Lunch on me?"

"Sure. Let me know when you're back in town."

"Deal. Thanks again."

As the line goes silent, I stare at the phone in my hand for a moment, and a familiar weight settles on my shoulders.

Before I can return my focus to the screen, there's a sharp knock on the office door. When I ask the person to enter, Sam appears, his dark-blue shirt straining slightly at the buttons. I immediately wait for him to comment about the state of my desk, and right on cue, he stops in front of me, looking down with a mix of amusement and disgust.

"How do you get anything done in this chaos, Sarah?" he asks, not waiting for an answer as he settles into the chair opposite mine. The wooden frame creaks.

I shrug. "Some people thrive in chaos, Sam."

He doesn't laugh at my joke. Instead, he leans forward, his expression turning serious as he gets ready to skip the small talk. "Have you thought about what we talked about? We need something big, Sarah. Something that will make the *Gazette* shine again."

Is he going to pester me every day now?

He stands up again. "Are you working on something interesting, something that will give me the push to make you a senior editor?" His eyes bore into mine.

I nod just as an image of Drew flickers across my mind. My brother's wife. The woman I know is a murderer. "Yes, Sam. I'm working on something big. Trust me."

Sam stares at me for a moment longer, then nods, seemingly satisfied. "Good. Don't let me down." With that, he turns and walks out, leaving me slumped in my chair, anxiety churning in my stomach.

Melody deserves justice, and I need a story that will catapult me to the top at the *Gazette*, a stepping stone to bigger newspapers or even the magazine industry. After the dust has settled, and with Drew behind bars and out of Mark's life, I'd feel better about leaving this sleepy town, knowing that he's safe from her.

As the day drags on, I try to focus but my mind keeps drifting to tonight's dinner, which Mark tried to cancel but I talked him out of it. Drew fed him some nonsense about grieving a friend that recently died, but I know what is really up with her.

No, tonight has to happen.

By the time the day ends, the office is mostly empty. The smell of cleaning products is starting to overpower the usual office smells as the janitorial staff begin their work. Sam and the others have left, but I spot Lori filing some papers on her desk. When she sees me getting ready to leave, she hurries over.

"Hey, Sarah, do you have a minute?"

No, I don't, but I force a smile. "Sure, Lori. What's up?"

She fidgets, glancing around before leaning in. "Did you get a chance to talk to Sam about me? I know I don't have a lot of experience, but I thought, you know, since I helped with that thing..."

I shake my head, cutting her off. "Not yet, Lori. It's a tough business. You can't expect to move up so quickly, especially without a degree." When her face crumbles, I feel a sudden pang of guilt, so I soften my tone. "But I do have a meeting with him on Monday to discuss it. Just don't get your hopes up too much, okay?" I squeeze her shoulder. "I'll do my best."

Her face lights up again, and she nods. "Thank you so much, Sarah."

I give her a tight smile and finally head home to get ready for dinner. But before that I pick up a little gift from Bliss & Twine, a beautiful bouquet of flowers I had specially made. A surprise for Drew.

At home, I change into the simple black dress I wore to Melody's funeral two years ago and apply my makeup with extra care.

Then finally, the doorbell rings and I glance out the window to see a police car parked in my driveway. A smile tugs at my lips as I head downstairs to open the door for my plus one. I don't normally bring a date to our family dinners, but this one is different.

# THIRTY-SIX

## DREW



I step inside the house after an evening jog on the beach, closing the door behind me and kicking off my shoes. Mark said he had a new client and he'd be home later, but someone is in the kitchen.

"Mark?" I call out. There's a clatter of pots and as I round the corner, I'm greeted by the sight of my husband bustling around, wearing the Santa Claus apron I got him last year at a fair. It's bright red with the words "Kiss the Cook" emblazoned across the front in bold white letters. Despite my mood, I can't help but smile.

"Hey, you're home early," I say, trying to keep my tone light. "What's all this?" I gesture to the ingredients scattered across the counter, fresh vegetables, spices, and chicken breasts.

Mark looks up, his face lighting up with that boyish grin that first captured my heart. "I decided we should go ahead and still have the family dinner." He avoids my gaze as he stirs a pot of sauce on the stove. "Sarah and I really think you need this."

My smile fades, replaced by a blooming wave of irritation in my chest. "Honey, we agreed yesterday to postpone the dinner," I say, trying to keep my voice calm. "I told you I wasn't feeling up for it after hearing the news about my old friend."

He pauses, turning to face me, his eyes sympathetic. "I know, but I thought maybe it would help take your mind off things."

Anger flares up in me and it comes so hot and fast that my entire body feels like it's burning. "Mark, my friend died," I snap, my voice rising. "You really think having dinner with your sister is going to make me feel better?"

Mark's face falls and he reaches for a rag to wipe his hands. "Look, I don't know how else to help you. I just thought being around family might be good for you."

Family. That word burns in my chest. "I can't do this tonight. I don't want to be around Sarah."

Mark's eyes narrow, but he doesn't say anything as he removes the bubbling pot from the stove. Finally, he sighs before approaching me and pulling me into a hug. "I'm sorry, baby. I didn't mean to upset you. But it's too late to cancel. I already told Sarah, and she's bringing a friend."

My heart skips a beat, and I pull away. "A friend?" Sarah has never brought a friend to our dinners before. It's always just been family, except for Lori who sometimes tags along with Jason. "Is it a date?"

Mark shrugs. "No idea. You know how Sarah is. She's never introduced any of her boyfriends to me. She just said she was bringing someone. Oh, and I told Jason too. He's bringing Lori."

Panic surges. "Jason's coming?" I manage to choke out.

Mark nods. "Of course. Why do you look surprised?"

A sharp pain shoots through my belly. I can't let my son come here tonight. If Sarah calls the cops in the middle of dinner, I don't want Jason to see me being arrested. I can't let him go through that, seeing a parent being led away by the cops like I did as a child.

Nobody recovers from that.

"I... I need to go change," I stammer, turning on my heel and fleeing upstairs.

Once in the safety of our bedroom, I close the door and lean against it, breathing heavily.

Grabbing my phone, I dial Jason's number.

"Mom? What's up?" he asks from the other end.

"Jason, sweetheart." I swallow hard and tighten my grip around the phone. "It's about dinner tonight. It's been canceled. You don't need to come over."

There's a brief pause. "Really? Cool. Well, Lori and I will go to the movies."

I close my eyes. "Go ahead and enjoy your evening, okay? We'll see you soon."

"Sure, Mom. Thanks for letting me know."

I hang up and sit on the edge of the bed before stripping off my clothes and stepping into the shower, turning the water as hot as I can stand it. The scalding heat helps to ground me, to wash away the fear and discomfort, if only for a moment. And it could be my last shower in the privacy of my home.

As steam fills the bathroom, the rose and eucalyptus from the shower gel soothes me slightly, but the knot in my stomach remains tightly wound. When I finally step out of the shower and wrap a towel around myself, I feel suddenly dizzy, and when I attempt to catch myself by grabbing onto the vanity, I knock over one of my favorite bottles of perfume, which shatters on the tile floor, sending shards of glass and a cloud of fragrance into the air.

I curse under my breath, bending down to clean up the mess. A sharp sting on my thumb makes me wince, and I notice a small cut oozing blood.

"Drew?" Mark appears suddenly in the room and hurries to my side. "Hey, it's okay."

I nod, unable to speak. He guides me to a padded stool and

fetches the small medical kit we keep in the bathroom cabinet. His touch is gentle as he cleans the cut and applies a Band-Aid, his brow furrowed in concentration.

Once the mess is cleared up, he comes to stand behind me and massages my shoulders.

"I'm so sorry you're going through this," he says and that's all it takes for the dam to break and for me to start crying, big, ugly sobs that rock my entire body. Mark turns me around and pulls me into his arms, holding me tightly. "Everything is going to be okay."

I pull back slightly, looking up at him with tear-filled eyes. "Mark, if you ever found out I did something really terrible, would you leave me or stop loving me?"

He places a finger under my chin and looks into my eyes. "Where is this coming from? Drew, there's nothing you could ever do that would make me stop loving you. Nothing."

His words should comfort me, but they only make the guilt and fear intensify inside me. Maybe I should tell him now, just go straight-out and confess everything before Sarah has the chance. But before I can gather the courage, the doorbell rings.

He kisses the top of my head and hurries downstairs to answer the door. I missed my chance.

Drawing in a deep breath, I force myself to stand, get dressed, and follow him downstairs, trying to appear calm and composed even as I feel like I'm dying inside. When I enter the living room, the first person I see is Sarah, standing there with a smug smile on her face. In her hand is a bouquet of white and yellow roses, the petals glistening with what looks like tiny crystals. And next to her, is a police officer.

# THIRTY-SEVEN

Sarah's smile is too bright as she presses the bouquet of flowers into my hands. "Drew, I saw these at Bliss & Twine and thought they might brighten up the place and cheer you up," she says, her voice sickly sweet.

It's an exact replica of Melody's wedding bouquet; I recognize it from the photos that used to adorn this house. Mark catches my eye, and I can see he recognizes it too.

My eyes flick to Sarah's date, a cop in full uniform with broad shoulders, a calm face and dark-brown eyes. His short black hair is neatly combed, and his uniform is immaculate.

"Drew, this is Officer James Carter, my friend," Sarah says, her smile never wavering. "James, this is my sister-in-law, Drew."

I can barely manage a nod. "Nice to meet you."

"Nice to meet you too." James's voice is deep and commanding and his handshake is firm, his skin rough against mine.

Soon we're seated around the dining table. The flowers are where Sarah wanted them, right in the middle, and I can't stop staring at them. I heard Mark exchange words with her in the kitchen earlier, but as usual he gave in to her ridiculous protests of innocence as she claimed she hadn't realized they matched Melody's bouquet.

When we start eating, Sarah leans into me. "Drew, I'm so sorry about your friend. I wanted to check on you, but I've been so busy with work. I'm working on an explosive story at the paper."

"Oh really? What's it about?" Mark asks. He picks up a bottle of water and pours all of us a glass.

Sarah waves a hand and pierces a baby potato with a fork. "I can't talk about it yet, but it's going to rock Stoneview."

Mark chuckles before turning to James, asking him about his job. When I hear that he works in homicide, my stomach churns. The chicken on my plate looks delicious, covered in herbs and spices, and the garlic bread is warm and buttery, but it all tastes like sand to me.

"Are you okay, Drew?" Sarah studies my face with fake concern. "You look a little pale."

I nod, forcing a smile. "Just a little tired. But it's... I'm fine." I reach for my glass of water and take a huge gulp.

"Officer Carter, how long have you been in the police force?" Mark asks, reaching for the bottle of water and refilling my glass before holding my hand tight under the table.

James takes a sip of water, his brown eyes calm and observant. "I've been with the force for about fifteen years now. It's a challenging but rewarding job."

"Wow, fifteen years," Mark says, clearly impressed. "That must have been quite a journey. Any memorable cases?" From the looks of it, Mark is just happy to see his sister with someone that must have so much potential that she brought him over to dinner.

He has absolutely no idea what's going on here.

James nods, his expression thoughtful. "Plenty. One that stands out was a cold case I helped solve a few years back. A young woman went missing, and her body was found years later. It took a lot of digging and some good old-fashioned police work to finally bring her killer to justice."

Dessert comes and goes, and still, Sarah hasn't made her move.

"Oh, Cassey, could you pass the wine?" she says suddenly.

My stomach drops, and when Mark looks at her in confusion, she slaps her forehead. "Oh my God. How silly of me. I'm sorry, Drew." She shakes her head. "I was talking to a colleague about a photographer named Cassey earlier today. She's supposed to be good. Since you're also a little into photography, maybe you've heard of her?"

"No." I clear my throat and avert my gaze. "No, I haven't." Before I can stop myself, I blurt out, "I'm so sorry, I'm not feeling well. I need to go lie down."

Before anyone can protest, I get to my feet, swaying slightly as my real name repeats inside my head.

Mark helps me upstairs and lays me down, brushing the hair from my forehead.

"I'm sorry, my love." He presses a kiss to my forehead. "Maybe this was too much for you. Just rest. I'll be up soon."

After he leaves, needing to do something, anything to stop the panic, I grab my phone and open the gallery app. I don't even realize what I'm doing at first, but my thumb moves automatically, scrolling through photos. The habit is comforting, almost like flipping through an old photo album.

Photos I've taken flash across the screen: the fox I spotted in the woods last time I went jogging there, its sleek red coat glowing in the dappled sunlight; the helmet at the memorial; several photos of the pond and the ducks, and a string of other random snapshots—leaves coated in frost, a perfect shadow cast by a lamppost. Each picture feels like a tiny anchor, grounding me in moments of peace.

And then I stop.

My thumb hovers over a photo I don't immediately recognize. It's from about a week ago when I'd taken the garbage out just as dusk was settling. I remember how serene the street had looked, bathed in the golden glow of the streetlamps, their reflections making the pavement shimmer. I'd stood in the middle of the road, compelled to capture the moment, but I hadn't looked at the photo afterward.

Now I zoom in. There, at the edge of the frame, partially obscured by shadows, is a figure. A person. My pulse quickens as I study the image, but it's too grainy to make out any details. At the time I'd thought I was alone.

I tell myself it's nothing. A trick of the light. Maybe someone was walking their dog, or just passing through. But the longer I stare, the less plausible it feels. The figure is standing. Watching?

Chewing a corner of my lip, I immediately think of the person I saw in the woods that day, wearing a hooded sweater, how I'd brushed it off as a coincidence. But now... now it feels deliberate. As if someone has been stalking me.

I shake my head, willing the paranoia to fade. "Stop it," I mutter aloud. "You're being ridiculous."

Still, I can't look at the photo any longer. I close the app and toss my phone onto the nightstand.

After what feels like at least an hour, I move to the window and watch as Officer Carter kisses Sarah on the cheek before getting into his car.

I'm sure they're not really dating.

As he drives away, I continue to watch Sarah as Mark joins her in our well-lit driveway, and their conversation seems to be growing heated, so much so that their raised voices begin to filter through the glass, but I still can't hear what they're saying.

Sarah stands with her arms crossed, her body language tense and agitated.

Then I see her throw her arms in the air before reaching into her bag and handing Mark a book. I recognize it immediately.

It's a book with a collection of my best photographs. The colors even from a distance are too familiar, too vibrant.

Okay, so that must be how she discovered my real name.

I watch as Mark stares at it, shaking his head.

Sarah jabs a finger at a spot on the cover while saying something. Then, as if in slow motion, I watch it happen. Mark sinks against his car, his legs seemingly unable to support him.

That's it. Sarah has just told Mark the truth, or at least, the part of it she knows. My life is being destroyed, and there's nothing I can do to stop it.

After what feels like an eternity, Mark pushes away from the car and turns back toward the house. He doesn't look at Sarah as he passes her, but his movements are deliberate, purposeful as he disappears inside.

I slide back into bed and close my eyes.

Downstairs, I hear the front door open and slam shut. Then Mark's heavy footsteps echo through the house, growing louder as he makes his way up the stairs.

## THIRTY-EIGHT

For as long as I've known Mark, I've never seen him this angry. His face is taut with rage and disbelief, and I can barely breathe as I wait for him to start the conversation.

His normally calm demeanor has completely vanished. He paces the room, holding the book, and I sit on the edge of the bed, my fingers gripping the sheets. I try to rehearse what I'll say to him once the accusations start flying.

His voice, when it finally comes, is a low growl, full of suppressed fury. "So," he says, stopping abruptly and turning to face me. "Drew is not your real name."

He's waiting for me to deny it, to say something that will make it all go away, but the photobook is proof.

When I say nothing, Mark's frustration boils over and he tosses it onto the bed, the pages fanning out to reveal my beautiful captures.

"That's a collection of photos you took, and the photographer's name is *Cassey*. Sarah says she found more proof that that's your real name." He buries both hands into his hair. "Please tell me there's some kind of explanation for this."

The room is heavy with silence until finally, I shake my head. "No, there isn't. My name used to be Cassey."

Mark turns on his heel and hurries out of the room. Moments later, I hear the front door bang shut.

The house grows darker as the evening drags on without him coming back home.

The sounds of the outside world filter in through the open window: the distant crash of waves against the shore, the rustling of leaves in the breeze, the chirp of a cricket.

Finally, I pull out our wedding album and lift open the heavy leather cover.

I flip through the pages and watch the photos bringing back memories of our wedding day in the botanic garden at the Glass Parlor.

It was a small, intimate ceremony, and we were surrounded by nature. The scent of blooming flowers had filled the air, mingling with the saltiness of the ocean breeze. Even now I remember the feel of Mark's hands in mine, warm and steady, as we exchanged vows. The sound of laughter and clinking glasses as our very few guests toasted to our happiness. The way the sunlight filtered through the trees, casting a golden glow over everything, I thought it would be fine, that by marrying him I wasn't making a big mistake, even though Jason insisted that I was.

In one photo, we're standing beneath a canopy of flowers, Mark's eyes locked onto mine with a look of pure love. I can almost hear the soft murmur of the promises we whispered to each other. In another, we're laughing, our faces lit up with joy. I run my fingers over the glossy images, and my heart aches with the memory of that perfect day.

Sarah was invited, of course, but she didn't attend. I close the album with a sigh, my fingers lingering on the cover for a moment before I put it to the side.

Once Mark discovers what I did to him, he'll turn me in to the police, and who would blame him?

This is my chance. I have to leave before he returns. Before I can stop myself, I pull out a duffel bag from the closet and unzip it to throw random clothes into it. Dresses, jeans, sweaters. I don't have time to think about what I'm packing, just grabbing whatever my hands touch.

I also pack one of Mark's shirts and stuff it into the bag. The familiar scent of his cologne is a cruel reminder of what I'm about to lose.

Next, I get my toiletries from the bathroom. I was foolish to think even for a second that this would ever work, that I could live a fairytale life after everything that happened.

Done packing, I write a quick letter to Mark, a few lines of apology and not much of an explanation, because where do I even start?

But just as I'm carrying my luggage downstairs, ready to put it in the trunk before getting the lottery ticket, the front door opens and Mark stands there, his hair soaked. He must have gone for a long swim in the ocean.

"What are you doing?" There's no trace of his earlier anger.

"I'm leaving." Without looking into his eyes, I heave my bag onto my shoulder.

He shakes his head and takes the luggage from me. Then sits me down on the stairs. "Not without telling me why you changed your name."

I take a deep breath and start from the beginning, weaving lies as I go because the truth will cut him too deep. I allow the words to just pour out, hoping they will be enough to buy me time. I can't give him everything, but I need to give him something, some- thing to steer him away from the pain, for now. I speak fast, letting it all out before he responds and attempts to fill in the holes.

"I'm so sorry I didn't tell you this, but my childhood was

tough. My father was an alcoholic. One night, he came home very drunk after losing his job, got into an argument with my mother and shot her."

Years later, I can still clearly remember what happened that night. I see my father walk through the front door after work while I was eating dinner, macaroni and cheese. I can see the drunken stagger in his step, the wild look in his eyes. I remember my mother's face, pale and terrified as she ushered me into the closet, pressing a finger against her lips, begging me to stay quiet. I can still hear her screams, then the pop of the gunshot followed by deafening silence.

I remember slowly crawling out of the closet and running out of the house through the kitchen back door. At that moment, I still didn't know that my mother was dead, running to get help not knowing that it was already too late. The neighbors called the cops.

The flashing lights of the police cars still haunt me to this day. My dad was cuffed, his eyes meeting mine for the last time before he got into the squad car, his expression one of confusion as if he didn't understand why he was being taken away. It was a sight that burned into my memory, one that I will carry with me for the rest of my life.

At my mother's funeral, I just stood there feeling a sort of detachment as I watched people cry for her, people who didn't know her as well as I did but seemed more affected by her death than me. I was just numb and the only emotion I recognized in my body was pure undiluted hatred for my father, emotions too strong and terrifying for a ten-year-old to feel.

Mark listens, clenching and unclenching his hands as he stares at me. "Oh Drew, that's awful. I'm so sorry. Why didn't you tell me all this? You always said you were estranged from your parents."

I blow out a breath and shrug. "I don't know. I guess I wanted to pretend the past never happened." I bite onto my bottom lip to stop it from shaking as hot tears slide down my cheeks.

He sighs, the weight of my words sinking in. "Is your father still in prison?"

I shake my head. "He was released on parole about two years ago, but he died shortly after, a heart attack, I heard."

"But when did you change your name and why?"

"I did it just after his release," I respond, running my hand up and down my arm. "Hearing about his release and death just brought up too much pain from the past. It felt like a nightmare was being resurrected. I couldn't live with Cassey—the name he gave me—anymore. It was a constant reminder of what he had done to us, to my mother." The memories wash over me again, making me shudder involuntarily. "After he died, I just wanted to start over completely, to bury the old me and begin again as someone else. The only way I could do that was by completely distancing myself from my old identity. Mark, I want you to know me as Drew, not Cassey."

I look over at him, finding his gaze fixed on me, his eyes full of understanding, but a long silence stretches between us before he reaches out and pulls me into his arms. "Okay. Promise me you'll never keep secrets from me again."

I say nothing as I hold on to him.

What Mark doesn't know is that my car—the one that hit his wife, which the police never found—was registered under the name Cassey Bell.

# THIRTY-NINE

It's early on Saturday morning, not even seven yet, and Mark is not in bed, probably out for a swim. I still can't believe he forgave me after finding out about my old name. He held me all night, whispering that if I never want to speak about my father again, we don't have to, but that he's there for me if I ever want to talk about my past.

Sitting up in bed, a pounding headache makes me nauseous, the kind of dull throb that starts right behind the eyes and spreads outward. I need fresh air.

I should probably have still left last night, but I couldn't do it. The thought of leaving Mark tore at my insides. I just feel that I need to hold on to him for as long as I can, to never let go until I have no choice.

I get dressed and head downstairs to put on my sneakers. Outside, the fresh air helps clear my head a little. I need a burst of adrenaline that only a hard run can provide. I need that moment of clarity that comes with physical exhaustion, when all other thoughts fall away and only the sound of my own heartbeat remains.

As I jog along the familiar path through the woods, my feet

pounding rhythmically against the dirt, I feel a sense of calm settle over me. Soon I find myself at my bench by the pond again, and after sitting for a while, I pull out my phone and snap a few photos. Then I continue my jog, which, without me even thinking about it, leads me to Melody's memorial, even though I know I should stay far away. But this time there's someone there, on their knees at the base of the tree.

It's Mark, shoulders slumped and head hanging low. My heart aches and I pause, unsure if I should approach him or give him space to grieve. I watch as he reaches out, his fingers removing the wilted flowers and decaying leaves from the memorial site, something I usually do, my little ritual. Slowly, he reaches to his side and replaces the faded blooms with vibrant white and yellow ones. I recognize them even from where I'm standing.

He finally stands up and his movements are sluggish as he brushes the dirt from his knees. After taking a moment to collect himself, he turns and walks away in the opposite direction. I wait until he's out of sight before stepping out from my hiding place. I approach the memorial, and my heart sinks further as I stare at the bouquet, wondering if maybe he did this for me, that he removed it from the house so I wouldn't see it again and get upset. This memorial is the closest thing we have to Melody's grave.

I wonder if the bouquet has stirred up his grief, reigniting his anger toward the person responsible for her death.

I don't want to imagine what he would do to me if he knew.

# FORTY

## SARAH



Driving past Mark's house on my way to work on Monday, I catch a glimpse of Drew through the large kitchen windows, acting as if everything is still the same, like she still belongs in Mark's house and life. As I watch, Mark comes up behind her, puts his arms around her waist and plants a kiss on the side of her neck. A lump forms in my throat, and my stomach lurches.

I guess they decided to spend the morning together, having breakfast like one happy family. How could Mark do this after what I told him about her on Friday, that his wife is a fraud and uses a different name? He's been avoiding me all weekend as well, choosing to bury his head in the sand. But I need to be patient, to wait for the right moment to make her pay.

I'm almost at the end of Elm Grove, when I snap and turn the car around again. Without hesitation, I come to a stop in Mark's driveway.

Normally, I would ring the bell before using my own key, but this time I unlock the door and walk right in, bumping straight into Mark who looks like he was headed upstairs. He's still in his pajamas and his hair is rumpled from sleep.

His face hardens the second he sees me. "What the hell, Sarah? Didn't think it was necessary to knock or ring the bell?"

I don't flinch as my eyes meet his. "We need to talk."

He hesitates, glancing over his shoulder. "Can it wait? Drew is making breakfast. We can—"

"No, it can't." I grab his arm and pull him outside onto the porch.

Mark looks at me, concern and frustration in his eyes. "What's this about?"

"You know what it's about. What are you going to do about Drew now that you know she's not the woman you married?" I demand, my voice rising with anger.

Mark's face hardens, and he crosses his arms. "She's my wife, Sarah. She's been through a lot, and we talked about it. I won't abandon her. There's more going on than you think."

I bet. I can only imagine the lies she told him when he confronted her.

I feel a surge of rage. "Whatever she told you, she's lying to you, Mark. I showed you proof that she's a liar, and you're just letting her stay here?"

Mark's eyes flash with frustration. "People make mistakes, Sarah. You don't know the whole story."

"And you do? You're blind, Mark! She's manipulating you."

Our argument escalates until we're both shouting. Finally, I can't take it anymore. I turn on my heel and return to my car. As I drive off to work, fuming, I force myself to calm down. It's fine. Mark doesn't have to do anything because I'll handle it my way.

When I arrive at the office, I find Sam sitting at my desk. His arms are folded over his big belly, a steaming cup of coffee in front of him.

Not him again. I just don't have the energy to deal with him or anyone else right now.

"Morning, Sarah," he says, his tone impatient. "You know why I'm here. I'm tired of waiting for you to come up with a hit story for the newspaper. You're dragging your feet, and I have people breathing down my neck."

I swallow hard, knowing I have to give him something. It's time.

"Sam, do you remember two years ago when my sister-in-law died? She was hit by a car, and the driver fled the scene and was never found."

Sam's eyes narrow, and he leans forward. "I remember. What are you getting at?"

Excited and nervous, I drop into the seat opposite him, on the other side of the desk. "I think I know who the hit-and-run driver is and I'm working on that story as we speak. I just need a little more time."

Sam's skepticism is palpable, but he nods. "How much time are we talking here?"

"I should have something by my birthday," I say, thinking quickly. "July thirty-first."

He raises an eyebrow. "Are you sure you want to write an article that affects your family?"

I nod. "My brother deserves to see justice done for the death of his wife."

Sam looks intrigued, even excited. "And where are you getting all this information?"

I wink at him. "Sit back and allow yourself to be surprised. I know what I'm doing. It will be epic."

Sam would want concrete evidence, I know. I'm going to have to get it.

He leaves my office, grinning from ear to ear, and I hope for the next few days he'll leave me alone.

As soon as he's gone, I pull out my phone and text Mark,

telling him that since my birthday is next Tuesday, I want to throw a last-minute birthday dinner party this Friday. I invite him, Drew, and Jason to come. He's surprised because I normally don't celebrate my birthdays since they remind me so much of our parents, but he thinks it's a wonderful idea.


After calling a party planner and going through the details of my last-minute party, the rest of the day drags on and I tackle mundane tasks related to my job. I review articles, edit submissions, and coordinate with reporters. The office buzzes with the usual activity, phones ringing, printers whirring, and the constant hum of conversation.

I keep glancing at the clock, willing the hours to go by faster, and finally after work, I drive to the Senior Living Center to visit Mrs. H. and check on Trina's mom. She looked very poorly when I dropped off her rather pricey medication the morning after Trina called me.

It's six-thirty when I arrive and the place is bustling with staff and volunteers moving about, helping residents with various activities. I wave at a few familiar faces. Edna, who's wearing a bright-red cardigan she knitted herself, is chatting with another resident, Mr. Collins, who she admitted once to having a crush on. Mr. Jacobs, with his ever-present pipe, is deep in conversation with one of the nurses and when he sees me, he gives me a little nod.

I nod back, but it's Mrs. Grayson who catches my attention. She's sitting at one of the tables with a cup of tea, looking better than the last time I saw her. Her cheeks have more color now, and there's a new sense of strength in the way she carries herself today.

I wish life could repair itself as quickly as the body can heal. If only it were as simple as mending a wound, stitching up the fractures. But here I am, still stuck, waiting for the right moment to fix everything that's been broken. We can only begin to heal as soon as I get Drew out of our lives, which might be sooner than she expects. Much sooner.

I find Mrs. H. by the window in the shared living room, gazing out at the sun setting over the distant horizon. Her frail form is hunched over a walker, her thin white hair neatly combed back. She turns her head as I approach and her wrinkled face breaks into a bright smile.

"Ah, dear girl, it's so good to see you," she says.

I sit down next to her, and we begin working on a jigsaw puzzle I find on a nearby shelf next to a stack of board games and well-worn novels. It's a scenic picture, a countryside bursting with greens, purples, and blues.

We chat as we fit the pieces together and Mrs. H. tells me about the nephew who came to visit her.

"He said he might come and get me to go and stay with him in Kansas City next month." Her hands fumble with a puzzle piece. "I've never been to such a large city before, it's a bit daunting. But he showed me photos of his two adorable children, Laila and Oliver."

I'm not sure if it's true that her long-lost nephew would want to take her out of the place she calls home, but the thought of one day coming here and not seeing Mrs. H. sits heavy in my chest. Still, I plaster on a smile and offer words of encouragement. "Change is hard, but sometimes it's necessary." I offer her a reassuring smile.

I remind myself one day if I find a new exciting job, I might leave Stoneview as well.

Maybe getting rid of Drew is not just about her—maybe it's about me finally reclaiming control over my own life. My birthday party will be the last event she will attend with all of us pretending to be one happy family.

By the time dinner rolls around, I'm already thinking ahead, not just about the party, but about everything that comes after it. Bringing myself back to the present, I help several of the residents to the dining hall, where the tables are set with crisp white linens and cheerful flower arrangements from the garden. Almost everyone is seated, chatting animatedly.

I join the staff in serving dinner, placing plates of food in front of the residents. The chicken is golden-brown, the vegetables vibrant and steaming. Conversations flow around me, snippets of stories and laughter.

After dinner, we gather in the common room, and I sit at the piano after everyone begs me to play.

As my fingers touch the keys and play "You Are My Sunshine," some residents even start to sway, and I feel myself relax. Then as soon as my mind is free to think, the perfect idea of how to destroy Drew comes to me.

When I finally leave, the sky is clear and bright with moon and starlight. Before I start the car, I pick up my phone to call Molly Winters, a friend who works at the local TV station.

Her voicemail kicks in, and I leave a quick message. "Hey Molly, it's Sarah. Call me back when you get a chance. I have a favor to ask you—something that could benefit both of us."

As I hang up, my phone vibrates. I glance at the screen to see another incoming call—Lori. I hesitate for a second before answering.

"Sarah, I found something else!" Lori's voice is breathless and excited. "I know what the mountain photo in Jason's apartment means. This could change everything."

# FORTY-ONE

## DREW



The salon energy is buzzing as we get ready for our VIP guests. There's the familiar sounds of chatter and hairdryers, and the TV on the wall that blares out the morning news. Maggie is sweeping up hair clippings near the front and the delivery boy, Tom, arrives with our weekly supplies.

"Morning, Drew!" Veronica calls out, her voice cheerful as always.

"Morning, Veronica," I reply, trying to infuse my voice with some enthusiasm.

"Hey, Drew, I thought you'd like some caffeine before the rush starts?" Tia asks, coming over with a cup of coffee.

I take the cup gratefully. "Thanks, Tia."

We move to the back to set up the refreshment table, pouring orange juice into paper cups and arranging the snacks.

"You sure you're okay?" Tia asks again, her voice low. She already asked me a few minutes ago.

"I'm fine," I insist, though we both know it's a lie.

Before she can press further, the front door opens, and our

VIPs start to arrive. Martin beams when he sees me, his scruffy beard and unruly hair looking even more unkempt than usual. I wave him over.

"Hey, Martin! Ready for your makeover?" I ask, guiding him to my station.

"You bet, but remember, just a cleanup."

"Got it." I start to wash his hair. "So, any big plans today?"

"Actually, yeah," Martin says, his excitement palpable. "I have an interview for a postman job. Can you believe it?"

"That's fantastic!" I'm genuinely thrilled for him.

"Yeah, a good man gave me a new shirt and pants, so I'll look professional." He grins.

As I work, he talks about the responsibilities he'll have if he gets the job. But soon, my thoughts drift back to my own troubles. Martin notices my distraction and asks, "You okay, Drew? Anything I can do to help?"

His offer nearly brings tears to my eyes. "No, Martin, but thank you. You're a good friend."

After I finish, he surprises me by pulling out a five-dollar bill. "I know I don't have to pay, but I can give you a tip, right?"

I want to refuse, knowing he needs it more than I do, but I see the pride in his eyes. "Thank you, Martin. It means a lot."

The rest of the day passes in a blur of haircuts and small talk. As I'm about to leave at 4 p.m., Tia stops me. "See you tonight?"

"Tonight?" I frown, not remembering any plans.

"For Sarah's birthday party. She invited me and said she wanted you to have a friend there," Tia explains.

Shock and fear tighten my chest. Why would Sarah invite my friend? I didn't even want to go, but Mark insisted, and I didn't know what to say.

Instead of heading home, I drive to Sip & Snack, where I find Jason behind the counter.

"Hey, Mom! What's up?" he asks, wiping his hands on his apron as he comes over.

"Can we talk outside for a minute?" I ask, trying to keep my voice steady.

We step out to my car, the afternoon sun casting long shadows on the pavement. Once we're seated, I take a deep breath. "Jason, there's no easy way to say this. I'm thinking of turning myself in tomorrow."

Jason's eyes widen. "What? Why?"

"I think someone knows. It would be better if I turn myself in instead of waiting for them to do it," I explain.

Tears fill Jason's eyes, and he looks like the little boy he once was. "I don't want you to go to prison, Mom. You should run instead. I'll go with you."

"No, Jason. Running won't solve anything. We'll always be looking over our shoulders. It's time to face the consequences. I want to spend tonight with you and Mark. Then tomorrow, I'll go to the police."

He shakes his head, refusing to accept my decision. "Don't do this. Please promise me you'll wait. We'll find another way."

Unable to handle the hurt in his eyes, I place a hand on his cheek and lie. "I promise." But deep down, I already know what I have to do.

After our talk, I drive to the shops to find a last-minute present for Sarah. On the way, I pass the police station and park across the street.

I sit in the car for a long moment, my heart pounding. The building is a hulking presence across the street, its windows dark and uninviting.

Taking a deep breath, I push open the car door and step out.

My legs heavy, I reach the sidewalk in front of the station and a tremor runs through my body. The station's glass doors are solid, their reflections showing a version of myself I barely recognize.

I shiver as I imagine what it would be like to walk inside. The sterile, white walls. The flickering fluorescent lights. The room where I would sit and wait for the fingerprints, the mugshot.

I take a step back, retreating to the edge of the sidewalk, closing my eyes and trying to steady my breathing.

The sound of a car honking jolts me from my panic. I look up, seeing the concerned faces of pedestrians. They glance at me briefly, curiosity flickering in their eyes before they move on.

I draw in a breath and think of Jason's tear-streaked face, of his desperate plea for me to find another way. I think of Mark, who's waiting at home for me. I think of people like Martin who face their own battles with quiet bravery. I think of the ticket I found.

## FORTY-TWO

Sarah is dressed all in black from head to toe. Her silk dress is a classic figure-hugging number, the deep obsidian fabric shimmering subtly under soft light, and the stilettos on her feet are polished to mirror-like perfection. A black velvet choker is curled around her throat, showing off a single, gleaming teardrop-shaped onyx pendant.

Though she looks stylish and classy, her outfit reminds me of someone going to a funeral rather than to a birthday party.

"Happy birthday," I say to her, my fingers brushing hers as I hand her the present, the scarf inside carefully folded.

"Thank you, Drew." She grins and draws me into a hug that feels more like a spider ensnaring its prey. "You really shouldn't have."

She steps back and offers us champagne, grabbing two flutes from a nearby tray, even though she knows I don't drink. Both Mark and I grab glasses of orange juice from another tray instead. Unperturbed, Sarah shrugs and starts drinking from one of the flutes. Then she breezes off to welcome and mingle with her other guests.

As the party hums along, she pulls Mark aside, saying she

has something important to tell him. She glances around briefly, her smile faltering as she leads him toward a quiet corner near the bar. My brow furrows as I watch them. There's something about the way she's gripping his arm, the way her lips move in quick, hushed words. Whatever she's saying—it's serious.

I can't hear a word, but from where I stand, I see Mark stiffen. His posture shifts, shoulders tensing. He shakes his head once, as though trying to brush off what she's telling him. But Sarah doesn't let up. Her fingers tighten on his arm, her expression pleading.

Mark takes a step back, his jaw clenched, his eyes darting toward me, then the floor. He runs a hand through his hair.

Eventually, he steps away. His fists are clenched, and his jaw is set hard. Then, as though flicking a switch, his expression softens and he walks over and smiles at me.

"Let's get some air." His voice is unnaturally calm as he takes my arm.

Once we step onto the terrace, the moon's silvery glow reflects off the seawater, and a cool breeze blows in from the ocean.

"What did Sarah want to talk to you about?" I ask nervously.

Mark's face tightens for a moment and he lets out a short, forced laugh. "Something ridiculous," he mutters, pausing as if searching for the right words. His fingers run through his hair, and he looks down at the glass in his hand. "It was about Shoreline. Nothing important. Don't worry about it."

I frown, but I don't push him. Not now.

"I know you didn't want to be here, but you still came." He takes a sip of orange juice. "Thanks for that."

"Sure." I lift my glass. "Let's just enjoy the party." This is not just a party. It's a goodbye.

Jason and Lori show up on the terrace when we're about to head back inside.

His sandy-blond hair is tousled and his gray eyes are shadowed. He's wearing a simple blue shirt that hangs loosely on his lean frame and he has the sleeves rolled up. Lori is in a sleek, chiffon cream dress that reaches a few too many inches above the knees and her hair is pulled into an elegant updo, strands of her brown hair falling gracefully around her face. No matter what I think of her, she is a stunning girl, and she and Jason do look good together.

Mark and I hug them both and then Jason pulls me aside while Lori stays back to chat with Mark. We walk to the far corner of the terrace, away from prying eyes and curious ears. Jason rests his elbows on the railing, looking out at the sea.

"Thanks for not doing it." His eyes meet mine and the fear I see in them breaks my heart.

"You asked me not to turn myself in, and I won't. But I'm thinking of leaving tomorrow. Alone. I don't want to run. But I have to do something, Jason."

"Are you sure someone knows? How do you—"

"Someone has been stalking me and leaving threatening clues. I think that person is just waiting for the right time to expose me."

Jason rakes a hand through his hair, exhaling sharply. "Do you think it's Sarah?"

When I don't respond, he nods slowly. "Fine. I'll come with you tomorrow. We can—"

"No." I reach for his hand and hold on tight. "I will not allow you to do that. You are doing well here and there's no need for you to disrupt all your progress for me."

Jason's face hardens, a stubborn set to his jaw. "You don't get to decide what I do."

"Please, I don't want you to run with me, Jason." I shake my head, desperation coloring my voice.

"But it's my choice," he replies. "You are my mother, and I won't let you do this on your own."

I pull him tightly to me and whisper into his ear, "Honey, I want you to stop worrying about me. I want you to live your life independently of me, have a good future." I pull away again and wipe away a tear sliding down his cheek. "Look, I came into some money. In about an hour, meet me at your apartment and I'll give you the details."

The post office is closed for the weekend, but I need to leave. I can't wait until Monday to claim the money and I might end up in jail very soon anyway. I'll just have to give Jason the ticket directly and have him claim it as his own, and hope he spends it wisely.

Jason's eyes widen. "What money? Where did you get—"

"I'll tell you all about it later. I want you to have it. You can use it to create your future here or anywhere else. Now we better go back before they start wondering where we are. See you later."

Jason nods slowly. His grip on my arm is firm, protective even, as we navigate through the throng of guests.

We find Mark and Lori enjoying the canapés in the living room, but before I can join Mark, I bump into Tia, who just arrived.

As always, her hair and entire look is colorful and exotic. She's wearing a vibrant, multilayered dress of oranges and fuchsias that makes her look like a living sunset, and large, round earrings of hammered gold dangle from her ears, catching the light when she moves.

She has also decided to wear her hair in its wild state today, the curls piled on top of her head in what should be a chaotic nest, but on her, it looks majestic, almost regal. She turns to me, her dark eyes sparkling with warmth, and an infectious smile playing on her lips.

"Looks like Sarah went all out," she says, grabbing a glass of champagne. "I'm not complaining, though. Enjoying the party?" She moves closer and studies my face. "You look a little pale."

"Of course, I'm having a good time," I lie, offering her a smile that doesn't quite reach my eyes.

But Tia knows me too well. Her keen gaze lingers on my hands, which betray me by shaking as I tighten my fingers around my glass. With a small gesture that feels monumental, I steady my grip, but not before a few drops of juice escape.

"Oops," I mutter, setting down the glass before anything else can spill.

"Everything okay, Drew?" Tia's brow is now creased with genuine concern.

"Fine," I insist. "Just... fine."

She's still wondering whether to believe me when my phone vibrates in my clutch purse. Looking for a distraction, I pull it out and read a message from a number I don't recognize.

*Hope you're ready for tonight's surprise.*

My breath catches inside my throat, and I find myself leaning against a nearby wall as my eyes search for Sarah in the crowd. I find her talking to a woman who looks a little familiar, but my mind is too scattered right now for me to place her. The person who sent me the message can't be Sarah because she's not even holding a phone in her hand.

Tia reaches out to grasp my wrist. "Drew, are you sure you're okay?"

I don't get to answer because Sarah suddenly calls out for everyone's attention. Moving to stand by the fireplace, she addresses her guests.

"I appreciate you all for coming tonight. I know you're here to celebrate my birthday, but there's something else, someone else, who deserves our remembrance." She pauses for a moment before continuing. "Tonight, I want us to honor Melody Reynolds, my dear sister-in-law and best friend who left us way too soon. Some of you probably knew her."

I can barely hold myself upright anymore. But Tia's arms are around me, holding me together. "It doesn't mean anything," she whispers. "Don't let her get to you."

The blood is rushing so much in my ears that I don't really hear much more of what Sarah says. But I do hear her ask if Mark wants to say a few words about his late wife, which he declines firmly but politely.

I'm still a mess when we all gather in the dining room. The long table is elegantly set with white plates, sparkling silverware, and crystal glasses. A large centerpiece of white roses and lilies sits in the middle of the table. The rest of the room is equally festive, with shiny silver streamers hanging from the ceiling and glittering balloons scattered throughout. I take my seat next to Mark, feeling the weight of everyone's eyes on me.

The clink of cutlery against china grates on my nerves as Sarah speaks. "I was the one who introduced Melody to Mark," she says to the woman I saw her with earlier, who I now recognize as Molly Winters, the reporter for the local TV station.

"Are you okay?" Mark's hand finds mine under the table, offering me something to hold on to.

"I need some air," I mumble, standing abruptly.

In the sanctuary of the bathroom, my phone buzzes again. Another message.

*Meet me in the basement at 9:10 p.m.*

My fingers tremble as they tap out a reply.

*Who are you?*

## FORTY-THREE

After ten minutes of me hiding out in the bathroom, I slip out and lock myself inside the guest bedroom upstairs, which used to be Mark's.

The double bed in the center is neatly made with plain, white linens, but the headboard is decorated with small stickers that peek through the edges of the bedding, most of them dinosaurs and spaceships. A couple of the stickers have faded, but their outlines are still visible. On the wall above the bed, a framed poster of a starry night sky hangs slightly askew.

A wooden toy chest sits against one wall, but it has been repurposed as a storage bench. A simple desk and chair stands in one corner, a place where Mark must have spent countless hours doing his homework or sketching out his dreams. The only thing on the desk is an old sports trophy, collecting dust. It's clear the space isn't used much. It hasn't been disrupted by Sarah's messiness. The air is dusty and a cobweb is swaying gently in the corner above the tiny built-in wardrobe.

I'm shaking all over. Sinking onto the bed, I catch my breath for a few minutes before heading back downstairs. I don't plan on staying at this party. I don't care what that text asked me to do. I'm going to get Jason and leave. In a few minutes, I'll give him the lottery ticket and I'll be on my way out of Mark's life.

To my relief, Jason is the first person I see in the living room where the guests are now enjoying the post-dinner chatter with more champagne, and he rushes over to me.

"Mom, are you okay?" he whispers. For once, Lori is not glued to his side, which makes things so much easier. I can't see Mark or Tia, who are probably searching for me, so we can slip out quickly before they notice we're gone.

I grip his arm tight. "Not really. Come with me."

"But—"

"NOW!"

Jason obeys, but as we push through the throng of people, with me almost knocking over a floating tray of champagne flutes carried by one of the people catering for the party, I hear Sarah's voice announcing that she has some good news to share. When I glance over my shoulder, I see the large flatscreen TV above the fireplace flicker to life.

The murmurs in the room quickly quiet down to whispers as the local news channel comes on. Then there's total silence as Melody's face fills the screen, her smile frozen.

My heart lodges in my throat and I will my legs to move, but they feel paralyzed.

Molly Winters, the same woman I saw earlier at the party, announces, "We have breaking news. After two years shrouded in mystery, the hit-and-run case of Melody Reynolds is on the verge of closure."

The walls are pressing in, the air thinning.

"Mom," I hear Jason say, but he sounds far away.

"Sources close to the investigation have informed us that the identity of the person responsible will be revealed in tomorrow's local papers."

My pulse starts to hammer against my temple. Next to me, Jason looks petrified, his eyes wide as he watches the broadcast.

The screen flashes to a picture of Melody's memorial site, the place I have been visiting for two years now. Then bile shoots up my throat and my feet carry me to the guest toilet, where I spew my entire dinner out.

The bathroom tiles are cool against my knees and I press my forehead against the edge of the porcelain sink.

Then, as if the nightmare couldn't get any worse, my phone buzzes again. I don't want to look, but I have to.

*Don't even think about leaving. Go to the basement now. If you try to run, you'll regret it. Think of your son.*

# FORTY-FOUR

My legs are wobbling as I rise from the floor. I open the door a crack and peer out into the hallway. It's empty, silent except for the distant hum of voices from the living room. Are they still watching the news? Melody's face, her frozen smile, flashes into my mind.

The door to the basement is at the end of the hallway, and every fiber of my being screams at me to turn back. But I can't. Whoever sent that text is watching me. If I don't do what they say…

I can't even finish the thought.

As I near the basement door, my fear escalates, turning my breath shallow and quick. The air feels colder here and the hair on the back of my neck prickles. My hand hovers over the doorknob, and for a split second, I consider turning around, heading back to the living room, to the warmth of the lights and the presence of people.

I twist the doorknob and open the door just enough to slip inside. The narrow staircase looms before me, and I hesitate, reach up and remove the key from the lock. My fingers are slick with sweat, and the key slips slightly as I pull it out, but I manage to hold onto it. I wouldn't want anyone locking me in.

The basement is dark, the only light coming from a single bulb hanging from the ceiling. The smell of dampness and dust fills my nostrils as I take a step forward. As I reach the bottom of the stairs, I feel another wave of nausea wash over me, but I force myself to keep moving. The space is made up of rows of shelves lined with boxes and old furniture covered in white sheets. But it's what's on the far wall that stops me dead in my tracks.

A shrine. That's the only word for it.

The entire wall is covered in photos, newspaper articles, and other mementos, all meticulously arranged like some kind of twisted collage. My eyes are drawn to the center of it all, where Melody's death certificate hangs, framed and pristine, as if it's the crown jewel. Photos of her are everywhere—smiling, laughing, posing with Mark. There are even photos from their wedding day, Melody in her white dress, Mark looking dashing in his tuxedo.

But it's not just Melody's face that haunts this wall.

Near the top is a blown-up black-and-white photo of me. Someone has scrawled across it in thick, angry red letters: MURDERER.

My knees buckle, and I stagger back, clutching the edge of an old wooden table for support. The room is suddenly spinning around me, and the air is too heavy to breathe. I can't tear my eyes away from that word.

I'm going to faint. I can feel it, the darkness creeping in at the edges of my vision, the world tilting dangerously beneath my feet. I need to get out of here, but my legs refuse to move.

Finally, I manage to tear my eyes away from the shrine and turn, desperate to flee, to put as much distance between me and this cursed place as possible. But as I spin around, I come face to face with Sarah. She's standing at the bottom of the stairs in the dim light.

I stumble back, bumping into the table again. The key I took from the door is still in my hand, clutched so tightly that the metal digs into my palm, but it's useless now.

Sarah steps forward, her presence filling the room.

"Where do you think you're going, Drew?" Her voice drips with venom. "It was you. You ran Melody over," she hisses, "and then you had the audacity to marry her grieving husband. What kind of monster does that? Don't even try to deny it because I have evidence."

"Sarah, I—" The words die on my lips. What can I say? That it was an accident? That I never meant for any of it to happen?

Her smirk tells me she's already judged and sentenced me. "Tomorrow, everyone will know who you really are and what you did. Mark will know the truth."

She doesn't need to elaborate. I saw the news on TV, the promise of a revelation.

I swallow hard and take a shot at reasoning with her. "Sarah, please." My voice quivers. "What do you want from me?"

"The truth," she hisses. "You killed Melody, and that's why you like to visit her memorial during your little jogs. I've been watching, you know, and at first, I didn't understand why you would do that, but now I know. Come on, confess to what you did."

It wasn't my imagination; someone really was stalking me all along. She was the figure standing in the shadows in the photo I took of the street, the person in the woods. Trying to sound brave, I scoff, "You seem to know everything already."

Sarah's lips curl into a smirk as she sinks into the tattered sofa across the room, the springs creaking under her weight. Her eyes never leave mine. "Yes, I do know it was you. Jason told me everything." Her voice is calm as she fishes out her phone and plays a recording.

Within seconds, my son's slurred words fills the space between us.

"Here's the deal," she continues, pausing the damning audio. "Confess now, and I'll let you run. I'll just let you disappear forever. Everyone will know what you did, but by the time that happens, you'll be long gone."

The offer hangs in the air, heavy and suffocating. A head start before my life implodes. A chance to flee the wreckage.

"Or," she adds, "I tell everyone upstairs right now. Including Mark."

Panic claws at my throat.

"Sarah... please—"

"Decide, Drew." She rises from the sofa and crosses the distance between us. "Confess. You were the one driving the Nissan that hit Melody when she fell into the street."

"Wait... Nissan?" The thick air of the basement chokes me as I fixate on the one glaring inconsistency that turns everything on its head. "And did you say Melody fell?"

The police never knew what kind of car it was. And nobody said anything about Melody falling.

"You were there that night, weren't you, Sarah?" I whisper.

# FORTY-FIVE

## SARAH

Two Years Ago

I'm standing in the driveway of my house, the rain falling in sheets around me. I'm soaked to the skin, my hair sticking to my face, and all I can think about is the woman standing a few feet away from me, her back turned as if she's got nothing to say for herself.

Melody. My sister-in-law. My best friend.

I stare at her, my heart clenched tight with rage, my fingers curled into fists at my sides. It's like a knife twisting deeper with every second that she stands there, not looking at me. She doesn't even have the decency to turn around and face me after what she's done. The rain washes over her too, but she just stands there, shoulders hunched, like she's the victim in all of this.

"Say something!" I finally snap.

She turns slowly, her face drawn and pale, her eyes shadowed with something that I hope is guilt. Her blonde hair is plastered to her head, her clothes clinging to her frame, but no, she doesn't look guilty. She looks at me like she's tired, like this is all just too much for her.

"What do you want me to say, Sarah?" Her voice is dull and it infuriates me even more. "I didn't plan for any of it to happen. It just... did."

"Nonsense!" The word explodes out of me, raw and broken around the edges. "You didn't just trip and fall into bed with *my boyfriend*, Melody. You chose to do it! You chose to betray Mark, and to betray me!"

She flinches at that, and for a split second, I think I see something real in her eyes—regret, maybe? But then she looks away. "I'm sorry, okay? It was a mistake. One stupid mistake."

"A mistake?" I echo, almost choking on the word. "Do you have any idea what that one mistake is going to do to Mark, how it's going to destroy him?" As devastated as I am to hear that my best friend slept with my boyfriend, I can't even start to imagine how Mark will feel when he hears about this. Melody is everything to him. "You think he will be able to handle knowing that the woman he loves has been sleeping with someone else behind his back?"

She shakes her head, tears mixing with the rain on her cheeks. "He already knows, Sarah. I told him before coming over here. And no, he didn't handle it well." She wipes her eyes with the heels of her palms. "I didn't mean to hurt anyone. I didn't mean for any of this to happen."

"But it did happen, Melody!" I shout, my voice cracking as my emotions boil over. "You've been lying to him, to both of us, and now you just want to brush it aside like it's nothing?"

"It's not nothing," Melody shoots back, her voice sharp as she turns to face me fully. "Do you think this is easy for me? Do you think I wanted this? Mark and I... we haven't been happy for a long time. I stayed with him because I felt guilty. But it's not fair to him, Sarah. He deserves better."

"He deserves you!" I scream, the words tearing out of me

like shards of glass. "Mark loves you. He would move mountains for you, give you everything. And you... you just throw it all away because you're too selfish to see what's right in front of you! How good you have it."

The rain is pounding harder now and my whole body is shaking with the force of my anger and the cold seeping its way into my bones. Melody looks at me, and I see the tears in her eyes, but it only makes me angrier. How dare she cry? How dare she act like she's the one who's been wronged?

She pushes back her shoulders and wipes at her face with the back of her hand. "I'm going to tell him that I want a divorce, Sarah. We don't belong together. Not anymore."

"Don't you dare." I take a step closer to her, cutting through the curtain of rain separating us. "Don't hurt my brother more than you already have."

"I'm sorry, but I can't keep living this lie. He deserves to know that I've been unhappy, that it's over." She stops talking and starts walking toward the pavement, heading to the house she shares with the man she betrayed.

Before I know what I'm doing, I run after her, grabbing her arm and gripping it tight. "You're not going anywhere," I say, my voice low with the intensity of my emotions. "You're not going to leave my brother, to ruin his life. You will stay in that marriage and fix what you've broken."

Melody tries to pull away, but I tighten my grip, my nails digging into her skin. "Let go of me, Sarah," she says, her voice shaking with something resembling fear. "Let go of me right now."

But I can't let go. I'm too angry, too hurt, too consumed by the thought of what this betrayal will do to my brother. The man who has already sacrificed so much for her, the man who loves her more than anything in this world.

"Let go!" she screams, finally wrenching herself free, but the momentum sends her stumbling backward, right to the edge of the curb.

"I'm going home." She wipes the rain and tears from her eyes. "And like I said, I'm going to tell Mark that I want a divorce. He deserves the truth, even if it hurts him." She turns again to walk away, but I can't let her go.

I reach out again, grabbing her arm tighter and spinning her around to face me. "You can't just break his heart and leave!"

"Sarah, let me go!" Melody struggles to free herself again, but I don't let go this time. I can't. All I can see is red. The thought of Mark's devastated face if she leaves him like this is eating away at me.

"I said let me go!" she screams again, finally stumbling backward into the street, her eyes wide.

And then it happens.

It's as if everything slows down, the sounds of the storm fading into the background as Melody falls into the path of an oncoming car, a bright-red Nissan. The headlights cut through the rain, blinding me, and the screech of tires is barely audible over the roaring in my ears. For a split second, Melody's eyes lock with mine. I see the terror swimming in them as she realizes what's about to happen.

"No!" The word rips out of me, but it's too late.

The car slams into her with a sickening thud, and she's thrown into the air like a rag doll before crumpling to the ground, motionless.

I stand there, frozen, my arm still outstretched, my breath caught in my throat as the car speeds off, its taillights disappearing into the night.

I can't move. I can't breathe. All I can do is stare at Melody lying still in the middle of the road, the rainwater pooling around her body, her hair spread out like a halo.

"No... no, no, no," I whisper and take a shaky step forward, then another, until I'm standing over her. I drop to my knees, the cold water soaking through my jeans, but I don't feel it. All I can see is Melody's pale face, her eyes closed, her chest still, the blood. My best friend.

Suddenly nothing else matters. My anger has fallen away completely, and all I am left with is a deep, permanent sorrow.

"Mel... please... I'm so sorry. Please, please come back." I reach out, my hand hovering over her, but I can't bring myself to make contact. She's so still, and a part of me is terrified that if I do, I'll confirm what I'm too afraid to admit.

Scared and not knowing what else to do, I step away from her. Before I can stop myself, before I can think straight, I'm running back to my house, my feet splashing through puddles. I can't stop shaking, can't stop the panic clawing at my throat.

I fumble with the door and nearly trip over the threshold as I run inside. Then I collapse onto the hallway floor, curling into a ball. My body shakes with sobs I can't hold back, and I squeeze my eyes shut as if that will make it all go away.

# FORTY-SIX

I don't know how long I lie on the floor, sobbing, but eventually, I hear the distant wail of sirens. The sound cuts through the fog in my mind, and I freeze, my breath catching in my throat.

They're coming. They're coming, and I don't know what to do.

I stay where I am, curled up on the floor, listening to the sirens getting closer, then fading away. Time stretches on, but I can't move. I can't do anything but listen to the rain and the beating of my own heart, pounding so hard it feels like it might burst right out of my chest.

Then, after a long time, I hear the distant ring of my phone.

The sound jolts me back to life and I scramble to my feet, my heart lodged inside my throat. I left the phone in the kitchen, where Melody and I had been having dinner. An innocent dinner that had spiraled into a nightmare. Everything had been fine until she confessed, until she told me she had slept with Lucas, my boyfriend of two years, my longest relationship.

In the kitchen, my hands are shaking so badly that I almost drop the phone as I pick it up. I stare at the screen, seeing

Mark's name flashing there. I don't want to answer, but I have to. I have to act normal. I have to pretend like everything's okay.

"Hello?" My voice is barely a whisper, shaky and weak.

"Sarah..." Mark's voice cracks, and I've never heard him sound so broken. "I'm at the hospital. Melody was hit by a car."

"Oh my God... Mark, I—Is she...?" I trail off, not sure what to say, not sure how to pretend I didn't know this already.

"She's in surgery," he says, his voice thick with tears. "They don't know if she's going to make it."

I press a hand to my mouth, trying to hold back the sobs that are threatening to break free. "I'm coming," I manage. "I'll be there as soon as I can."

I don't even remember how I get to the hospital. The drive is a blur and all I can think about is Mark's voice, the way he sounded so lost, so devastated.

When I finally arrive, I rush inside, barely registering the people around me, the sterile smell of the hospital, the bright, artificial lights that make everything seem too harsh.

Mark is waiting in the hallway outside the operating room, his face pale, his eyes red-rimmed and hollow. He looks up when he sees me, and for a moment, he looks like he's about to collapse. I rush to him, pulling him into a tight hug.

"She's in surgery," he repeats, his voice breaking. "They said it's bad, Sarah. Really bad."

I hold him tighter, trying to find the right words, but they all stick in my throat. What can I say? How can I comfort him when I'm the reason she's here?

We sit in the waiting room for hours, the silence heavy between us. Mark keeps his head in his hands, not speaking, just waiting, hoping for some kind of miracle. I can't look at him, can't bear to see the pain in his eyes, the guilt gnawing at me.

Finally, a doctor comes out, her expression grim. "Mr. Reynolds," she tells Mark, "your wife is stable, but she's in a coma. We'll have to wait and see how she responds in the next few days."

Mark nods numbly and I just sit there, frozen, as the reality of what I've done crashes over me.

Eventually, they let us into the room to see her. Mark hesitates at the door, then pushes it open, and we walk in together. The room is cold, sterile, the air thick with the smell of antiseptic.

Melody's face is pale, her eyes closed as tubes and wires connect her to the machine that is keeping her alive.

Mark collapses into the chair beside her bed, taking her hand in his, his shoulders shaking with silent sobs. I step outside to give them a moment, and after Mark leaves the room to collect himself, I reenter.

"I'm so sorry," I whisper to Melody as I stand at the foot of the bed. "I never meant for this to happen."

I squeeze my eyes as anger burns its way up my neck. If the driver of that car had not been speeding, Melody would never have been run over. They would have seen her and swerved in time. It's not my fault, it's theirs.

Opening my wet eyes again I continue to stare at her still face and in that instant, a horrible thought crosses my mind. What if she wakes up? What if she remembers what happened? What if she tells Mark everything?

Disgusted with myself, I shake my head, trying to banish the thought, but it lingers, dark and poisonous. I should want her to wake up. I should want her to recover. But the truth is, a part of me is terrified of what will happen if she does.

*Please don't wake up*, I think, the words forming in the darkest corner of my mind.

No one else knows what happened tonight. No one but me and Melody. And if she never wakes up, she can never tell.

I stare at her, watching the rise and fall of her chest. It's too shallow, too faint. There's a suffocating stillness in the room, as if the world has stopped turning for just a moment. My hand hovers above the plug. If I pull it, it will end and she will never wake up, and my secret will be safe.

I take a deep breath, steadying myself. This is the only way. There's no going back from this. With a swift motion, I disconnect the life-saving machine.

The room falls into an eerie silence, the hum of the machine gone. Soon after, Melody's chest stops rising and falling.

It's done. My heart skips a beat, but I don't move—paralyzed. And neither does Melody.

I wait a little longer, holding my breath, hoping for something—anything—that tells me this isn't as final as it feels. But nothing happens, and the stillness settles in, absolute and cold.

As the reality of what I've done hits me, fear sweeps through me. What if there's a silent alarm somewhere, alerting the staff? The longer I stand here, the more certain I am that someone will walk in. What if they find me? What if they know what I've done?

No. I can't do this. I'm not a murderer. Maybe it's not too late. Maybe this can be undone.

I glance at the plug, the thin cord still disconnected. But before I can reconnect the machine, I hear a soft movement from the doorway. I turn, my mouth dry, and there, standing in the doorway, is a nurse, Trina according to her name tag.

"What on earth?" Before I can respond, Trina is halfway across the room. She grabs the plug from me and with a calm, practiced motion, she reattaches the machine, and the monitors hum back to life. Then she meets my gaze, her expression impassive. "Get out. Now."

I don't speak. I don't know what to say. So, without a word, I rush out of the room.

Instead of going to the waiting room, where Mark is, I run to the nearest bathroom, locking the door behind me. My breaths come in jagged gasps as I lean against the sink.

What did I do? My mind replays the moment I disconnected the machine, the brief spark of hope that Melody might never wake up. I pray it didn't work.

*She has to be okay*, I think as I grip the edge of the sink. *Maybe they can save her.*

I wait there for what feels like hours, hoping the tightness in my chest will loosen. But when I finally gather the strength to leave the bathroom, the world outside is colder and when I reach Melody's room, Mark is kneeling on the floor just outside her door, his body slumped, his sobs echoing down the hall. A doctor stands beside him, his hand resting gently on Mark's shoulder.

My heart sinks like a rock. I killed my best friend.

The doctor steps away from Mark, shaking his head. "I'm truly sorry for your loss," he says before walking away.

I stand there, numb and unable to move. I don't even know how to comfort Mark when I'm so weighed down by my guilt.

Then, out of nowhere, that nurse—Trina—appears again. She walks toward me with a calm, purposeful step and then pulls me aside, guiding me down the hall to a more secluded spot. When she speaks, her voice is low, almost a whisper.

"I saw what you did," she says.

I open my mouth, but no words come out.

Trina tilts her head. "Don't worry, I'm not here to turn you in. Not yet." She folds her arms across her chest. "But you're going to help me with something, or I'll tell your brother and the police everything. Meet me tomorrow for coffee at Honeywood, at one p.m. I want to make you a deal."

# FORTY-SEVEN

## DREW

Sarah's face crumples and she steps back, her eyes wide.

"You must have been there that night," I repeat with more confidence. "You saw what happened. The police never revealed the car that hit Melody. And no one ever said that she *fell*. She could have just been crossing the road."

"Shut up, Drew," Sarah hisses. "Just shut up!"

But I can't. I won't. Even if I'm just throwing spaghetti at the wall at this point to see what sticks.

"No, I will not shut up." I move back until my body is pressed against the cool wall. "How do you know about the Nissan and Melody falling?"

"Stop talking." She lunges forward, her fingers clawing at the air like talons.

"Did you see it happen?" I dodge her grasp, but before my eyes focus on her again, I notice a small, blinking red light in one corner on the shelf.

Oh my God. She's filming me. She brought me down here

so she can get everything I say on tape. I wonder if the video is streaming live somewhere. Are the police watching this?

I bet Sarah never thought anything could go wrong with her perfect little plan, did she? She's so angry that she forgot about her own camera, but I will use it to my advantage. As of this moment, I still haven't confessed to anything, but she might.

"Why are you so angry, Sarah?" I press, pushing her to the edge. "It makes me wonder if you did more than watch what happened to your best friend. Were you involved, maybe?"

The words leave my mouth, and suddenly, my mind snaps back to Melody's memorial. The helmet. That red message scrawled across its pristine surface, that stood out from the rest. My pulse quickens as my gaze drifts to the word MURDERER painted on the wall and its bold red lines seem to pulse in the dim light. And then something clicks—the way the capital E is written. The slight slant to the right. The unique way the letter R also curves, only slightly, at the end.

My hands tremble as I reach into my purse and pull out my phone. My thumb swipes through the gallery, hunting for the photo I took at the memorial. When I took those photos, I never thought there would come a time when they would be useful.

"What are you doing?" Sarah demands, her voice cracking as she watches me.

Ignoring her, I keep searching.

Then I find it. The photo of the helmet, the messages written in various colors, and there, clear as day, the one in red: *I'M SO SORRY FOR WHAT HAPPENED. I WISH I COULD TURN BACK TIME AND YOU'D STILL BE HERE.* I zoom in.

When I read the message on the helmet, I didn't immediately suspect it was from Sarah because normally, she prefers to write in cursive and not in block letters. Now I look at the word MURDERER on the wall again, the identical Es and Rs. She definitely wrote it, and if a handwriting analyst had both samples, they would be able to confirm it.

"I said, what the hell are you doing?" Sarah's voice cuts through the silence again, more insistent, desperate even.

I hold the phone up and read the message aloud: "*I'm so sorry for what happened. I wish I could turn back time and you'd still be here.*" My voice shakes as I meet her panicked gaze. "I know you wrote this, Sarah. What are you sorry for exactly?"

Her eyes flicker to the screen for a split second, and then she lashes out. With a sharp cry, she knocks the phone from my hand, sending it skidding across the floor.

And that's all the confirmation I need.

"Shut your damn mouth!" she spits, her voice shaking with what sounds like fear. Then suddenly, she lunges again, and this time, her fingers make contact, wrapping around my throat with a grip that's shockingly strong.

I gasp, my hands instinctively flying up to grab at her wrists, trying to pry her fingers away, but she's relentless. The pressure on my windpipe increases, cutting off my air supply, and the room begins to spin.

Sarah's wild eyes bore into mine, and for a moment, I truly believe this unhinged woman is going to kill me.

I struggle against her, kicking out with my legs, trying to push her off, but her grip only tightens. My vision blurs at the edges, and I can feel the darkness closing in, threatening to pull me under. My lungs burn, screaming for oxygen, and a strangled sound escapes my throat.

"I said shut your mouth..." she hisses through clenched teeth, her voice low and dangerous. "You don't know what you're talking about."

But I do know. I know there's something here, something she's hiding, and I can't let it go. Even as the world begins to fade, I can't let her win.

"Sarah," I manage to choke out. "Don't..."

"You killed Melody and now you will pay with your life." Her breath is hot on my face.

My vision blurs, the edges going black as the room spins. Just as the darkness closes in, a sudden force slams into Sarah, knocking her off me.

I collapse to the floor, gasping for air, my throat burning as I suck in ragged breaths. It takes a moment for the world to right itself, for the spinning to stop. When I finally look up, Jason has Sarah pinned down, his strong arms holding her wrists to the floor.

"Get off me!" Sarah screams, thrashing beneath him, but Jason doesn't budge.

"Jason!" I rasp as I struggle to sit up.

"Mom, stay back!" Jason yells, his focus entirely on Sarah. "Don't you dare touch my mother again."

Sarah continues to struggle, but she's no match for him. He may be young, but he's bigger, stronger, and right now, determined to keep her from doing any more harm to me.

"She killed Melody," Sarah hisses. "She deserves to pay."

Jason's jaw tightens, and for a moment, I see a flash of something in his eyes—pain, guilt, something deep and dark. "No, she didn't," he says, his voice low and controlled. "You're blaming the wrong person, Sarah."

Sarah's struggling slows, confusion clouding her features. "What are you talking about? You told me everything."

"No," Jason says, his voice like steel. "You think you know what happened, but you don't. It was—"

"Jason, what are you—" My question dies on my lips.

"It was me, Sarah," he chokes out. "I was driving that night, in my mother's car. I lied when I told you she caused the accident because she drilled it into me, she told me that if we were ever suspected that's what I should say, that she did it. But it was me. I killed Melody."

"Jason, no." Tears cloud my eyes as I gaze at the blinking light in the corner of the shelf.

## FORTY-EIGHT

"I've lived with it every day," Jason continues, his eyes on me as his shoulders shake with the force of his sobbing. "You protected me, Mom, and I'm so grateful but I can't hide anymore. Not when it's destroying your life." As though he has lost all strength, he lets go of Sarah and draws his knees to his body, rocking back and forth. "I will go to the police to confess everything." He looks up for a brief moment, his eyes locking onto Sarah. "But there is something else. When I saw you just now, attacking Mom, I had a flashback to what I saw that night. You said Melody fell into the road, but she didn't. She was pushed right in front of the car." He points at Sarah. "You pushed her."

He drops his head and continues to cry again. The strength he showed moments ago has crumbled and now he looks so small, so broken.

But there's no time to process this. No time to comfort him, to tell him it's going to be okay, that we'll figure this out together. Because even as Jason breaks down, Sarah's eyes flash with something dangerous, a realization that quickly turns to rage. I know then that she will do everything it takes to make sure the whole truth does not come to light.

"You saw nothing." Her voice is a whisper at first, but then it rises, filled with venom. "You killed her, you murdered my friend."

Jason doesn't answer, his body shaking as he continues to rock back and forth, his face buried in his hands. The guilt is eating him alive, and it's too much for him to bear.

She scrambles to her feet, her eyes wild with fury. I can see her muscles tensing, her hands curling into fists. She's about to lose control again, and this time, I don't know if I can stop her.

"Sarah, please," I plead, my voice barely audible. "Don't do this. We can talk about this. We can—"

But she's not listening. Her eyes are locked on Jason, who still hasn't moved, still hasn't looked up. It's as if he's accepted whatever punishment she's about to dish out. Like he thinks he deserves it.

Before I can react, she lunges for an iron rake leaning against the wall. I hadn't even noticed it before, but now it's the most dangerous thing in the room. My heart lurches as I see her fingers curl around the handle, her knuckles turning white.

"Jason, run!" I scream and his head snaps up at the sound of my voice, his eyes wide with fear as he sees Sarah coming at him with the rake. But he doesn't move. It's like he's frozen in place, unable to do anything but watch as she raises the weapon above her head, ready to bring it down on him.

In that split second, something shifts in his eyes, and he pushes himself up from the floor, meeting Sarah head-on. He grabs the rake with both hands just as she swings it down toward him.

The two of them struggle and the sound of metal scraping against the concrete floor echoes through the room as they wrestle for control of the rake. Jason's face is contorted with effort, his muscles straining as he tries to wrench the weapon from Sarah's grip.

"Let go, Sarah!" he grunts, his voice strained. "This isn't going to solve anything!"

But Sarah is beyond reasoning. Her eyes are wild and unseeing as she fights with everything she's got.

I can see the desperation in Jason's eyes, the way he's trying to hold back, to not hurt her, but she's not giving him a choice.

With a sudden burst of strength, he manages to twist the rake out of Sarah's hands, sending it clattering to the floor. But before he can even catch his breath, Sarah is on him again, her hands clawing at his face, trying to push him back.

Jason stumbles, his foot slipping on the cold concrete floor, and he turns to run up the stairs. But Sarah is right behind him and before he's out of her reach, her fingers grab at his shirt, pulling him back with a force that sends both of them tumbling down the stairs.

I scream as they fall, the sound of their bodies crashing down the stairs reverberating through the room. They hit the ground hard, and for a moment, everything goes still.

My breath catches in my throat, the world slowing to a painful crawl as I stare at the tangled mess of limbs on the floor. Jason's body is sprawled out, unmoving. I can't tell if he's hurt, if he's breathing, if—

And then he moves, groaning as he pushes himself up on his elbows. His face is contorted with pain. "Mom...? Mom, are you okay?"

I rush forward, my heart in my throat as I kneel beside him and reach out to touch his face. "Jason, oh God, Jason, are you okay?"

He nods and tries to sit up. "I'm fine... I'm okay..."

But then his eyes widen, and he freezes. His gaze is locked on something on the floor next to him. I follow his stare, and the sight that greets me makes my blood run cold.

Sarah is lying on the floor, her body twisted at an unnatural angle, her eyes wide open but unseeing. And beneath her, I see it—the iron rake, its sharp prongs protruding from her, slick with blood.

"Oh my God..." I whisper.

Jason stares down at her, his face pale, his eyes wide with horror. "Mom... I didn't mean to... I didn't... She..."

His whole body is convulsing. I can see the guilt, the fear, the absolute terror in his eyes as he looks up at me, silently begging for reassurance, for something to make this all go away.

But I don't have the words. I don't know what to say, how to make this right. All I can do is pull him into my arms, giving him a quick but firm reassuring squeeze.

When I release him and look up, I see Mark standing frozen on the landing.

Suddenly, his grief-stricken voice cuts through the air. "What have you done?" He rushes down the stairs and drops to his knees beside Sarah.

"Sarah! Wake up!" he shouts and presses his fingers to her neck with shaking hands, desperate for any sign of life.

For a moment, nothing happens, then, just as the silence becomes unbearable, Sarah's eyes flutter open. They drift slowly until they find Mark. "S... sorry," she murmurs, her voice laced with pain before her eyes drift shut again.

## FORTY-NINE

How do I tell my husband that my son ran over his first wife and I kept it from him for two whole years? How do I explain that it was an accident, that Jason was young, drunk because his first love had dumped him, and he was driving my car without permission?

These are the questions that swirl in my mind as I stand with Tia's arms wrapped around me, watching the police car take my son away. Jason called the cops himself, his voice steady as he assured me and Lori, who couldn't stop crying, that it was the right thing to do, that he would be fine, and that I no longer had to lie for him.

He made me promise not to follow him to the station. I've never seen him more determined to take responsibility for his actions, something that should make a parent proud but it only makes me sad.

Right behind the police car is the ambulance, rushing Sarah to the emergency room. When I saw her close her eyes on that basement floor earlier, I was certain she was dead. But apparently, the EMTs were able to find a weak pulse. To be honest, I'm not sure whether to feel relief or disappointment.

The sounds of the sirens fade into the distance, leaving nothing but an eerie silence behind. The guests from Sarah's party have also trickled away, whispering among themselves, their faces pale with shock. Tia remains by my side, no questions asked. I can't believe there were times I had doubted her.

Now that it's just us, I can't hold it in any longer. The weight of everything that has happened crashes down on me hard and I sink to the ground. Right there on the sidewalk, my knees hit the concrete, and the tears that I've been holding back finally break free.

My sobs are violent and uncontrollable. Each one tears through me with a strength I didn't know I had left. I press my palms against the pavement, feeling the rough texture against my skin as I cry out every bit of grief, guilt, and fear that has built up inside me over the last two years.

With tears in her eyes, Tia crouches beside me and wraps her arms around my shoulders, pulling me close. She doesn't say anything, doesn't try to hush me or tell me it's going to be okay, because she knows it's not. Instead, she just lets me weep until there's nothing left inside me. Tia had rushed into the basement just seconds after Mark found us, and her screams had signaled to everyone else that something was wrong. Unlike Mark, she rushed to Jason and me and asked what happened as she helped me to my feet and up the steps. Somehow, I found the strength to tell her, using as few words as I possibly could, and she found out the rest as the police questioned us.

The sky above us seems to be darkening even more, but I can't seem to move. I don't want to move. I just want to stay here, on this sidewalk.

But then, as my sobs start to subside, something shifts inside me. I can't just sit here and wallow in my misery. There's still something I have to do.

With a sudden surge of determination, I push myself up. My legs are shaky but they manage to hold me upright.

"I need to find Mark," I whisper to Tia, my voice hoarse from crying. "I need to explain."

She hesitates for a moment, then stands up with me. "Okay. Let's go find him."

We walk the short distance to my house, Tia's arm still around me as if she's afraid I might crumble again at any moment. But I'm holding it together now, driven by the need to find my husband, to try and make him understand.

When we reach the driveway, though, my heart drops. Mark's car is gone. Is he with Sarah at the hospital?

We step into the house and it feels empty and hollow, like all the warmth has been sucked out of it. I head straight upstairs, my feet moving as if on their own as I make my way to our bedroom. But when I open the closet door, the sight that greets me stops me dead in my tracks. Half of his clothes are gone and the hangers swing lightly. One of our suitcases is missing too. I call his cellphone, but it's switched off.

He's gone.

The realization hits me like a physical blow, and I stagger back, clutching the doorframe for support. My legs give out, and I collapse to the floor. The strength drains from my body as the tears start to flow again.

Tia is beside me in an instant. "Drew, listen to me," she says gently. "Maybe it's for the best that Mark takes some time away. He needs to process everything that's happened. You both do."

But her words barely register. All I can think about is that he's gone. After everything that's happened, I'm the one who should have left, not him. This is his home and I'm the stranger that lied to him.

While my world is crumbling around me, piece by piece, Tia stays with me. Her presence is the only thing keeping me from completely falling apart.

"I'm so sorry," I finally find the courage to say. "I'm sorry you wanted to find out what happened to your friend and I knew... I didn't—"

"Yeah, how could you not tell me?" Tia wipes her eyes and looks at me with hurt in her eyes. "I needed to know, Drew. All this time, I thought it was Mark who had something to do with Melody's death. I just needed evidence, something I could take to the police. I couldn't bear to be in the same room as him."

Her words hang in the air, and I feel the guilt twisting deep inside me. "I wanted to protect my son." I sniff. "Wouldn't you do the same if you were a mother?"

Saying nothing, she stares at me for a long, agonizing moment, then shakes her head and walks to the window, looking out into the night. She presses a hand to her forehead. "Melody was my friend, Drew, and it tortured me that the person who killed her never got punished for it. And now I find out it was your son, and you never said a word. Tell me, how am I supposed to forgive that?"

"I know. I'm so sorry." Her words are like daggers, and I don't even try to defend myself.

Tia paces the room, tears sliding down her cheeks.

After what feels like an eternity, she stops and looks at me again. "I need a moment," she says, her voice hollow. Then, before I can say another word, she walks out, leaving me alone in the crushing silence of the room.

When she finally returns, her face is calmer, though her eyes are red. She stands in front of me, arms crossed and her expression guarded. "What you did was wrong. And I'm telling you right now, I don't know if I can forgive you. But I'm here—for now—because despite everything, I care about you. But don't think that means I can forget what you've done."

I nod, blinking back tears when she sits down next to me and reaches for my hand, squeezing it tightly, but says nothing.

"Is that why you became my friend?" I ask after a long silence. "To find out about Mark?"

Tia hesitates, her expression pained, but then she nods. "At first, yes, that was the plan," she admits. "But then I got to know you, Drew. I came to love you and care for you, and that's why I'm still here right now, with you."

Her words hit me like a wave, and my heart aches in ways I never expected. "Thank you. I don't deserve your kindness."

"Melody was my friend," Tia continues, her voice cracking. "But so are you. And if I were a mother, maybe I would have done the same thing."

Her love and her understanding cuts through the wall of guilt and grief surrounding me, and I break down again, collapsing into her arms. We hold each other tightly, her tears mixing with mine as we sit together, two broken souls tangled in the mess of love, loss, and forgiveness.

Even though Tia is still angry with me, she insists on spending the night, refusing to leave me alone, and I'm too broken to argue. So, we go through the motions of getting ready for bed—with her wearing a pair of my pajamas—but I know I won't be able to sleep tonight or many nights in the near future, not with my son going to prison.

Tia eventually falls asleep beside me, but I lie wide awake, staring at the ceiling, thinking about Jason and how scared he must be. Since Sarah was also involved in Melody's death, maybe we can fight this.

And then, a thought pierces through the fog in my mind. The lottery ticket. I sit up suddenly, my heart pounding. I have to claim the prize. Jason will need a good lawyer, and God knows what else. If I have any chance of helping him, of fixing this mess, I need that money.

Careful not to wake Tia, I slip out of bed and tiptoe downstairs, every creak of the floorboards sounding like a thunderclap in the stillness. I grab a flashlight from the kitchen drawer and make my way to the garage.

My beam of light sweeps over stacks of boxes until I spot the one I'm looking for. I lift it to the floor and kneel beside it, my hands trembling as I sift through the contents: a battered action figure, a tiny pair of sneakers, a photo of Jason grinning proudly with a missing tooth. But as I dig deeper, a hollow feeling grows in my chest.

It's gone. No teddy bear.

Panic surges through me as I frantically search the surrounding area and some of the other boxes, including Melody's. It has to be here. I know I left it here. But it's not.

Sarah, then. She must have followed me and found the hiding place.

She took it. Just like she took everything from me.

The flashlight slips from my grasp, clattering to the ground as I sink to my knees. My son is going to prison and there's nothing I can do about it.

FIFTY

On Saturday morning, the day after my life imploded, Tia leaves for work before seven, promising that as soon as she's done, she'll come right back to our house.

*Our house.* It never was, and now it never will be. The more time Mark has to think about what happened, the more he'll realize he can't forgive me—not after all the lies I've told him.

I try calling him again. His phone is on now, but even though it rings, he doesn't pick up. The call goes to voicemail.

"Mark, I'm so, so sorry," I whisper, then hang up because how do you properly apologize for something this big over the phone? What we need is a face-to-face conversation, one that will probably destroy us even more, but it has to happen.

After hanging up, I find myself putting on my jogging clothes, something I've done out of habit for so long that I do it without thinking. But there won't be any jogging for me today— or for a while. Not along my usual route, anyway. It would break my heart too much to pass by the café where Jason worked and not be able to go inside and see him, or to catch a glimpse of his familiar face through the window. And I can't go back to Melody's memorial site either. If it didn't feel wrong before, it certainly does now.

But the main reason I can't go jogging, or do anything else, is because I need to see my son. There's not much I can do for him without money to bail him out or hire a lawyer, but I need to see with my own eyes that he's okay after spending the night in a jail cell.

Last night, after finding that the lottery ticket was gone, I snuck into Sarah's house—using the spare key Mark keeps with us—and searched for it, but I didn't find it. It was difficult to go back there, but I needed to know if it was hidden somewhere. I searched every room except the basement. Just the thought of going back down there made me want to throw up.

Not knowing if they'll even let me see Jason, I'll still go to the police station. I don't bother showering or changing into other clothes. Instead, I grab my purse and head downstairs, but before I can reach the last step, the doorbell rings. I come to a halt and my heart jumps to my throat. I immediately imagine Sarah standing on the doorstep.

Frozen, I wait a few heartbeats, expecting her to use her key and walk right in, as she always used to. But the bell rings again.

Sarah, if she miraculously survived the night, won't be coming here anytime soon. She'll be in the hospital for a long time. And even when she's discharged, she might be heading straight to prison for pushing Melody into the road in front of an oncoming vehicle.

Anger boils up inside me when I think of how she was on her high horse all this time, telling me and everyone how close she and Melody used to be and how I would never measure up. And all along, she was hiding this huge, deadly secret. You'd think that since she was guilty, she'd want Melody's case to be forgotten and left to go cold, but I guess she saw a way to get me out of Mark's life and grabbed it. Or perhaps she was deflecting, desperate to put the blame on someone else.

She was so confident that no one saw her that night that she didn't see the risk—didn't know she'd expose herself. The only reason I hope she pulls through is so she can pay for what she did.

The bell rings a third time before I spring into action and move toward the door. It could be the police with more questions about that night, trying to find out what I know. They questioned me last night before Jason was taken away, but I know that was just the beginning.

The person I least expect to see standing in front of my door is Martin.

I'm so startled to see him that I take a step back. He looks more disheveled than I've ever seen him, his shoulders hunched forward. In his arms, he's holding a small shoebox. And is it possible that his hair has gone even grayer since I last saw him?

"Martin, hi. What are you doing here?" I glance behind him, half-expecting to see the car that drove him here. But all I see are my neighbors' curtains twitching as they peer out at my house, hungry for gossip. The whole town must have heard by now. I can literally feel their eyes on me.

"I'm very sorry to show up unannounced." Martin shifts from one foot to the other. "Do you mind if... Can we have a talk?" His voice is tired, as if the weight of the world is pressing down on him.

I glance at my watch. "I'm actually on my way to—"

"Please, it's important. I won't be long."

Without a word, I open the door wider. As soon as he enters, I shut it again, locking out the nosy neighbors. Instead of leading him to the living room, I show him to the kitchen and watch as he looks around nervously, probably not used to being in such a nice place.

I offer him a seat at the kitchen table, and when I ask if he wants something to drink, he shakes his head. So, I sit across from him, wondering if he's here because he found out what happened last night and wants to see if I'm okay. The thought warms my heart. I could use all the friends I can get right now because I know the next few weeks and months will be devastating.

"I heard about your son, Jason." Martin puts the box he brought with him between us on the table.

I blow out a breath and nod. "How do you—"

"It's a small town, and people are talking." He wipes his eyes with his hands and looks away for a moment before looking back at me. His concern touches me. I've told him bits and pieces about Jason, but not nearly enough to warrant this reaction. And now I'm not sure how to react myself.

"It means a lot that you came, Martin." I reach out and squeeze his rough hands. "But I really need to get to my son. What did you want to talk to me about?"

Martin doesn't answer immediately. Instead, he pushes the shoebox toward me. I hesitate before opening it, wondering if he brought me money to help out, something I could never accept from him. "Martin, you shouldn't have—" I start to say, but my words trail off as I lift the lid and see a plain white envelope with my name written across it in block letters above my old address. But the envelope is not stamped.

"What...?" My voice falters as I lift the unopened envelope, only to find many more like it underneath. At the bottom of the box is a photo of a little girl with pigtails and a gap-toothed smile holding a knitted doll. That little girl is me.

I hold up one of the envelopes. "What... Where did you get these?"

Martin doesn't meet my eyes as he answers. "I wrote them in prison, but I didn't have the courage to send them to you." He wipes the sweat off his forehead with the back of his hand. "Drew, I'm your father."

## FIFTY-ONE

I stare at Martin, my mind struggling to process what he just said. My father? No, it can't be. My father is dead.

I was ten years old when he went to prison, twenty-seven years ago, and I never kept any photos of him. Over time, I did my best to erase the memories of his face from my mind.

Back then, he was always well-groomed, with closely trimmed hair and a neat beard. Seeing him now, with his bushy gray beard and wild, unkempt hair, it's no wonder I didn't recognize him. Suddenly, it all makes sense—why he refused to let me cut his beard or hair. He didn't want me to recognize him.

"You're lying," I manage to choke out, barely able to breathe. "My father is dead. After he was released..."

Martin shakes his head, his eyes filled with regret. "I was very sick at the time. I almost died, but I didn't. And when I survived, I knew it was a sign. A sign that I needed to find you, to make things right."

A rush of emotions overcomes me—confusion, anger, disbelief. Memories flood back—memories of the man I hated, the man who shattered our family, the man who ruined my life. And now he's sitting across from me, telling me he's the same man I've been sharing my breaks with, the same man I confided in about my family problems, the man I called my friend. He lied to me. He manipulated me into getting close to him.

Tears blur my vision as the full weight of his betrayal crashes down on me. "I can never forgive you," I say, my voice shaking and my words drowning in tears.

Martin's face crumples, and he falls to his knees in front of me. "I know I don't deserve your forgiveness, but I'm begging you. There's nothing I wouldn't do to make it right."

My heart aches with the raw, searing pain of old wounds reopening. "You can't make it right," I say, my voice breaking. "You killed my mother. You took everything from me."

"I know." Martin's tears are streaming down his face. "I know, and I'm so sorry. I stayed away because I knew you wouldn't want me back in your life after what I did, what I will never forgive myself for. But I had to make sure you and your son were okay. I was devastated when you told me you weren't happy. I wanted to tell you who I was, but... you once told me you were glad your father was dead. I thought it was better to stay in the background, to help you from a distance." He pauses, his breath hitching with emotion. "That's why I left you the lottery ticket."

Struggling to breathe, I swallow hard. "It... It was you?"

"Yes. I used to go to the post office every week to play. It felt like a game, something fun to do. One time, when I bumped into your colleague there, I even convinced her to give it a shot. You never know, right?"

"Tia?" I press my fingers to my forehead, the memory surfacing. "She mentioned that someone convinced her to play the lottery."

"That was me." He blows out a breath. "When you confided in me about your financial problems, I started playing the lottery even more, hoping for a miracle. I didn't think it would ever happen, but then... it did. I won. And the only thing

I could think about was helping you, fixing the mess I made of your life. But I couldn't give the winning ticket to you in person. I knew you'd never accept it from me. You hate me—and you should. So I sent it to you anonymously."

His words crash over me, leaving me gasping for air. The room starts to spin around me, and I press my fingers to my temples, trying to piece it all together. "You... you really left me that ticket?"

He nods, his expression filled with both guilt and hope. "I thought it would be enough, that it would make your life easier. But then you didn't claim the money. Day after day, I watched and waited, but nothing. I don't understand. Why didn't you claim it?" He lifts his hand to touch mine before, thankfully, changing his mind and pulling back before I reject him. "I just wanted to fix things for you, in any way I could. Please, take the money. Let me do this one thing for you."

His words echo in the silence, but I'm too numb to respond. My mind reels with shock and the unbearable weight of everything he's just revealed. I should probably be thankful for what he tried to do for me, but all I can feel is the searing heat of my anger. Sure, he may have thought he was helping, but nothing can change what he did. It doesn't erase the pain he caused, the years of suffering. He took my mother away from me. No amount of money can undo that.

"Too much has happened and I know you might never forgive me, but I love you and I think you should get professional help. I can see you're suffering and the only way you can find freedom is by confronting the past, making peace with it."

My head snaps back as I glare at him. "You left that note on my car, didn't you?" When he says nothing, I almost laugh out loud. Does he really think me talking to a stranger would make the nightmares he created go away? "Look, I can't do this," I whisper, standing up so quickly that my chair almost crashes to the floor. "I can't handle this right now. You need to leave."

Martin looks devastated, but he nods, pushing himself up from the floor. "I understand. But before I go, please, let me be there for my grandson. I've been through what he's about to go through. I just want to help."

I don't know what to say. Then just as we're about to leave the kitchen, I catch sight of Mark's car pulling into the driveway through the window and my heart leaps into my throat, panic rising inside me. "You need to go," I urge Martin. "Now."

# FIFTY-TWO

I barely have a moment to catch my breath before Mark walks in, barely acknowledging Martin's presence. My heart stutters as I see him for the first time since last night.

Mark looks like a man who's been shattered. His clothes are wrinkled and disheveled, as if he's slept in them—or more likely, not slept at all. His shirt is untucked, his shoes scuffed, and his hair is a chaotic mess. But it's his face that breaks me: eyes red-rimmed, swollen, and glassy with unshed tears. His jaw is clenched so tightly I can see the muscle twitching in his cheek.

He doesn't say a word as he pushes past me. I follow him into the living room and watch as he drops onto the couch, his head falling into his hands. His broad shoulders hunch forward, and for a moment, he just sits there, completely still.

I remain rooted to the spot, unsure what to do, where to go, or what to say. I slowly move toward the couch, but I can't bring myself to sit beside him. Instead, I choose the far end, keeping a safe distance, because I know he doesn't want me close—not now, maybe not ever again.

The silence stretches on, suffocating, and I struggle to find my voice, to say something—anything—that might bridge the gap between us. But every word I think of doesn't feel enough. I clench my hands in my lap, my nails digging into my palms.

Finally, I gather the courage to speak. "Mark, I'm so sorry. I should have told you..."

He looks up suddenly, and the fury in his eyes is like a blow to the chest. His face is contorted with anger and pain, and his gaze pierces through me.

"Sorry?" His voice is rough and raw, like he's been yelling or crying—or both—all night. "What exactly are you sorry for, Drew? That you lied about your name? Or maybe you're sorry you didn't tell me that your son—my stepson—ran over my first wife? Or is it that you're sorry you were ready to take the fall for him so he wouldn't have to face what he did? Tell me, Drew, what are you sorry for exactly? Because there's too damn much to count."

Tears are streaming down my face but I can't look away from him. His eyes are blazing with pain, but beneath that, I can see the deep, aching sorrow that's tearing him apart.

"I'm sorry for everything," I whisper, the words tasting bitter on my tongue before I release them. "I should have told you everything from the start. I did what I did because I was so scared for Jason. I didn't want him to go to prison. I told him to say I was the one driving if it ever came out. I was just trying to protect my son... I was just being a mother."

That night, long after he fled Elm Grove, Jason crashed my car into a tree. Surprisingly, not much damage was done to the vehicle, but he broke his leg, and that's how we ended up in the same hospital as Mark, where I lied to the doctors, telling them he had been in a motorcycle accident.

We didn't even live here. After Jason's girlfriend broke his heart, I took him on a road trip to Stoneview because he was spiraling. He used to love road trips, and I thought a couple of days in this pretty little town I'd photographed once would do him good. I never thought we would end up staying. I never thought it would come to this.

I swallow hard, trying to keep the tears at bay, but they're already burning my eyes and blurring my vision as I look at the man I love, whose life I've destroyed.

Mark's expression softens for a brief moment. But the anger quickly returns, hardening his features, and he shakes his head.

"Protecting your son… at what cost, Drew?" His voice is laced with bitterness. "You lied to me. You manipulated your way into my life after my wife died. Did you do it out of guilt? Out of some twisted sense of duty? Did you ever even love me? Or was it all just a way to make yourself feel better for what you did?"

The tears trickle down my cheeks as I shake my head. "No, Mark, it wasn't like that. I never planned any of this. I didn't mean to fall in love with you—I just wanted to help you, to be there for you. But somewhere along the way, it happened, and I love you. I love you more than anything, and I'm so, so sorry…"

But he's not listening. He's barely holding it together, I can see the tears welling up in his eyes, threatening to spill over. It's the worst pain I've ever seen on anyone, and it's all my fault. I did this to him.

"I can't do this." Mark jumps to his feet so fast that I recoil inside. His face is twisted in agony, and he looks down at me like he's seeing a stranger. "I'm finding it very hard to believe anything you say. I need to go. I don't know when I'll be back—if I'll be back."

His words strike me with a force that leaves me breathless. He's leaving, and there's nothing I can do to stop him. Nothing I can say that will make it better. Feeling helpless, I watch as he turns to walk away from me, from us, his movements stiff, like he's forcing himself.

But just before he reaches the doorway, he pauses, and when he speaks again, his voice is cold, detached. "Do you remember at the party when Sarah wanted to speak to me? She told me that Jason's father didn't die in a car accident, like you told me when we bonded in the hospital... It was a skiing accident. You lied to all of us about that too, just to manipulate me." He sighs and pinches the bridge of his nose. "I didn't want to believe Sarah then, but now that I know who you really are, I see she was telling the truth. You thought it was a way to get close to me, to act like our pain was the same. That's what Sarah thinks. What she thought." I watch as tears fill his eyes and then he clears his throat. "For your information, Sarah didn't make it last night. She died on the way to the hospital. Your son murdered my wife, and my sister."

# FIFTY-THREE

## DREW

Four Years Ago

Before I even realize what I'm doing, my hands are pummeling against Dean's chest, pushing him back. "You don't get it! You don't know what you're putting us through!"

I can't stop. Each strike is fueled by a whirlwind of pent-up anger and pain. He tries to hold my wrists, but my fury is like a wild animal, roaring and clawing to break free.

Deep down, I know he isn't my father, but right now, he is the closest target for all my unresolved hurt. I feel like a crazy person, but something inside me has taken over, and I can't stop.

"Why won't you listen to me?" I scream, my voice cracking. "How dare you destroy our family like this? You're just throwing it all away!" The words pour out in a torrent of bitterness.

Every time my fist connects with his body, I punish him for my father's sins, for every night I spent hiding from a man I thought never truly loved me. Dean is now my scapegoat, and I unleash years of frustration on him, my hands landing with an intensity I didn't know I was capable of.

He stumbles backward. "Stop this! This isn't—"

But I'm not listening. "You think you can just drink and act like everything's fine? This isn't who you are! You're ruining us!"

I push him again, and we don't notice how close we are to the edge of the slope, the steep drop that lurks just behind us.

With one final shove, my hands connect with his chest, and he goes tumbling over the edge. Time freezes as I watch in horror, his body slipping away from me, spiraling down the mountainside. My heart races, and my breath catches in my throat as panic sets in.

"Dean!" I scream, my voice echoing into the vastness. I rush to the edge. The slope is steep and icy, far too dangerous for me to scramble down after him. All I can do is watch in horror as he falls, helplessly aware of the sharp rocks protruding from the snow below.

I can't breathe as I see him hit something hard. "No!" I shout. My heart is frozen, and I flail my arms, dread overwhelming me. "Someone, please!" My voice cracks with panic as I see my husband lying motionless below, fighting the urge to throw myself down after him.

Finally, I see a couple of skiers in the distance, their laughter and chatter echoing off the mountainside. "Help! My husband fell! Please!" I'm not sure if they hear me, but I cling to hope as I watch the scene unfold below.

When the rescuers finally arrive, I'm frozen in place, eyes glued to Dean's still body. They rush to assess the situation, checking for a pulse.

"Dean, please," I whisper, tears streaming down my face. My heart feels like it's shattering, each piece cutting deeper as the reality sinks in. I stagger back, away from the edge, away from the terrible sight of the man I love lying motionless on the icy ground. The world around me blurs as I struggle to breathe. It feels surreal, as if I'm watching a scene from a horror movie.

"Help him!" I scream, my voice raw with desperation. "Please, save him!" My heart races, each beat pounding like a drum in my ears, drowning out the panicked whispers of the rescuers and the distant voices of other skiers. All I can see is Dean, and all I can feel is the weight of my guilt crashing down on me like an avalanche.

The rescuers work in a flurry, their movements quick and practiced, but it feels like a blur. All the while I'm standing there, helpless and terrified. Finally, one of them looks up and I know immediately. My husband is gone.

"No! He can't be," I whisper to myself. "He can't be dead. I'm so sorry. I didn't mean to! I just—" My sobs come hard and I bury my face in my hands, feeling the warmth of my tears mixing with the cold of the snow beneath me.

A group of onlookers gathers, but I barely register them. All I can see is my husband, the only man I've ever loved, lying there, unmoving. "He can't be gone," I repeat. "He just can't be."

As the rescuers prepare to transport him, each move they make feels like a knife twisting deeper into my chest. I should be with Dean, holding him, not standing here, watching.

"Please, God, please," I plead. "Not now. Not like this. Not him." But my words are met with silence, the only response is the wind howling around us, mocking my desperation.

When they finally manage to lift him up and load him onto a stretcher, I feel the world tilt beneath me. I want to run to him, to scream that I love him, to beg him to come back, to say I'm sorry. But my legs feel like lead, and I can't move.

"Mom!" My son's voice cuts through my fog of despair, and I turn to see him standing a few feet away, his expression a mix of fear and confusion. "What's happening? Did someone get hurt? Where's Dad?" Then he sees the stretcher as it's pushed past, and his face crumbles. His eyes meet mine, filled with questions I can't begin to answer.

"Oh God, Jason..." My words are a broken whisper as I stumble toward him. "Your dad..." But the words die on my lips, replaced by a strangled sob. "It was an accident. He fell."

I can see the doubt in Jason's eyes, the way he searches my face for the truth. "But—"

"He was drunk, baby, and he slipped," I say, pulling him to me.

Jason never did find out the truth of exactly what happened that day. But a few years later, after Melody died and I met Mark, when we had started our lives over again, I sat Jason down and suggested that going forward we should tell everyone that his father died in a car accident. "This was all over the local papers, and they mentioned that he fell because he was drunk. I don't want him to be remembered like that. Let's not taint his memory."

But in truth, I wanted to say it was a car accident not only to distance myself from the truth, but also because it gave me a way to connect to Mark. Telling him that both our spouses died in car accidents gave us a common bond, a shared pain that seemed to cement our budding relationship.

The thing is, after telling the lie so many times, I made myself believe it too.

Now the years of deception have finally caught up, unraveling the perfect world I had carefully stitched together.

I deserve to be behind bars just like my son.

# FIFTY-FOUR

## DREW

The car is filled with a palpable sense of relief. I glance at the rearview mirror and catch Jason's eye in the backseat. He's smiling—actually smiling—for the first time in what feels like forever.

Lori sits next to him, holding his hand tight, her eyes, like mine, bright with tears of joy. In the front passenger seat is the man I choose to continue calling Martin. I watch as he leans back and smiles softly out at the road.

My worst nightmare, the thing I've been anxious about for months, didn't happen, and my heart swells with gratitude. Today, the judge ruled that Jason won't go to prison.

Three months ago, I hit rock bottom, watching as my son was arrested and charged with something I feared would destroy him, destroy his life and mine. At the time, I didn't have the money for a good lawyer who could fight for him, and the weight of that nearly crushed me.

But then, in a twist of fate, Hannah Howard, the florist,

walked into the salon, just as she had promised she would when I saw her at the Pilates class.

I hadn't expected much from the visit, just a casual chat while she got her hair done. But like everyone else, Hannah had heard about what happened to Jason, and she asked, with genuine concern, if there was anything she could do to help.

The memory of that moment is still fresh in my mind, the moment I broke down right there in the salon, sobbing uncontrollably. In my desperation, I begged Hannah to ask her husband, Nathan, if he would represent Jason. I openly told her that I had no money, nothing to offer but my gratitude. I didn't think anything would come of it, but three days later, Nathan showed up at the salon, asking to speak to me.

He told me that he believed Jason deserved another chance, that everyone makes mistakes. I had heard of Nathan's reputation—he doesn't lose many cases he takes on—but given the charges Jason was facing, I didn't have much hope.

But Nathan delivered on his promise. He did what seemed impossible. He prevented Jason from going to prison, to be sentenced to probation instead. Nathan presented evidence of my son's good character and lack of prior criminal history. But the heart of his defense was that Melody's death wasn't solely Jason's fault, that Sarah Reynolds pushing Melody was the direct cause of the accident, making her the primary responsible party, if she had lived to face trial.

There was no concrete evidence to prove that Sarah really did push Melody, especially since Jason's memory that he saw it happen was fuzzy. Not even my photo of Sarah's writing on the helmet helped, but it didn't matter because the truth Nathan uncovered was far more chilling. Sarah hadn't just pushed Melody in a fit of rage—she'd made sure she died. She murdered her best friend and sister-in-law.

During Jason's trial, a woman by the name of Trina Landon was brought in as a witness.

Trina, a woman who said she needed to clear her conscience, had been working as a nurse at the hospital the night Melody died and said she saw Sarah pull the plug. She even shared a short video clip she took.

Then Trina started talking about how she had blackmailed Sarah after Melody's death, that she forced her to put her mother in the Stoneview seniors' home, demanding that she pay for her mother's stay there and her medical bills, all the while threatening to expose Sarah's involvement in Melody's death if she didn't comply. Trina had text messages and emails between the two of them, confirming everything.

Sarah was guilty as hell, but Nathan still had to convince the court not to send Jason to prison. When it came to Jason fleeing the scene, Nathan argued that it was a reaction of panic and fear, not a conscious decision to evade responsibility. And somehow, he convinced the court.

Now, as we drive toward Jason's apartment, where I've been living for the past three months, the atmosphere in the car is almost surreal. We're all talking excitedly, voices overlapping in the best kind of chaos. With this second chance in his pocket, Jason is planning to go back to school, and Lori is already talking about how we can celebrate this coming weekend.

My eyes wander to the girl I never trusted or approved of when Jason first started dating her. But she has proven herself during these dark months. She visited Jason every chance she got while he was in jail as I could not afford bail, and she never wavered in her support. I realize, with a small pang of guilt, that I like Lori—more than I've ever admitted to myself.

I shift my gaze to Martin, the man I used to hate. He's cleaned himself up—shaved his beard, cut his hair, even gotten the job he had applied for at the post office. He's trying, in his own way, to make amends. I don't know if I can ever fully forgive him for what he did, but I know one thing, that people make mistakes, some of them huge, and everyone deserves a second chance. Nathan Howard reminded me of that.

Martin isn't the drunk who raised me and killed my mother anymore. He's a man who is doing everything to redeem himself. I don't think I will ever call him Dad again, but we will be okay. And it's good to know that Jason has someone else who loves him by his side.

I still wonder where Sarah put the lottery ticket. If I had found it, I would have collected the money and given it to Jason to start his new life.

As we pull into the parking lot of Jason's apartment complex, my heart suddenly squeezes. I notice a familiar car parked on the other side of the road, Mark's sedan.

I haven't spoken to my husband since the day he told me of Sarah's death, but I've noticed him at all the court proceedings. He kept his distance and left soon after each session, but I saw him. After staying in his house for a week following Sarah's death and hearing nothing from him, I packed my things and moved into Jason's apartment. The house we shared just didn't feel right anymore.

I can barely move or breathe as I watch him approach us. He looks tired, older, and his face is harder than I remember. Clearly, he has grieved a lot in the past months and I feel like reaching out and pulling him into a hug. But instead, I brace myself, expecting him to be furious, to serve me divorce papers on the spot.

I hold my breath as he stops in front of us, his gaze lingering on Jason, then shifting to me. The silence is long and thick with anticipation.

Then, in a voice raw with emotion, he speaks. "Drew, I want you to come home."

The words take a moment to register, and when they do, I can't hide my shock, barely able to stand as my knees weaken. But before I can respond, Mark turns to Jason, pulling him into an unexpected hug. I watch as Jason stiffens, then slowly relaxes, returning the embrace.

"I forgive you, son," Mark says quietly. "You made a mistake and I... I forgive you."

Tears well up in my eyes. This is not the outcome I expected at all. It's more than I dared to hope for.

As Mark releases Jason and steps back, his eyes meet mine again and he wraps his arms around me. "Let's try to be a family again," he whispers.

# EPILOGUE

## MARK



The sun is just setting and I'm sitting alone in the home office, my eyes locked on the video footage playing on the screen, Sarah's footage that she captured the night Jason confessed in her basement. The police found it inside her house, which is now mine, and a friend of mine in the department made a copy for me.

Watching my sister on screen, the weight of everything settles heavily in my chest, and I don't regret not going to the funeral. She pretended to mourn the loss of my wife, all the while hiding the truth, hiding her betrayal. Sarah wasn't just a liar; she was a murderer. I feel sick, betrayed by the one person I should have trusted the most.

I press my hands flat against the desk, my fingers splayed, trying to calm the shaking.

Breathe, I tell myself, but the tightness in my chest won't let me. How could she, my own sister, do this to Melody, to me? I ball my hands into fists, fighting the urge to throw something, to destroy something—anything. The anger claws at me, but it's the sickening feeling of betrayal that hurts the most.

For the last two years, I've been haunted by the thought that my wife had killed herself, threw herself in front of a moving vehicle. I remember that night vividly, the confrontation when I discovered her affair. I was awful to her, my words sharp enough to cut. She had left the house in tears, and I believed she stepped in front of that moving car deliberately. I had no idea she went to Sarah's place for dinner, and then that my own sister, and her best friend, had pushed her into the street.

All this time, I've carried so much guilt. I thought I was trying to redeem myself by donating to the church and going to confessions, but it was never enough.

After several deep breaths, I'm finally calm and able to think clearly. But I can feel the heat behind my eyes, the pressure that's been building for months. I pause the video on an image of Jason, tears streaming down his face as he confesses what he did to Melody, how he slammed into her and drove off.

Reaching for the notebook sitting beside me, I flip through the pages filled with meticulous notes, plans, and detailed sketches of a car.

In the back of my mind, the details swirl: how I tinkered with the brakes, just enough to make it look like an accident. A slight adjustment that will fail when it matters most. It's all there, laid out in black and white. The plan I've been working on for a while thanks to the help of the dark side of the internet.

But as I stare at the pages in front of me, I know I have to do something about them. My hands tremble as I rip them from the notebook, tearing them one by one before feeding them into the shredder. Each page disappears, reduced to thin strips of unrecognizable paper.

When the notebook is empty, I close it and shove it back into the drawer, now nothing more than a hollow shell. I sit there for a moment, the heaviness of it all pressing down on me.

But I push it away, forcing myself to get up and go downstairs to my family.

Drew, Jason, and Martin, the father-in-law I didn't know I had, are already standing by the front door, ready for us to go to Tia's engagement party. Even though she's been engaged for three years, she and her fiancé never celebrated. Drew said the party signals they're finally ready to move forward, and they've even set a wedding date.

Jason is wearing a crisp blue shirt with beige slacks and Drew is wearing one of my favorite dresses on her, a deep red number that clings to her in all the right places, with a cream shawl covering her shoulders. And Martin is wearing a gray suit that looks a little too large for him.

"Mark," Drew says, "we need to leave now or we'll be late."

I force a smile as I join them, slipping into the role I've been playing for a while "You three go ahead," I say casually. "I've got something to take care of first, but I'll meet you there."

"All right then." Drew gives me a long hug, her arms wrapping around me tightly, and she plants a kiss on my cheek. "Don't be too long." Her eyes search mine as if she can sense that something is off. But I keep my expression steady, and reassure her with another smile.

I watch them leave, standing in the doorway as Drew's car pulls out of the driveway. They wave, and I lift my hand in return. Then I watch until the car disappears around the corner. The moment they're out of sight, I let out a deep sigh and close the door.

"It has to end this way," I whisper to myself. "Goodbye, Drew."

From my pocket, I pull out the lottery ticket that Drew had hidden from me, staring at it for a moment. I found it in Sarah's car.

When Sarah pulled me aside at the party, she told me there

was something she wanted to show me in her car after the celebration. "More proof that your wife is a liar," she'd said.

A few days after her death, her words kept echoing in my mind, urging me to search her car thoroughly. When I lifted the trunk floor, I noticed a hidden compartment and, inside, a teddy bear that Drew once told me had belonged to Jason when he was a child.

I picked it up, examining it closely, wondering why Sarah had it. The blue and white coat it wore felt soft in my hands, and I brushed my fingers over the seams. As I lifted it, I noticed a zipper hidden beneath it.

I unzipped it and found the lottery ticket tucked neatly inside, undeniable proof that my wife *is* a liar.

And this lottery ticket is a fresh start for me, offering me a new life somewhere far away. I still have time to claim the prize.

As I turn and walk back into the house, my plan feels more real than ever. There's no turning back now. Soon, all the secrets, all the lies—they'll go up in flames.

And for the first time in what feels like years, I feel something close to peace.

# A LETTER FROM L.G. DAVIS

Dear reader,

Thank you for diving into *The New Marriage*. Writing this book was a deeply personal journey, especially as it was written during a challenging time in my life due to health struggles. Immersing myself in Drew and Mark's world gave me purpose and strength, and I poured my heart into every twist and turn of their complicated relationship. I hope you found the suspense, secrets, and surprises just as gripping as I did while writing them.

It was also so much fun to return to Stoneview, the setting of my Broken Vows series. Revisiting this world felt like coming home, and I hope you enjoyed seeing some familiar faces along the way.

As always, my goal is to create a world where tension is palpable and every turn leaves you questioning what's real. I wanted to craft a story that would keep you on edge, and I hope it did just that.

If you enjoyed *The New Marriage*, I'd be so grateful if you'd consider leaving a review. Your thoughts and feedback are incredibly important to me and help me continue writing stories that connect with readers like you. If you'd like to stay updated on my upcoming releases, I'd love for you to join my email list. You'll be the first to hear about new books, exclusive content, and all the exciting news.

*www.bookouture.com/l-g-davis*

Your support means everything to me, and I'm truly thankful for it. I can't wait to share more stories with you in the future.

Warmly,

Liz

www.lgdavis.com

 facebook.com/LGDavisBooks

 x.com/lgdavisauthor

 instagram.com/lgdavisauthor

# ACKNOWLEDGMENTS

Writing *The New Marriage* has been both a rewarding and challenging journey. There were moments during the writing process when I wasn't sure I could finish, but the support of so many incredible people made it possible. I am deeply grateful to everyone who stood by me along the way.

To the entire Bookouture team—thank you for your unwavering dedication and professionalism in helping bring this book to life. Your support and hard work have been invaluable. I feel so fortunate to be part of such a talented and encouraging team.

A special thank you to my editor, Rhianna—your patience, insight, and belief in me were a lifeline throughout this process. Even during the most difficult times when my health made everything feel overwhelming, you were there to offer both guidance and understanding. I couldn't have asked for a better editor, and I'm so grateful for everything you've done to help shape this story.

And, of course, to my husband, my anchor. You and our two beautiful children have been my steady rock, offering endless encouragement and love. You are my constant source of strength, and I can't thank you enough for standing by me and believing in me, even when I struggled to believe in myself. This book is as much yours as it is mine.

Finally, to my readers—thank you for your continued support. Your feedback, reviews, and encouragement are what make this all worthwhile. Knowing that my stories resonate with you fills me with gratitude, and I look forward to sharing more of my work with you in the future.

With all my gratitude,

Liz

PUBLISHING TEAM

**Turning a manuscript into a book requires the efforts of many people. The publishing team at Bookouture would like to acknowledge everyone who contributed to this publication.**

### Commercial
Lauren Morrissette
Hannah Richmond
Imogen Allport

### Data and analysis
Mark Alder
Mohamed Bussuri

### Editorial
Rhianna Louise
Melissa Tran

### Copyeditor
Donna Hillyer

### Proofreader
Emily Boyce

### Marketing
Alex Crow

Melanie Price
Occy Carr
Cíara Rosney
Martyna Młynarska

**Operations and distribution**
Marina Valles
Stephanie Straub
Joe Morris

**Production**
Hannah Snetsinger
Mandy Kullar
Jen Shannon
Ria Clare

**Publicity**
Kim Nash
Noelle Holten
Jess Readett
Sarah Hardy

**Rights and contracts**
Peta Nightingale
Richard King
Saidah Graham